Sept 7

"You're not really planning to walk home with me."

"Why wouldn't I?" Alia continued shrugging into her shoulder holster.

Landry swallowed hard. He'd never been drawn to needy women, and Alia was a prime example why. She damn well protected herself, and he found that way sexier than a damsel in distress.

Beads of sweat were gathering across his skin, and they made his voice thick, even though he tried to hide it with teasing. "What's the plan? If we get mugged, you'll hold them off while I run for help?"

Her gaze was warm and heated him from the inside out. "I don't know how fast you can run."

"Doesn't matter. I only have to be able to outrun *you*."

She smirked. "Not likely. I'll tell you what, if we get mugged, I'll handle the bad guys. Then you can thank me later."

He knew exactly what form he would want that thank-you to take. Blocking the image from his mind, he snorted. "I think getting to kick bad-guy butt in front of me would be reward enough for you."

***

Dear Reader,

Bayou Hero is a story close to my heart. That kind of sounds as though the others aren't, but that's not the case. It's just a matter of connecting with this story in different ways than I do with the others. I've always heard the advice "Write what you know," to which my usual response is, "Write what you want to write about—that's what research is for." But when I do write what I know—whether it's a place where I've lived, a pastime I've indulged in or my experience as a military spouse—that special bond is there.

Being a navy spouse, and with my husband being a former cop, I couldn't avoid getting exposed to the Naval Criminal Investigative Service during our military years, especially since my husband worked with them the last several years. I always wanted to do an NCIS book, and *finally* here it is. And it's set in New Orleans, my favorite city in the world (outside of Oklahoma, of course), and has a hero and a heroine whom I've adored spending time with. I hope you enjoy NCIS, New Orleans, Landry and Alia as much as I have.

Marilyn

BAYOU HERO

Marilyn Pappano

HARLEQUIN®ROMANTIC SUSPENSE

Recycling programs
for this product may
not exist in your area.

ISBN-13: 978-0-373-27902-9

Bayou Hero

Copyright © 2015 by Marilyn Pappano

Marilyn Pappano has spent most of her life growing into the person she was meant to be, but isn't there yet. She's been blessed by family—her husband, their son, his lovely wife and a grandson who is almost certainly the most beautiful and talented baby in the world—and friends, along with a writing career that's made her one of the luckiest people around. Her passions, besides those already listed, include the pack of wild dogs who make their home in her house, fighting the good fight against the weeds that make up her yard, killing the creepy-crawlies that slither out of those weeds and, of course, anything having to do with books.

Books by Marilyn Pappano

Harlequin Romantic Suspense

Copper Lake Secrets
In the Enemy's Arms
Christmas Confidential
"Holiday Protector"
Copper Lake Confidential
Copper Lake Encounter
Undercover in Copper Lake

Silhouette Romantic Suspense

Scandal in Copper Lake
Passion to Die For
Criminal Deception
Protector's Temptation
Covert Christmas
"Open Season"

Visit the Author Profile page at
Harlequin.com for more titles

Even if every single book doesn't say so, they're all for you, sweetie. I couldn't do this without you.

Chapter 1

The Greek Revival mansion sat a hundred feet back from Saint Charles Avenue, separated from the street by a six-foot-tall wrought iron fence. The house was stately, the lawn perfectly manicured and the very air around it smelled sweeter, or so it seemed to Alia Kingsley as she snagged a few feet of curb space and climbed out of her car.

The only things more out of place than her in New Orleans's Garden District this summer morning were the vehicles that overflowed the mansion's brick-paved drive and clogged the side street. New Orleans Police Department cars, marked and unmarked; an ambulance, its paramedics standing idle; a van from the coroner's office; sedans bearing US Government tags; and trucks carrying the logos of the local media outlets.

Yellow crime-scene tape kept the reporters and curious neighbors at bay. Alia flashed her credentials to the young cop standing guard at the end of the drive, and he lifted the tape so she could pass. "Who's in charge?"

"Not me. I'm crowd control," he said with a shrug. "Ask one of the detectives."

With a nod, she followed the drive up a slight incline. Another uniformed officer stood guard at the back door of the house. A short distance away, a sailor, his face as colorless as his summer whites, sat at a patio table, a handkerchief pressed to his mouth. He was talking to Jimmy DiBiase, college football star turned cop and, more importantly in her opinion, if not his, her ex-husband.

This wasn't a good start to her week.

When Jimmy saw her, he left the table and met her halfway. "I was hopin' you'd catch this."

"Yeah, we work so well together," she said drily.

"We did a lot of things good together."

"Are you sure that was you and me, or maybe one of your girlfriends?"

He had the grace to flush at that, though if he truly felt any regret it didn't show in his voice. "Aw, sweet pea, we ain't ever gonna work things out if you don't give ole Jimmy a break." With that Southern drawl and broad grin of his, he managed to make the two of them working things out sound almost reasonable. Lucky for her, at 8:10 a.m. without nearly enough caffeine in her system, *reasonable* didn't put in an appearance on her list of things to be.

She gestured to the mansion behind him. "Whose house?"

"You don't know?"

Obviously someone with money and, considering the official navy vehicle in the driveway and the kid in uniform, someone with enough rank to rate a driver. But she didn't start her days, or her cases, making guesses, so she waited for Jimmy to tell her. He did so with great pleasure.

"Honey, you are a special guest at the family home of Rear Admiral Jeremiah Jackson Junior."

She knew the name, of course. A special agent with the Naval Criminal Investigative Service couldn't spend more than a day at the New Orleans office without hearing Admiral Jackson mentioned. He was nothing less than a legend—tough as nails, hard-line, a leftover from the days when being an officer and a gentleman meant something. His career had been long and illustrious, his navy commands as shipshape as any and more than most.

"Is he the victim?" she asked, gazing at the back of the house. Windows marched across each of three stories in perfect symmetry. The admiral liked order in his job as well as his home. She knew his type well. Her own father, Rear Admiral Charles Kingsley, Retired, was just like him.

"Him. His housekeeper. Her daughter. The gardener."

Alia's breath caught in her chest. "How old was the daughter?"

"Mid-twenties. Had Down syndrome."

Four homicides. The spotlight would be shining brightly on this case. "Did the housekeeper live in?"

"Had quarters right there." He nodded toward the nearest corner of the house.

"And the gardener? Did he live here, too?"

"She. No. She just liked to get an early start before the day got too hot."

Alia shifted her gaze to the lawn. The grass was clipped, the sidewalks, driveway and beds neatly edged. Flowers bloomed profusely, and the pots spaced evenly across the patio contained plantings so healthy they looked fake. The gardener's dedication to her job had been admirable...though it had cost her her life.

Finally she looked at Jimmy again and asked the important question. "How did they die?"

"Stabbed. Once each on the employees, in the chest. The gardener also suffered a blow to the head. We figure she walked in and surprised the killer, so he knocked her out, then killed her. The old woman was found in bed, the daughter on the floor beside her bed."

"And the admiral?"

Jimmy hesitated. "In his bed. When I came out to talk to the driver, the ME's investigator was still counting the wounds. He was up to twenty-seven."

Three people efficiently killed and one overkilled. It was safe to assume he'd been the real target, and the others had merely been in the wrong place at the wrong time. Jeez, how could being asleep in your own bed be the wrong place at the wrong time?

"You wanna go in?"

She could think of a hundred things she'd rather do, but she nodded and followed him to the back door, where the officer standing guard offered them both gloves and protective booties. The door was an old-fashioned one made of wood with a nine-paned window looking out. The pane closest to the knob was broken out.

The door opened into a space that did double duty as mudroom and laundry room, and then into a kitchen. The house might be two hundred years old, but the kitchen was definitely of the twenty-first century. Appliances, surfaces, cabinets—all were top-of-the-line and pricey. The commercial-grade stove and the refrigerator alone cost more than everything in her little house combined.

The smell of coffee coming from the maker on the countertop made her mouth water. "Is that on a timer?"

"Yeah." It was a crime scene tech who answered. "No help there."

Jimmy came to a stop beside the body facedown on the kitchen floor. "Constance Marks, age twenty-four. That's her blue pickup out there. Self-employed, worked for the admiral, his daughter and some of their friends."

Constance was slim and tanned, wore shorts with a lot of pockets and sneakers with good support, and her blond hair was matted with blood on the crown. More blood stained her shirt and seeped onto the cream-and-white tile of the floor. All that outdoor work had given her solid muscles, which hadn't mattered a damn in the end.

"The servants' quarters are down here." Jimmy led the way through a door between the refrigerator and the wine cooler. Several doors opened off the hallway— a pantry, a closet—and at the end was a living room, kitchen, two bedrooms, and a bath. The rooms were small, the furnishings good but worn. Judging by the kitchen, no expense had been spared in the main house, while none had been wasted here.

Crime Scene Unit techs were at work in both bedrooms. The smells of blood and bodily waste were strong in the air, competing with the scents of furniture polish and antiseptic cleaner. Jimmy stopped in the doorway on the right. "Laura Owen. She put up a struggle—broke the lamp on the nightstand and knocked a pillow off the bed. She has defensive wounds on her hands."

Laura lay on her side, a pair of thick-lensed glasses

broken next to her. She was short, chubby and her face bore the distinctive features of Down syndrome. Her nightgown was white cotton, sleeveless, covered with pastel bunnies, and a ragged stuffed rabbit lay on the floor near her, its floppy ear just touching the blood.

"What kind of guy kills a mentally disabled kid just for being here?" Jimmy asked with a shake of his head.

"You think a low IQ should be a disqualifying condition for murder?" The CSU techs snickered. "Then you'd be safe, wouldn't you?"

Alia turned across the hall to the other bedroom, and Jimmy followed her. "Wilma Owen. Killed in her sleep. No defensive wounds."

Wilma Owen was in her late sixties, maybe early seventies, her hair white, her face bearing the lines of long life and troubles. If not for the blood that turned much of her bedding red, she would appear peacefully asleep.

Alia stepped back as two ME's investigators came in with body bags, then she and Jimmy returned the way they'd come. "Any sign of forced entry besides the broken glass in the rear door?"

"No. And that lock's not double-keyed, so someone could get in there easily."

They walked through a swinging door into the formal dining room, filled with antiques. Jeremiah Jackson might have spent his life serving his country, but there'd been no need. His ancestors had amassed a fortune before the Civil War and had been among the few to hold onto it postwar. Jeremiah could have lived in luxury without ever working a day.

First question of a homicide investigation: who stood to benefit from the victim's death?

They left the dining room for a broad hallway, easily bigger than some of the rooms. The rugs underfoot were old and valuable, the furniture costly, the art objects rare. And the man who'd owned it all had worked seventy and eighty-hour weeks, deploying for months at a time, missing important family events, being an absentee husband and father for thirty years.

As they approached the elaborate front door, she gestured toward the alarm keypad nearby. The light glowed green. "Was the alarm set?"

"We're guessing not. You know how many people invest in fancy alarm systems, then not use them. Somebody like Jackson probably thought he was above common crime."

There was a certain level of arrogance to anyone who attained the rank of admiral. The admiralty was small and select, theoretically only the best of the best. She could well imagine Jackson believing he was invulnerable, especially in his own home. Alia's father had a bit of that smugness, but her mother kept it under control.

Jimmy turned up the stairs, and she followed. On the landing halfway up, she stopped to study a portrait. It was an oil and showed the admiral, a mere commander at the time, in his choker whites with his family—wife, son, daughter. Jackson appeared stern but proud, the wife fragile. The daughter, nine, maybe ten years old, stood next to her father and smiled brightly, while the son, almost a teen, looked remote. Withdrawn.

It could be difficult, growing up the only son of an ambitious, hard-ass career officer. It had been tough for Alia at times, being an only child. Such fathers tended to have expectations of their children, and they didn't take disappointment lightly.

"What about the family? You mentioned the daughter."

"Mary Ellen. Married to Scott Davison, lives a couple streets over, has two daughters."

"The son?"

"Jeremiah the third. Goes by Landry, his mama's maiden name. Works at a bar down in the Quarter and lives above it. Doesn't visit the old homestead often."

The esteemed Rear Admiral Jackson's only son tended bar. Yeah, growing up had definitely been tough for Jeremiah III. "And the mother?"

"Camilla. A bit of a mystery there."

She waited for him to go on, but he was gazing at the portrait. He'd always had an eye for the ladies, even those old enough to be his own mother, one of the reasons he and Alia were no longer married.

"What's the mystery?"

"Huh?" He jerked his attention from the painting. "Oh. She hasn't been seen for three, four weeks—no one's really sure how long. The admiral told his neighbor she was visiting relatives. His daughter said the same. Gossip says she ran off, alone or with a boyfriend, or that she's in a private hospital somewhere. They say she never was very strong, and that she drank to get through the times her husband was gone." After a reflective moment, Jimmy finished. "Maybe it was the times he was home she needed help."

That was one thing Alia had no experience with. Her father may have worn the silver stars in the family, but her mother was the boss. She had a strength that no three admirals could match and was proud of it. She'd taught Alia to be strong, too—one of Jimmy's complaints about her. She'd never needed him, he'd said, and he was probably right.

"Where do you learn all these things?" she asked as they started up the last section of stairs.

"Hey, I'm a detective. Finding out stuff is what they pay me for." Then he relented. "As important as Jackson is in navy circles, he's that and more in New Orleans society, which means the gossip is plentiful. You just have to know who to ask."

It was easy to find the admiral's bedroom: it was the one where personnel swarmed, collecting evidence. Alia paused before reaching the doorway, taking quick short breaths through her mouth. Seeing the awful things that one human being could do to another never got any easier.

Two steps took her to the doorway, one more inside. The room was huge: sitting area in front of a fireplace; a delicate writing desk overlooking a front window; a massive bed; a door opening into a bathroom and closet. It was one of Louisiana's quirks that old houses traditionally lacked closets, but this one was an exception.

The furniture, the art on the walls, the knickknacks on tables, the Middle Eastern rugs—all costly. It was overdone for Alia's tastes, too cluttered, too much pattern and color and far too rich, but the room looked exactly what it was: a personal space for a wealthy couple in a lavish mansion.

If one could dismiss the blood.

It was a lot of blood, an entire life's worth. It covered the admiral's chest, saturated the sheets, soaked the mattress. There were small splatters on the wall, the shade of the lamp on the night table, the pristine white pillowcase on the opposite side of the bed, a few drops on the floor. Blood was slick. It made knives slip in wet grips, often causing killers to cut themselves. Would some of this blood belong to the killer?

Finally she forced herself to focus on the victim. He was a few inches shorter than six feet, broad shouldered, barrel-chested. At one time he'd been solid muscle, but living the good life of the admiralty had put some extra weight on him. His hair was white, thick, and his blue eyes were open, staring sightlessly toward the ceiling. Had his attacker been the last thing he'd seen in life? Had he known him? Had he known the reason for his death?

"The splatter is cast-off from the knife." Jimmy gestured to the deadly blade still sticking out of Jackson's chest. "It's a butcher knife from downstairs."

"Time of death?"

"About 5:00 a.m., best guess. We'll know more when we get him on the table," answered the coroner's investigator. "He was likely asleep. Didn't even get his hands up to defend himself."

"So someone comes here, breaks in without a weapon and kills four people?" *What's wrong with this picture?* It wasn't a burglary gone wrong—too many small items of great value left in place. It wasn't a planned murder. No one on a mission to kill would come without a weapon. That left a crime of passion or a killer too disorganized to plan. A killer with serious psychological problems. "Is anything obvious missing?"

"Don't know," Jimmy said. "The daughter's going to come over tomorrow, after the bodies have been removed, and take a look around. She's here four, five times a week according to the neighbor."

He gestured to the door, and she went back into the broad hallway.

"Remember when you served me with divorce papers, you said that was the end of us?" He grinned that big ole grin. "Guess you were wrong about that. Sweet pea, we're gonna be working this case together. You're gonna be my partner."

Landry Jackson had driven to the Garden District intending to go straight to his sister's house, but he hadn't been able to resist stopping at the family home. He'd parked a few blocks over, added a baseball cap to help the dark shades for a bit of camouflage and had been standing in the shade of a crape myrtle for the past half hour, just one more among the neighbors, reporters and the morbidly curious milling around. A few of the older neighbors seemed vaguely familiar, but he doubted any of them remembered him or would recognize him if they did.

There were whispers that confirmed what Mary Ellen had told him in her hysterical phone call earlier, that the admiral was dead. They didn't stir any emotion in him, not even the relief he'd always expected to feel once the old man passed. Certainly no sadness. No regret.

His shrink's voice echoed from years past. *You don't owe him anything. Being a parent doesn't automatically entitle a person to respect or love or anything else.*

In the Jackson household, being a child didn't entitle a person to those things, either.

He stared at the house where he'd grown up, too much, too fast, and tried to summon a few happy memories. They were there. They just didn't want to sneak out into the light at the moment. Mostly, he remembered relief every time the admiral went away, dread every time he came back. Mostly he didn't want to remember anything, good or bad.

A murmur went up around him as two people started down the driveway toward the gate. The reporter next to him was muttering into his cell phone, and Landry listened without much interest. "Primaries appear to be Jimmy DiBiase with NOPD, and the woman is NCIS. Uh, Leah, Lina. No, Alia. Alia Kingsley. Huh."

Landry was familiar with DiBiase from the news, the paper and his regular partying on Bourbon Street. He didn't think he'd ever seen Alia Kingsley, though he could have and just skimmed right over her. Her hair was stark black, tightly braided, her features average with a hint of the East—Filipina, maybe, or Japanese—and her navy skirt and jacket with light blue shirt and ugly heels were just slightly this side of flattering. Did she not know how to dress to suit her less than curvy body or did she downplay her looks deliberately?

They stopped in the middle of the drive to talk to a group of men in suits—NOPD detectives, NCIS agents— who all listened while Kingsley spoke. Her gaze roamed dismissively over the media—they showed up for every major crime—and settled briefly on the others. Landry was turning away when it reached him, like a laser between his shoulder blades. He couldn't resist glancing back at her, their gazes connecting for an instant, then he slipped through the crowd and headed to his car.

His skin was damp with sweat by the time he'd jogged the few blocks to Miss Viola's house, whose driveway he'd borrowed. The old lady was waiting on her porch, a mug of hot tea on a table next to a half-eaten slice of buttered toast and a bottle of cold water. "Well?" For an eighty-one-year-old woman, she put a wealth of meaning into that single word.

Bypassing his car, he climbed the steps and leaned

against the railing near her. She offered the bottle, and he drank half of it before answering. "They're not releasing any information yet, but the rumors appear to be true."

"Jeremiah Jackson Junior is dead." Miss Viola wasn't any sorrier than he was, though she'd known the admiral his entire life. "This much fuss for just him?"

"No. Apparently the Owens, too, and the gardener's truck was there."

"Poor Laura. And Constance…oh, she loved her work and was finally making good money at it. She takes care of my lawn, too, and she's meticulous." Miss Viola's gaze wandered across the yard as if realizing she would never see Constance in it again.

After a solemn moment, she said, "I understand why someone would kill Jeremiah, but why the others? Why Laura? The girl wouldn't have hurt a fly and couldn't have been much of a witness."

"You know the kind of people the admiral associated with."

"May they all rot in hell." After sipping her tea, Miss Viola waved toward his car. "Go on now and get over to Mary Ellen's. You don't know how this is going to hit her. Tell her to call me if she needs a thing."

"I will." Landry finished the water in another swallow, then set the bottle back on the table. He was halfway down the steps when she called out.

"Obviously you remember where I live. Come by once in a while. I miss your face."

He smiled fondly and repeated his answer. "I will."

It wasn't far from Miss Viola's house to Mary Ellen's. Like the Jackson house, it dated to the early 1800s and was large, gracious, the very image of a Southern mansion with its broad porches and tall columns. It sat in the middle of the block, large expanses of lawn on either side, an American flag flying from a bracket on one column, a small pink bicycle overturned on the sidewalk.

Landry parked behind his brother-in-law's Mercedes and took the side steps onto the porch. His knock at the door was answered so quickly that the housekeeper must have been hovering nearby. "Mr. Landry," she greeted him grimly.

"Miss Geneva."

"Your sister is in the sunroom." As an afterthought, she added, "I'm sorry for your loss."

Don't be. I'm not. But he politely thanked her. "Are the girls here?"

"No, Mr. Scott dropped them at a friend's house."

He nodded and headed down the wide corridor to the sunroom at the back of the house. He was sorry to have missed Faith and Mariela—they were the very best of the Jackson family—but glad they weren't here to deal with emotions they didn't understand.

The sun porch spanned the width of the house, enclosed on three sides with glass, with double doors that opened onto the porch and the yard beyond. Despite the heat of the day, the windows and doors were open, the ceiling fans overhead moving the heavy air in a futile attempt to provide cooling. Mary Ellen liked the heat. Sometimes she joked that she was just a tropical girl, but once, in a particularly melancholy moment, she'd told him that she could never get warm, no matter how she tried.

He understood the feeling.

She sat in a wicker rocker, arms folded across her middle, staring into the distance at something no one else could see. She did that a lot, and if questioned about it, she laughed and said her mind liked to wander. If she could see the stark, gut-wrenching look on her face at those times, she would probably never laugh again.

Her husband, sitting on a footstool in front of her, was first to notice Landry. "Mary Ellen, look, your brother's here."

She didn't look. Didn't give any sign that she'd heard Scott.

Scott met Landry halfway and shook hands. "I'm glad you came. Have you heard anything else?"

Breathing deeply of the flowering plants that filled the room, Landry shook his head. He would let the authorities tell them that the old man wasn't the only victim. She knew Constance and the Owens way better than he did, and he'd always been the one experiencing bad news. He didn't deliver it. "How is she holding up?"

"She's been like that since she called you. Hasn't cried a tear."

Scott sounded worried, but Landry wasn't. Tears were overrated. Their mother had cried thousands of them when they were still a family. So had Mary Ellen, and Landry had shed a few of his own. It hadn't changed anything. It hadn't made them feel better. There'd been no catharsis.

Navigating around furniture and plants, he crouched in front of his sister and took her hand in his. It was ice-cold. "Hey, Mary Ellen."

Her gaze shifted slowly, a millimeter at a time, until it connected with his. A wobbly smile touched her mouth, then slipped away. "It's true, isn't it, Landry? It really is true. Daddy's dead."

"Yeah, he is."

The tears that had concerned Scott welled in her

brown eyes, so much like Landry's, but didn't spill over. "I knew," she whispered. "I felt it all the way deep inside, but I kept thinking…"

That it might be a mistake. That it was never good to celebrate prematurely.

Though she seemed to be leaning toward mourning. Why? What had she seen in the admiral that made him worth mourning? Things had been no better for her than for Landry, worse even. She'd been fragile, like their mother, and in her eyes, her escape had been as bad as the situation she'd left.

But the concept of family had always been important to Mary Ellen. She heaped her family with love and respect and expectations; she forgave them anything. She stood by them no matter what. She'd even been trying from the day he left the family to bring him back into it. She'd succeeded only as far as the next generation. No way was he going to let the admiral drive him away from his nieces.

Mary Ellen's eyes widened as if she'd just thought of something, and her fingers tightened around his in a grip that was painful. *So much for fragile.* "Oh, Landry, how will we tell Mama? She'll be so heartbroken. He was her life."

Landry blinked. He'd never been sure their mother loved their father. Camilla was wellborn, but the family had fallen on hard times. Her daddy would have sold her to the highest bidder to hold on to the family property. Jeremiah, a mere ensign at the time, had been looking for a wife suitable to the illustrious Jackson family as well as his journey into the upper echelons of navy command. Landry had never figured their marriage for anything more than a business arrangement.

"Mary Ellen, we don't even know where she is." After too many years with the old man, Camilla had finally taken off. Miss Viola had been the one to tell Landry, calling him at the bar, asking if Camilla had discussed her plans with him. *You know I only see her twice a year.* From the time he'd left home, she'd always tracked him down on his birthday and at Christmas. He'd visited with her awhile at Mary Ellen's wedding—with the admiral glowering from a distance—and again when the girls were born. That was it.

Mary Ellen's expression turned wistful. "Every time the phone rings, I hope... The girls and I pray for her every night before bed." Her gaze slanted his way. "We pray for you, too."

Landry wasn't sure what to say to that. They'd gone to mass every week as kids, and he'd said a lot of prayers, but the only answer he'd ever got was silence. God's ears were obviously closed to some people's pleas, and he was one of them.

Ignoring her last comment, he watched her closely as he asked, "Did you know she was leaving? Did she say goodbye to you? Did she say anything at all to suggest...?"

He could see Camilla neglecting to mention it to *him*. Their mother-son relationship had run its course. But after Mary Ellen's years away at boarding school, the two had been close, especially once the babies had come along.

There were no shadows in Mary Ellen's eyes, no guilt or deceit crossing her face, just a wounded-deer look. "No. I never understood. But Daddy said..."

Like the bastard wouldn't lie? Rear Admiral Jeremiah Jackson Junior would be the last man to admit that his wife of more than thirty years had taken off for a better life. The disrespect would be more than his ego could afford.

Wherever Camilla was, Landry hoped she was happy. God knew, she deserved it.

Soft footsteps sounded in the hall a moment before Geneva appeared in the doorway. "Mr. Scott, the police are here. They want to talk to Miss Mary Ellen."

As Scott nodded, Landry pried his hand free of his sister's and stood, the muscles in his calves stinging in relief. He moved behind her, finding a spot to lean against the wall, grateful for the tall plants and busy wallpaper that would buy him a few minutes of time, and watched silently as Jimmy DiBiase came through the doorway. Following a few steps behind him was Alia Kingsley.

They introduced themselves to Mary Ellen and Scott, expressed their condolences, took a seat and began asking questions. *When was the last time you saw your father? Talked to him? Were at his house?* Landry listened to his sister's answer, one to cover them all: *I was at the house last night. Scott was working late, and the girls and I walked over to have dinner with him. We stayed until eight. I had to get them home for bedtime.*

If she'd forgiven their father, she was a bigger person than Landry. Granted, he wasn't big on forgiveness in general. He would have sooner killed the man than forgiven him—a sentiment better kept to himself under the circumstances.

The interview had gone on about five minutes when Landry made the mistake of exhaling and setting the delicate leaves of the plant beside him fluttering. Alia Kingsley's gaze cut his way, laserlike in its intensity, and recognition flashed in her eyes. She interrupted DiBiase in the middle of a question and bluntly spoke.

"You were outside the house earlier." The smooth skin wrinkled between her eyes as her gaze zeroed in on his face, cataloging it, he had no doubt, for future-suspect reference. "Why? Who are you?"

Mary Ellen glanced over her shoulder, her eyes widening, pink spots forming high on her cheeks. "Oh, where are my manners? I'm sorry. Sometimes he's so quiet, I forget he's around." Her smile fluttered, and so did her hands. "Special Agent Kingsley, Detective DiBiase, this is my brother, Jeremiah Jackson the third."

Chapter 2

As a sardonic smile slowly tilted the corner of Jeremiah III's mouth, it popped into Alia's mind that, unlike his sister, he had no manners. The air of quiet about him was almost predatory. He didn't look the son of Louisiana privilege. His shorts were khaki, faded and worn, and his Hawaiian shirt, though subdued, was still a Hawaiian shirt. It was difficult to tell if his unruly dark brown hair needed a trim or was expensively cut to look that way, but there was no missing the quality of his running shoes, the aged patina of his wristwatch or the distrust and *keep your distance* shimmering the air around him.

It was hard to believe the uncomfortable boy in the Jackson family portrait had grown into this confident man. But weren't her own middle school pictures proof that a person didn't stay gawky, clumsy and a misfit forever?

"Mr. Jackson—"

"Landry."

Her jaw tightened before she could stop it. "You were at your father's house. Why didn't you identify yourself?"

"To who?"

"The officer at the gate?"

"Why?"

"Surely you knew we would want to talk to you."

With easy, lithe movements the failed ballerina in her envied, he pushed away from the wall and moved to stand directly behind Mary Ellen. He rested one hand on the back of her chair, the other on her shoulder, and she reached up to cling to it. "I have nothing to tell you."

Alia ignored his flat statement. "When was the last time you saw your father?"

"A long time ago."

"How long? A year? Two? Ten?"

Landry and Mary Ellen exchanged looks. "Twelve years."

"You're sure of that?"

"It was my wedding," Mary Ellen supplied in a helpful tone. She struck Alia as the peacemaker, the giver, the one who wanted things to go smoothly for everyone else. Such a task could be exhausting work, especially with a father accustomed to command and a brother on the outs with him.

"No family Christmases since then?" Jimmy asked. "Funerals, christenings, anniversaries, birthdays?"

Landry didn't respond. He'd given his answer and was apparently satisfied that it required no explanation.

Mary Ellen's free hand fluttered. "Our family doesn't... Landry isn't big on formal events. He doesn't care about things like holidays and birthdays, except for my girls'. He never misses my girls' birthdays."

But he never saw his father then. Separate occasions, Alia guessed. The grandparents one day, the uncle next. What had happened between the admiral and his son that they couldn't set their problems aside for two hours for a child's birthday party?

"Did your father have any enemies?" Jimmy asked.

For the first time, Scott Davison spoke. "He was an admiral in the United States Navy. You don't reach that rank without making a few enemies along the way."

The higher in pay grade an officer advanced, the fewer the billets, the fiercer the competition. But Jackson's death hadn't been caused by professional envy. It had been much too personal for that.

Beside Alia, Jimmy shifted. "You know, Mr. and Mrs. Davison, Mr. Jackson, things'll go quicker if we talk to you separately. Why don't we—" he gestured to the Davisons "—stay here, and maybe Special Agent Kingsley could take Mr. Jackson into another room…"

Mary Ellen was quick to agree, to start a suggestion on which room, but her brother overrode her. "You like flowers, Special Agent Kingsley? Because my sister grows some of the prettiest ones around."

Alia glanced out the windows at the lush garden, catching a glimpse of Jimmy's mouth twitching in the process. The sunroom was only marginally cooler than the outside temperature, though at least the ceiling fans created a breeze. Outside she would swelter—no doubt the reason Jackson had suggested it.

As she stood, he made a gesture, long lean fingers indicating a set of open doors. Fingers and hands that bore a few scars and calluses but no cuts. No injuries where a blood-slick knife had sliced through skin.

Though a killer with any sense would have worn gloves. Even a crime of passion would have allowed a few moments for finding a pair in the house.

She took the steps down onto the patio, and sweat broke out along her hairline. She loved New Orleans—even kind of loved the humidity—but this was turning out to be one of the heavy, muggy days best spent over an air-conditioning vent. Already her shirt was clinging to her body, and tiny rivulets were rolling down her spine. She swore she could feel blisters forming inside her shoes, and she was already regretting her choice of a suit this morning.

Landry crossed the patio to the yard. With the first step, Alia's heel sank into recently watered grass. She put on her best blank expression, gritted her teeth and walked with him toward the nearest flower bed. "Do you know any of your father's enemies?" she asked evenly.

"Twelve years since I saw him," he reminded her. He'd shoved his hands into his pockets, his gaze on flowers that were, indeed, pretty: tall, strong and healthy, vibrant colors against lush grass and graceful trees.

"What about your mother?"

He tilted his head to one side. "They were married longer than I've been alive. If she were going to kill him, don't you think she would have done it sooner?"

Alia waited a beat before clarifying her question. "Where is your mother?"

"I don't know."

"When was the last time you saw her?"

"Christmas."

Six months ago. The only reason more than a week

passed without Alia seeing her own mother was the thousand miles between them. She could hardly imagine living in the same town, only a few miles apart, and having virtually no contact.

"Is she on vacation? Visiting family or friends? Doing a grand tour of Europe? Volunteering in the rain forests of South America?"

That earned her a sidelong glance but nothing more.

"She must be somewhere, Mr. Jackson."

"I don't know where." Before she could open her mouth again, he went on. "In case you haven't figured it out yet, my parents and I aren't close. Here's what I know about my mother's current whereabouts—one day about three weeks ago, Miss Viola called and asked if I knew she was gone. I didn't. We weren't due to see each other again until September. Mary Ellen confirmed that she was, indeed, gone, off to visit relatives. I asked her which relatives. She said the admiral hadn't told her." He raised both hands in a final *that's all you're gonna get 'cause that's all I know* gesture.

Alia gazed at a giant orange zinnia so brilliant that it made her eyes hurt. So Admiral Jackson had given his daughter minimal information, and she'd accepted it. Because that was how their relationship had always been? He'd dominated and she'd accepted?

Could Camilla be dead? Were the rumors true that she'd been institutionalized or had taken off with a lover?

Feeling Landry's gaze on her, she gently flicked a beetle from the zinnia, then resumed their slow pace. "Who is Miss Viola?"

"Viola Fulsom. She's my mother's father's second cousin three times removed or something."

In simpler words, family. In Louisiana, it didn't matter how many times removed; a cousin was a cousin. And yet in this particular family, father and son were estranged, mother and son virtually so. Father was dead, mother was missing, and son...

Was Jeremiah Jackson III a killer? Had he gone into his childhood home, taken a knife from the kitchen drawer and plunged it into his father's sleeping body more than thirty times?

Alia shuddered deep inside. It didn't matter how many cases she worked, how many crime scenes she saw or what gruesome details she noted in reports and photographs. She couldn't quite grasp the character flaw that made it so easy for a person to take another's life. She could read and talk and investigate, but she couldn't— wouldn't—crawl inside a killer's mind any more than she had to.

"Where does Miss Viola live?"

"Where everyone in our family except me has lived for the past five generations."

The Garden District, with its beautiful houses and wealthy families who sometimes hid more secrets than the darkest bayou.

Alia committed the name to memory. Members of the Jackson and Landry families couldn't hide in Louisiana even if they wanted to. Too much money to spend, too many parties to attend, too many decades of history to uphold. Miss Viola would be easy to locate.

They were approaching a set of fat-cushioned wicker chairs underneath the spreading branches of a live oak near the back corner of the lawn. A bit of breeze blew through there, redolent with the heavy scents of flowers and, fainter, from someone else's yard, food cooking over charcoal. The aroma was enough to remind her that she'd skimped on breakfast and it was nowhere near time for lunch.

After Landry sat in one chair, she took the other. The wicker was the expensive kind that didn't creak with every tiny movement. Crossing her legs, she allowed herself to wonder for a moment what it was like to own a place like this: luxurious, no expenses spared, decorated with antiques and high-end furnishings, wrapped in the long, sultry history of the old, sultry city.

Money doesn't buy happiness, her mother always said, and Alia had always thought it could certainly help. But the Jacksons proved Mom right: they had money, and they weren't happy.

"How long have you lived in New Orleans?"

Landry's head was tilted back, hands folded over his belly, eyes little more than slits. "All my life."

"Your family didn't accompany the admiral to his assignments?"

"Camilla Jackson move away from here, even temporarily? Saint Louis Cathedral would crumble to dust first." Then he did a lazy sort of shrug, so very careless and so very charming to a woman who was the charmable sort.

Thank God, Alia's weakness for charming scoundrels had died somewhere about the middle of her marriage to Jimmy.

"When the old man got orders," he went on, "he went, we stayed here, and he came home on weekends and on leave."

Staying home took all the fun out of the life. She'd been born in the Philippines, started school in Hawaii and finished it in DC, with stops in California, South Carolina, Florida and Virginia. Dropping in at the Pentagon after school had been a regular practice. She'd gotten a gift from the Secretary of the Navy upon high school graduation and even attended a dinner at the White House. "So you missed out on the whole navy brat experience."

"Jeremiah Jackson had no tolerance for bratty behavior."

She would bet he hadn't—not from his children, the sailors under his command or civilians like her who worked for his navy. "What happened between you two?"

She felt the instant he glanced at her. His eyes were still slitted, making it impossible to read their expression, and a small muscle twitched in his jaw. It didn't bother her; people in general didn't like being questioned, especially with suspicion. They tended to get annoyed or smug or tearful or angry, and she tended to stay on track. Stubbornness was one of her better traits, according to Jimmy.

But Landry could probably out-stubborn her. She knew he'd only answered her questions because she'd asked them here at his sister's house. If she had shown up at the bar or his apartment, he would have shown her right back out. She couldn't compel him to tell her anything important—couldn't compel him to talk to her at all—and he knew it.

"I think your partner's ready to go," he said in a slow drawl accompanied by a gesture toward the house.

A quick look showed Jimmy standing in the doorway to the sunroom, watching them with his hands on his hips. "If you think of something you're willing to share…" She rose, pulled a business card from her pocket and offered it to him. When he made no move to take it, she laid it on the arm of his chair, sliding one corner between the woven wicker. It fell through, landing crookedly on the lush grass. Neither of them picked it up. Instead, she cut across the lawn to the house and followed Jimmy inside, then out again through the front door.

Landry watched her until she was out of sight, then slumped lower in his seat and closed his eyes. After the time with her, he'd concluded she was deliberately downplaying her looks with the ugly clothes. In a predominantly male environment, maybe it worked for her, though he couldn't help thinking she'd have better luck if she did the opposite. What man wouldn't prefer to talk to her with a little style to the hair, an airy dress almost thin enough to see through, a little cleavage and sexy, strappy sandals to show off those long, lean legs? They'd tell her what she wanted to know—tell her everything they knew—just to keep her around a little longer.

He heard an engine starting out front, then pushed to his feet. Without picking up the business card, he headed for the house, glancing back only for an instant while climbing the steps. It tilted at an angle, caught between blades of lush green grass. He wouldn't forget her name, and if he ever wanted to talk to her, he could look up the NCIS office number on the computer.

Once she discovered that of all the people who'd hated Jeremiah, no one hated him as much as Landry, she would probably be looking *him* up.

The sunroom was empty. He ran into Scott, heading for the stairway carrying a heavy crystal tumbler filled with milk, warm, no doubt—Mary Ellen's go-to when she needed comfort. Their mother preferred gin, and their father had preferred—

Landry's stomach took a sour tumble that he did his damnedest to ignore. "Is she lying down?"

"Said she would." With his free hand, Scott combed through his hair. "The detective asked us to ask the relatives about Camilla—see if we can find out who she's visiting. I never wanted to say anything to Mary Ellen, but I never thought she *was* visiting family. If she is, why hasn't she called the girls at least once? And why wouldn't the admiral say who? Why the secrecy if it was just a regular trip to visit family?"

Because the admiral was a deceitful man. Landry knew some of his uglier secrets. God, he hoped they were the uglier ones, because he damn well didn't want to think about what could be worse.

"Where do you think she is, then?" His voice was level, but something new stirred deep inside for his mother: worry. Could something have happened to her? Was it coincidence that her husband was murdered just a few weeks after she disappeared?

Scott shifted uncomfortably, glanced up the stairs, then lowered his voice. "I think she left. Left him. Left the marriage. I think she hasn't called Mary Ellen because she knew she would beg her to come back. I think she didn't tell anyone where she was going so he couldn't find her."

Left. Landry had asked her to leave his father but only once. He was fifteen, desperately trying to figure out his own and Mary Ellen's futures, and Camilla had given him a sad, sorry look, murmured, *You don't understand, baby*, then taken a healthy sip of gin.

Left, when there was no one left to save except maybe herself.

"There's other theories." Scott glanced upstairs again.

"Seline Moncrief thinks she ran off with a man. Honoria Thomas thinks the admiral checked her into rehab for her drinking problem. Judge Macklin's wife is convinced that the admiral sent her away because he has no need for her now that he's retiring." He stopped, swallowed hard. "Had no need. Was retiring."

"I hadn't heard that. When?"

"A couple months. Said he'd done his service to his country and now he wanted to devote his time to his family, golfing and fishing."

Inside, Landry shuddered, grateful the old man's definition of *family* no longer included him. He'd had enough quality time with his father to last through eternity.

He said his goodbyes and covered half the distance to the door before Scott spoke again. When he turned, his brother-in-law was paused on the stairs.

"Mary Ellen said she would appreciate it tremendously if you would help her with the funeral arrangements tomorrow, but she'd understand if you said no."

Of course she'd take responsibility for the funeral. Who else would? Leave it to Landry, and he'd have the bastard cremated, then flushed down the toilet. But it wasn't left to him, and though he'd rather do anything else in the world—almost—he would help plan a respectful send-off for the admiral. Not because Jeremiah deserved it, but because Mary Ellen wanted it.

"Let me know when and where."

Scott nodded, and Landry was finally free to walk out of the house…where he found Alia Kingsley waiting on the porch. A glance at the street showed that DiBiase was gone, and there were no cars around that might be hers.

She'd put on a pair of sunglasses, the really dark kind

that made it impossible to see her eyes. He didn't trust people when he couldn't see their eyes.

Hell, he didn't trust most people even when he could see their eyes.

"Forget something?"

"I thought I'd go see Miss Viola now. I need an address."

He headed down the steps. "You're the police. Find her yourself."

"I can do that. But it's quicker if you tell me. Or—" she matched him stride for stride "—I can ask your sister."

"Mary Ellen's resting."

"Then it would be a shame to disturb her, especially after such a difficult morning."

Stopping beside his car, he stared at her, implacably calm and unflustered on the other side of the vehicle. "Three blocks that way." He pointed back the way he'd come. "At Saint Charles. On the left." Then he stated the obvious. "You don't have a car."

The faintest of smiles tilted the corners of her mouth. "It's still at the admiral's house. But I run five miles every day. I can walk three blocks." She turned and started to do just that.

He could let her go—should let her go—but the idea of her questioning Miss Viola alone made a muscle twitch at the back of his neck. The old lady knew all the family secrets. She also knew to keep them to herself. He trusted her on that. At least, he always had.

It was Kingsley he didn't trust.

"I'm headed that way. I'll give you a ride."

She stopped, maybe twenty feet away, and gave him a steady look. He would bet she didn't believe his plan to go by the Fulsom house was more than a minute old, but she returned to the driveway, opened the passenger door and slid into the seat. She rested her hands in her lap. Long fingers, no jewelry, unpolished nails. Was there no Mr. Special Agent Kingsley, or was she one of those people who preferred to not wear a wedding ring?

As he backed the car into the street, he waited for her to start with a new line of questions. She didn't. She didn't complain about the heat in the car, didn't ask him to turn on the air-conditioning for the short drive. For all she made her presence known, he could have been alone.

When he pulled into Miss Viola's drive for the second time that morning, she undid her seat belt and opened the door. "You don't have to get out. I can introduce myself."

"Right." He shut off the engine. Obviously she didn't want him interfering in her interview, but not quite as much as he didn't want Miss Viola letting anything slip.

They climbed the steps, and he rang the bell. A pretty redhead answered, let them into the foyer and left to get Miss Viola. He stood, hands in his pockets, and hoped his cousin was taking a nap, heading out the door to an appointment that couldn't wait or entertaining someone she wouldn't put off just to talk to a cop. The mayor would be nice, the governor even better. Both were frequent guests.

No such luck. A moment later she came into sight, a smile creasing her face. "This is my lucky day, seeing you again so soon after the last time." Her gaze shifted from him to the investigator, but he had no intentions of providing introductions. He wasn't here to make things easier for Alia.

"Ms. Fulsom, I'm Special Agent Alia Kingsley with NCIS. That's the Naval—"

"I know what it is. I watch TV. That Special Agent Gibbs is a fine-looking man, isn't he?" She sighed, then turned serious. "I assume you're here about Jeremiah."

"Yes, ma'am. Is there someplace we can talk privately?"

Miss Viola's frail hand fluttered in his direction. "Oh, honey, Landry knows everything I do. Jeremiah was his father, after all. We'll go into the library." She gestured to the door behind Alia. "The furniture is much more comfortable than the antiques in the rest of the house. Landry, will you bring us iced tea, please?"

Why couldn't she just ask the housekeeper to bring it? he groused. But for the most part, when Miss Viola asked, he obeyed. After giving Alia a sharp look, he went down the hall to the kitchen.

Landry didn't want to leave her alone with Miss Viola. Alia considered that as she followed the woman into the library. Was it just distrust? Or because, turning Ms. Fulsom's words around, she knew everything about Jeremiah that Landry did? Including what had come between father and son.

"You have a lovely home," she said as she took a seat in a black leather chair. The sides curved around, almost like a cocoon, and the cushions had just the right amount of give. It was quite possibly the most comfortable chair she'd ever sat in, and as a bonus, it swiveled and rocked, too.

"It is. I'd give you a tour, but the interesting parts are upstairs, and I don't go up there anymore. Broken hip. Last year. My children turned the ladies' parlor and a few other rooms into a bedroom suite for me, and I haven't been upstairs since."

Her stab at being social taken care of, Alia went right into her questions. Maybe she would learn something before Landry returned. "Ms. Fulsom—"

"Oh, call me Viola like everyone else."

Alia smiled politely. "Miss Viola, how long have you known the admiral?"

"All of his wo—" Viola stopped, grimaced, then finished. "Life."

What had she been about to say? His worthless life?

"You don't regret his passing."

"That would be unchristian of me, wouldn't it?" Then the woman shrugged. "I've been a good Christian my entire life. God will forgive me this lapse, don't you think?"

"Why did you dislike him?"

"Did you know him?" she asked in a manner that suggested that would be explanation enough. "The way he treated Camilla, the children, everyone he thought was somehow inferior to him—which included pretty much everyone he ever met."

Alia glanced toward the open doorway. "You know he and his son were estranged at the time of his death."

"A lot longer than that," Miss Viola corrected her. "The boy's been on his own since he was fifteen and would have been better off if he'd left ten years earlier."

"What happened between them?"

Miss Viola's gaze went distant while she fingered a massive ruby ring on her left hand. There was regret in her dim eyes, along with a touch of anger, a bigger touch of shame and definitely some sorrow. After a moment, she sighed. "Landry learned early on that he wasn't cut out for life in Jeremiah's home."

That could mean a dozen things. Had Jeremiah wanted Landry to follow in his footsteps? Had they disagreed on career, education, religion, the life expected of a Jackson in this city? Had Landry refused to kow-tow to his father, or had he demanded the old man treat Camilla and Mary Ellen better?

"In what ways?" Alia asked as voices—Landry's and the housekeeper's—sounded faintly down the hall. "What expectations did Jeremiah have that Landry wouldn't meet?" *Answer quickly, please*, she silently urged as the voices faded and a lone set of steps headed their way.

Again Miss Viola's gaze drifted before she gave her-self a shake and said, "You know how it is with children and their parents."

As the last word came out, Landry came in, carry-ing three tall glasses of iced tea. He handed one to his cousin, then offered Alia one. The glass was delicate, the kind of stemware her mother saved for special occasions, the tea freshly brewed, sugary and flavored with mint. As she savored a sip, he moved behind her, feigning in-terest in the books open on the ancient oak table there.

She asked Miss Viola a dozen more questions and couldn't help but notice that before she answered even the simplest one, her gaze went to Landry. Delaying to be sure she worded her answer just so or seeking his ap-proval before offering any answer at all? Alia looked at him, too, several times, but his expression never told her a thing. He could be part of the decor for all the overt interest he showed, but Alia was certain he was guid-ing Miss Viola.

Which made the interview pointless.

After a few more questions, Alia set her glass on a nearby table and stood. "I appreciate your time, Miss Viola. If I think of anything else, I'll stop by again." Preferably without any warning so Landry couldn't control the next interview.

"That would be fine." Miss Viola also stood. "If you give me a half hour's notice, I'll have Molly fix one of the desserts she's famous for. The doctor tells me to limit my sweets and fried foods and salt and fat, but heavens, I'm eighty-one years old and in perfect health. If I can't eat what I want, what's the point of making it to eighty-two?"

The three of them moved to the front door, where she and the old lady exchanged goodbyes. Alia walked outside, unsurprised that Landry followed her. He took the steps beside her before asking, "You want a ride to your car?"

What ulterior motive did he have for offering? Was he just making sure that she did, in fact, leave Miss Viola's house? Did he want to see the home where he'd grown up, where his father had died a violent death? Did he think she might offer him an under-the-police-tape visit?

Regardless of his motive, she accepted. With the temperature and humidity both hovering close to one hundred, the couple blocks' walk would sap a good chunk of her energy.

Again, the trip was made in silence. This time he didn't pull into the driveway, even though the young officer waiting there would have let them pass. He parked across the street and didn't even glance to his left.

"It's a beautiful house," Alia said, watching him closely.

His only response was the twitch of a taut muscle in his jaw.

"You haven't been here in twelve years?"

Another faint twitch. "Closer to seventeen."

"Miss Viola said you left home when you were fifteen. Was that the last time you saw the place?"

"Yeah."

"Going out on your own at fifteen…" Alia gave a shake of her head. At fifteen she'd thought she was grown-up and competent, but her parents had known better. She wouldn't have made it two days on the street all by her lonesome. "Why did your mother let you do that?"

"She had no choice." He glanced at her, then at the street ahead, and murmured, "He never gave any of us a choice."

The words were soft, not meant for her to hear, and the expression on his face was bitter, resigned. She knew from cases she'd worked that some parents lived to make their children's lives miserable, but she didn't understand it. Why bring a child into the world if all you intended to do was torment it?

Obviously Jeremiah Jackson had tormented his son.

And that made Landry a viable suspect in Jeremiah's death.

She asked the question she should have asked first thing back at Mary Ellen Davison's house. "Where were you between three and six this morning?"

He looked at her then, dark eyes locking on her face. There was no guilt in them, no emotion whatsoever, but that didn't mean anything. She'd met some skilled liars in her life—had even married one. Popular myths aside, there was no way to look at a person and know beyond a doubt that he was lying.

"I was at the bar. Got roped into filling in for one of my boss's poker buddies. I didn't get home until a quarter to six."

"So you didn't kill your father."

Again, he took a long time to answer, and again, his features were unreadable. "No," he said at last, breaking gazes with her, gesturing toward the passenger door, a clear sign he wanted her to get out.

She did so and was about to close the door when he looked at her again. "But I wish I had."

"Watch who you say that to." Closing the door, she circled behind the car to cross the street. The cop on guard was young, probably very new, hot and in need of a break. She smiled at him as she passed, climbed to the top of the incline, then grabbed a lawn chair and toted it back down. "No protocol says you have to pass out from the heat while you're on watch."

"Thank you, ma'am."

"Anybody been here who doesn't belong?"

"Reporters. Some of 'em are still taking pictures across the street."

She leaned past him to see the small pods of camera-wielding people on the far side of the street.

"Some people claiming to be relatives stopped by, too. Wanted to go in and get some precious little something-or-other the admiral or his wife promised 'em the last time they were here."

"Ah, families. Gotta love them."

She climbed the driveway again, studying the windows, the outdoor spaces, the lawn, the flowers, the detached garage. How well had the killer known this place? Had he been a regular guest? Had he lived for a time in one of those curtained rooms upstairs? Had he been a she, come back from her own disappearance to take revenge on the husband who'd cost her a son?

Once she was inside the house, she wandered through

the common areas downstairs before going upstairs. This time she ignored the admiral and Camilla's suite, turning the opposite direction. The first room she came to was a guest room—lovely, richly decorated. Across the hall was another, and next to it, a girl's room. This room was impressive and, judging from the pristine state and the faint scent of paint, recently decorated.

The admiral had two young granddaughters, just the right age to appreciate the whimsical colors and design of the room. Every girlie princess fantasy had been incorporated into the space, with enough toys and dress-up clothes to make any girl happy to move in.

The whole prissy/happiness/light room made Alia shudder.

Back into the hall and down to the last remaining door. The knob creaked when she turned it. It was one of those curtained rooms she'd noticed outside. It smelled stuffy, and a flick of the light switch illuminated a layer of dust everywhere. Pale blue walls, a single bed, a desk and wooden chair, a bookcase. No pictures on the walls, no linens on the bed, no television or computer or books on the shelves. No keepsakes. No clothes in the closet. No sign that anyone had lived in the room in the past twenty years.

Or, at least, seventeen.

They hadn't kept anything that showed a fifteen-year-old boy had lived here, hated here, plotted to escape from here.

Landry would probably be happy that they'd sanitized his memory from the room. After all, he sure appeared to work hard at sanitizing their memories from his life.

Chapter 3

As Landry lost sight of the Jackson home in the rear-view mirror, he took a few deep breaths of relief. Now he could go home. Push his family back into the dark little corner they belonged, at least until morning. Go back to being just Landry instead of Jeremiah Jackson III.

Blue Orleans, the bar where he worked, was located in the French Quarter, an old brick building that stood, faintly crooked, between a restaurant and a vacant storefront. The job came with an apartment upstairs and his own off-street parking. He pulled into the space that ended at an elaborate iron gate set into a matching fence and kept anyone without a key away from the courtyard and the apartments beyond. Beyond the fence, there was a fountain, flower beds and brick walkways that led to two doors downstairs and two sets of stairs, one for each place upstairs.

He took the stairs on his left, coming out on a long landing that had been a balcony in the original house. The brass numeral three that had fallen off the door long ago had left an impression of the number in faded red paint. In fact, *faded* was the best description for the entire building. What had been a pricey, showy home fifteen decades ago reminded him of an aging, wrinkled beauty queen: a ghost of its former loveliness but with its grace and gentility intact.

He'd just finished opening a few windows when his cell rang. After a glance at the screen, he debated answering long enough for the caller to hang up. A moment later, the phone beeped, signaling a voice mail. In the cool, dim light of his bedroom, he sprawled across the bed before playing the message, closing his eyes at the soft greeting.

"Landry, it's Dr. Granville. I heard the news about Captain Jackson… I guess I should make that Admiral. I understand he's been promoted since the last time I saw you. Anyway, hearing the news made me think of you, and I wanted to tell you if you need to talk—and you know, of course, that I think you should—I'm still here or I can refer you to someone else." The faintly accented voice paused before going on. "Take care of yourself through this, Landry."

He noticed as the message clicked off that she hadn't offered condolences.

Victoria Granville, blonde, British and beautiful, was a few years younger than his mother and knew him better than anyone, including his mother. Without her, he wasn't sure he would have survived being Jeremiah's son.

But he didn't need to talk to her now. He was okay with his father's death. His only care was a vague sort of relief. The admiral was dead. Now he could burn in the fires of hell, where he belonged, and Landry...

Landry was free. At last. Thank God.

He just didn't feel that way yet.

He dozed awhile, but his sleep was restless. Funny how things never changed. He was thirty-two years old, but in his dreams he was just a kid again, gangly, scrawny, and couldn't defend himself or anyone else. In that same realm, Jeremiah was always three times larger than life, menacing, cruel, willing to squash Landry like a bug. *No one will notice if you're gone. No one will miss you.*

Right back at you, old bastard, Landry thought as he changed into clean shorts and a T-shirt advertising the club. He'd begun working at Blue Orleans before he was old enough to legally set foot in the door, running errands, tending bar on occasion, helping to throw out the belligerent drunks. His boss, Maxine, had always counted policemen among her clientele; a few free drinks or a food run down the street for the best po'boys in the city made them overlook the underage help.

Tonight Landry hadn't been on the clock long before the first cop he could identify strolled through the doors: Jimmy DiBiase, still wearing the white shirt and dark pants, looking pretty wrung out. Landry's gaze automatically looked past to see if Kingsley was following him, but there was no sign of her.

"Give me something cold on ice." DiBiase slid onto the bar stool in front of Landry, lifted a handful of peanuts from the dish and cracked one.

"You wanna be more specific?"

The cop glanced over both shoulders, then said, "Water'll do."

Landry filled a tall glass with ice, then topped it off with his bottled water supply beneath the bar. He added a straw, a few wedges of lemon and lime, then set it down. "Where's your partner? I thought you guys were attached at the hip."

DiBiase smiled. "Nah, the divorce decree pretty much took care of that."

Landry couldn't have gone any stiffer without facing physical threat. Divorce decree? Special Agent Kingsley had been married to good ole boy DiBiase? It was a hard pairing to wrap his mind around. The beauty and the beast. The good, the bad and the ugly. She was cool, elegant, prettier than she wanted people to know, and DiBiase was a New Orleans homicide detective. You didn't have to say much more than that for people to get the picture.

DiBiase grinned. "Surprised you, huh? Hell, it surprised me back when she said yes. Not so much when she cut the ties and wished me to the depths of hell."

Now that part was easier to imagine. Alia in a fussy, lacy, girlie gown? Alia promising forever to DiBiase? Settling into life all lovey-dovey as Mr. and Mrs. and planning a future? None of those images would form. But kicking DiBiase to the curb, maybe with a particular level of viciousness? Yeah, he could see that.

DiBiase grinned again. "It was my fault. I can't even point any fingers her way, which is just as well since she'd probably break them." He took a drink, then said reflectively, "Hell, she'd have been justified shooting me a time or two, but she never threatened me with anything more than a stun gun. Believe me, nothing wakes a man up quicker than finding one of those pressed to his throat."

Landry filled an order for one of the waitresses, who smiled coyly at DiBiase while she waited. "You two work together often?" he asked when she left to deliver the drinks. Just making conversation. He didn't give a damn about either DiBiase or Alia Kingsley. He just wanted them out of his—and more importantly, Mary Ellen's—life.

"Nah. We're only doing it now because we've got civilians among the victims, although they tend to get lost in the admiral's shadow."

A lot of people had got lost in the admiral's shadow, pretty much everyone who spent any time with him. Camilla had once said he was the sun around which the world rotated. Her smile at the time, Landry remembered, had been sickly. Sad.

"Your sister's pretty shaken up."

The muscles in Landry's neck tensed. "She's got a soft heart. She cries over roadkill."

DiBiase chuckled, then turned serious in the space of a heartbeat. "I asked her for a list of your parents' friends. We'd like the same from you."

Landry filled an order for another waitress, who also smiled coyly at the cop while she waited, then traded full bottles of Corona for empties for the two guys sitting at the opposite end of the bar. When he returned to DiBiase, he said levelly, "I haven't been part of the family for a long time. I don't really remember any names."

Except for Jeremiah's special friends. He could recite those names in his sleep: a lawyer, the head of New Orleans's largest advertising firm, a university dean, an adviser to a governor. People hidden deep in memory, frequently appearing in bad dreams.

Maybe the dreams would stop when they were all dead, too.

"See what you can come up with," DiBiase said. Rising from the stool, he drained the last of the water, then headed out the door.

Or maybe the dreams wouldn't stop until *he* was dead.

With notes scattered around her, her laptop and tablet both on the coffee table and a bowl of buttered popcorn next to her, Alia looked up to give her eyes a break. The ceiling fan swirled slowly, enough to cool, not enough to mess up her piles, and an impossibly thin woman on the television talked in an impossibly cheery voice about the miracle bra she held in her hands.

A glance at the clock showed it was nine, which made it seven in Coronado, California, where her parents lived. She called them most Mondays, Thursdays and Saturdays, except when social plans interfered—her parents', not hers. She went on dates occasionally and had a girls' night out once a month. Otherwise, it was pretty much work all the time.

How am I going to get grandchildren at this rate? her mother good-naturedly complained.

Better adopt them, was Alia's usual response. It was her job to protect kids when she could, to get justice for them when she couldn't. Let someone else have them. Hell, she didn't even want a pet.

Wriggling out from under everything without upsetting it, she got to her feet and padded into the kitchen for a refill on her drink. Mornings, she mainlined coffee; during the day, she stuck with water; alone in the evenings, she drank Kool-Aid. Jimmy had given her a hard time about it until she'd put him in a wrist lock and brought him to his knees.

He'd learned not to get between a girl and her Kool-Aid.

With her glass in one hand, she grabbed a half dozen bite-size candy bars from the dish on the counter and headed back to the living room, where she traded the candy for her cell phone. Her mother answered after only two rings.

"Hey, *mamacita*."

Her mother sniffed. "That's *mę* to you, *chica*. Hold on. Your father's trying to take the phone away from me." There was an admonishment, then the sound of a door closing before her mom said, "I'm back."

"I take it Dad's seen the news."

"The news, the internet, his old navy shipmates' gossip loop. We saw you just for a few seconds on the national news. You looked thin."

"I am thin, Mom."

"Are you sleeping well?"

"Yes."

"Eating well?"

Alia looked at the empty wrappers on the coffee table: one hamburger, superlarge fries and two tacos, along with butter-stained napkins from the popcorn. "Yep." Was it her fault if her mother defined *eating well* as a balanced meal while Alia took it to refer to quantity?

Mom sniffed again. "We also saw Jimmy on that news clip. You keep your distance from him."

"Kind of hard, Mom. We're working the case together."

There was a moment of silence before Lisa sighed. "I don't know whether to be more worried about the ugly things you see or that you're looking for a crazed killer or that you're spending time with Jimmy DiBiase."

Knowing she couldn't reassure her mom about the first two—Lien Hieu Kingsley would never believe her daughter was grown enough to see ugly things or deal with ugly people—Alia said lightly, "I'm immune to Jimmy now."

"You loved him so much."

"I did. Until I didn't." It hadn't been easy, especially when she'd thought he meant the vows he'd taken, but trust and love could survive only so many betrayals. One too many, and her love had stopped. One moment it was there. The next it was gone, never to return.

"Uh-oh. Your father found me. You be careful, sweetie."

"I will, Mom."

Again, there was the soft sound of conversation before her father came on the line. "How are you, scooter?"

"Never gonna live down that name, am I?"

"Aw, but you were so cute with that toy scooter. You rode it everywhere you went, to meet me at the door, to the dining room, to the potty."

"I tell people you call me that because I ate scooter pies after every meal for years."

"Well, there is that." His chuckle was followed by a hesitation, then… "Are you assigned to the case?"

"Yes, sir." He'd never made her call him *sir.* There had been Daddy, then Dad and the occasional rank. But when it came to work, well, she was an NCIS agent, and he was an admiral. Retired or not, it was hard to shake the *sir.*

She would bet *sir* or rank had been the only titles Jeremiah Junior had accepted from Landry and Mary Ellen.

Finally she got to the point of tonight's call. "Did you know him?"

"There aren't that many admirals. You can't help but meet them all sooner or later."

"What did you think of him?"

"Jerry was a good officer. Hard-nosed. Strict. By the book, but fair. He never asked more of the people under his command than he gave himself."

"Did you ever meet his wife?"

"Hmm. Not that I can recall."

"She and the son and daughter didn't accompany him to any of his duty stations, but I thought maybe she'd shown up for some official functions."

"I remember him talking about his daughter like she was the prettiest, smartest, best daughter in the world, which was ridiculous since everyone already knew that was you. But I never knew he had a son. Huh. I would have figured any son of Jeremiah Jackson would have wound up in the navy himself."

Just like any son of Charles Kingsley's. Alia hadn't been willing to go quite that far, but she couldn't deny his approval had played a role in her application to NCIS.

Though he would have loved her no matter what career path she'd chosen. Could Landry Jackson say that about his own father?

She doubted it.

"It's gonna be one hell of a funeral," Dad said.

"I bet it will be." It would have been a spectacle even if he'd died peacefully in his sleep, between all the senior-ranking officers and Pentagon officials, the upper crust of New Orleans society and the city's love of a good funeral. But with the admiral brutally murdered, his daughter in shock, his son's presence unwilling, his wife's whereabouts unknown and law enforcement scrutinizing everyone in attendance, it just might be a circus.

"If you weren't working, I'd be tempted to come. Show my respects to Jerry. See New Orleans. See you. It's been a long time."

Alia smiled. She'd flown to California for Christmas and stayed nearly two weeks. Still, it was nice to know he missed her. "I'll let you know all the gaudy details. Maybe someone will collapse beside the casket and confess all."

"It would be convenient, wouldn't it? You watch out for yourself, okay?"

"I always do, Dad." She hung up, then unwrapped a candy bar. She bit it in half and let the chocolate slowly dissolve in her mouth while thinking about what her father had said. *Jerry was a good officer.* How much had Jeremiah hated being called Jerry? Likely someone who outranked him had first called him that, and others had picked up on it.

But the admiral hadn't been murdered because he was a good officer. His death had had nothing to do with the navy and everything to do with being a privileged man who felt entitled to whatever he wanted.

So what had he wanted that led to his death?

Alia was pulling out of her driveway Tuesday morning at a quarter to eight, with an oversize travel mug of coffee in the cup holder, a .40 caliber pistol and a Taser in their holsters, and a cream cheese–slathered bagel in her left hand. It was going to be another hot and muggy day, and she expected to spend little, if any, time in the office, so she'd dressed accordingly in a sleeveless blouse and skirt with a belt to hold her badge and weapons. A jacket, to cover the weapons, sat on the passenger seat.

The neighborhood where she lived consisted of three main streets: Serenity, Divinity and Trinity. It had gone through several phases in its history, from upper middle class to mostly slum, then back to respectability. Though some houses remained shuttered and decaying, in the past ten years new owners had given most of them new life. The gangbangers had been forced out, the local church was flourishing, and the neighborhood had its own market, preschool and two restaurants. They hadn't had a violent crime in their few blocks in three years.

Alia had talked to Jimmy while dressing, arranging to meet midmorning to trade notes from yesterday. First, though, she was going to surprise Miss Viola and find out if the old lady was any more forthcoming about the Jackson family without a Jackson in the room.

With the radio providing background noise, Alia took a bite of bagel, savored the oniony dough and the creamy cheese and wished she'd tossed a handful of candy bars into her bag. Breakfast, no matter what it was, was always more satisfying with chocolate.

Her mind wandered as she drove, mostly to the whereabouts of Camilla Kingsley. Landry had said she'd had no choice when he'd left home. *He never gave any of us a choice*, he'd muttered. What about now? At her age, had she earned the right to make a few decisions for herself, such as this trip out of town? When she heard the news of her husband's death, would she return home? Was she even alive to hear the news?

Maybe Miss Viola would tell her more than she'd volunteered yesterday.

The Fulsom home looked even statelier today. The

white columns and siding gleamed in the morning sun. The dew-dampened grass seemed greener, the pastels of the flowers overflowing the beds softer. Alia parked in the driveway, in the dappled shade of an oak, got out and glanced around. A tall wrought iron fence circled the backyard, and the flowering vines that grew over it blocked even a glimpse inside while perfuming the air with their sweet jasmine.

A dog barked across the street, and a lawn mower sounded nearby. A woman sat on a porch swing—mother or nanny—while a small girl played with dolls. Life as usual.

Alia climbed the steps, weaving past a pair of antique rockers, bypassing a breakfast table and two chairs, reaching the door. She would bet every area of the house, inside and out, offered little seating areas for private conversations, both good and bad.

At the door, she pressed the bell, listening to its deep tones echoing inside. She pressed her ear close to the wood of the door, straining for any answering response. No footsteps. No call for housekeeper Molly to answer the door with a plate of her famous desserts in hand.

Alia moved to the right, sliding behind a settee to look inside the nearest window of the library. Fingers cupped to the glass to deflect reflections, she noted the old oak library table, the chair where she'd sat, the shelves she'd faced. Her gaze swept to the left, through the open doors into the entryway: elegant stairs sweeping to the second floor, a painting of a Fulsom ancestor on the wall above a demilune table, a priceless chandelier casting more shadows than it banished…and a small pink-clad shape on the floor.

Her breath caught in her chest. The form was thin,

tiny, the pink a robe, one slipper to match, mussed white hair. The body lay mostly on a rug at the foot of the stairs, but the pale, frail hands were on the polished floor, fingers spread wide, the ruby ring catching a ray of light.

"Aw, Miss Viola," she whispered. "Damn…"

Turning her back on the window and retreating a few steps, she called Jimmy, then her supervisor. Maybe they would be lucky, and Miss Viola's death would be accidental. The old lady was eighty-one. Maybe she'd fallen, her heart had stopped or she'd suffered a stroke. Maybe it had just been her time. Maybe it wasn't related, just purely coincidental to the other murders.

But if they weren't lucky, the body count had just reached five. Were there more deaths to come?

Letting the scene process in the back of her mind, Alia began a walk around the house, looking for any signs of forced entry. Locating an unsecured gate into the backyard, she went through it, cell phone in one hand, pistol in the other.

She'd expected small elaborate gardens, an enormous swimming pool, a cabana or two, sprawling seating for fifty, a tiled or wood platform to support Miss Viola's favorite string quartet or for speech-giving at political fund-raisers.

The space was lovely, but beyond a modest red-brick patio down a few steps from the veranda, it was all garden: vegetable, shade, orchard and flowers. Standing on the patio, she identified tomatoes, cucumbers, zucchini, cantaloupes, herbs, lettuce, cabbage, an entire rainbow of bell peppers—enough produce to stock the market at the entrance to the Serenity neighborhood. What did an elderly woman want with such a large garden?

One of the doors leading into the house abruptly opened, and she spun around, bringing up her pistol.

"Don't shoot." Jimmy raised both hands in surrender. "I've got too much on my schedule to die today."

Grimacing, she holstered the pistol. She'd made it through their marriage without killing him, though he'd dearly deserved it on multiple occasions. Why do it now?

He waited, holding the door open. As usual, he wore a white shirt, black trousers and black tie, and she knew from experience that the black suit coat was in the car.

"Do you still own five white shirts, five black suits and five black ties?" she asked as she passed him, entering the coolness of the mudroom.

"Do you remember the stuff you get into on this job? Besides, sometimes I'm tired—"

"Or hung over."

"—and not really focused on choosing clothes. This way I always match." His tone turned more serious as he closed and relocked the door. "You saw the old lady?"

"Only from outside."

"Doesn't look any better inside, but at least it's not our concern."

Alia followed him through a kitchen she would sell Jimmy's soul for, then into the broad hallway. Yesterday she had stood right where Miss Viola's head rested,

She look so small and helpless. It was hard to imagine that less than twenty-four hours ago, they'd sat in the library and talked, that Miss Viola had extended her hospitality for another visit. And now...

Giving herself a shake, Alia took in the scene, so very similar to the day before. No sign of a break-in or a struggle, no sign of a burglary that had gone wrong. Like the admiral, there were too many valuable items just the right size for slipping into a pocket or a bag, including the huge ruby ring on Miss Viola's left hand.

Natural causes, she reminded herself. Not every death was a homicide, not all circumstances suspicious.

The coroner's assistant glanced up from his position next to the body. "Time of death was between midnight and 3:00 a.m. Head trauma. Apparently, she tripped coming down the steps. Lost her shoe there—" he pointed to the missing slipper lying crookedly halfway up the stairs "—got tangled in her robe and took a tumble."

...the interesting parts are upstairs, and I don't go up there anymore. Broken hip. Last year. I haven't been upstairs since.

"No," Alia murmured, then repeated in a stronger voice, "No. She didn't fall down the stairs."

"Why do you say that?" Jimmy asked.

"She broke her hip last year. Her kids fixed her a suite on this floor, at the back of the house. She didn't go upstairs."

"Maybe she was home alone, needed something, thought one time wouldn't hurt," the coroner's investigator suggested.

"No," Alia repeated. "She would have waited. If it was important, she would have called someone. She's got family and friends everywhere. And she never would have tried it in those slippy little shoes and a robe that's just waiting to trip her."

The men exchanged looks, then Jimmy asked the question that apparently they were all thinking. "Why would someone want to kill an eighty-year-old lady who lives in her house, grows her garden, goes to church and wouldn't hurt a fly?"

"This particular eighty-one-year-old lady is related by

marriage to the Jackson family. She knew all of Camilla's and Jeremiah's history. Miss Viola probably knew everyone in the neighborhood, city, parish and state who had a feud with the admiral, when and what about. I'm guessing she knew the secrets people wanted to stay buried."

"Well, hell. So odds of this being coincidence…"

"I thought you don't believe in coincidence."

Scowling, he rubbed the back of his neck. "I don't. I believe God's got a wicked sense of humor and Karma's a fire-breathing bitch."

The men laughed. Alia patiently pointed out, "You've got to admit—you tested their patience."

"Maybe. A little." Turning back to the other investigators, he shrugged. "Let's treat this like a crime scene until we find out cause of death for sure."

Alia's gaze went past him to the tall windows across the room that overlooked the driveway. The car parking next to hers was middle-of-the-road average, old enough to lay some claim on vintage and showing the scars and dings of a lot of miles. She'd ridden in it for a few minutes yesterday and had figured she would see it again. Just not here. Not now.

"Family," she muttered to Jimmy as she headed out the door. She met Landry and Mary Ellen at the far end of the porch, only a few steps from his vehicle. "You can't be here," she said firmly, blocking their way, realizing she would have to break the news, wishing she'd sent Jimmy instead. She hadn't had to make many death notifications, and she never knew what to say. Sweet-talker Jimmy always managed to find just the right words.

"B-but Miss Viola… All th-these police c-c-cars… What's happened?" Mary Ellen didn't look as if she'd rested last night. Her eyes were bloodshot, dark circles underneath them, and her chin was wobbling now. "Where is Miss Viola? Is she all right? We've got to see her. We've got to—Landry!"

There were no circles around his eyes, no sign that a single tear had fallen. He was dressed more formally today, in gray trousers and a blue button-down, with that same antique watch on his left wrist. A family heirloom, likely from the Landry side of the family. Had it come from the Jacksons, it would likely be buried in silt at the bottom of the Mississippi.

His mouth was hard, the look in his eyes even more so. "What happened?" His voice was low, soft as granite, devoid of emotion but, conversely, all the more touching for the lack of it.

"We don't know yet. Miss Viola…" Alia looked away, noticing in some distant portion of her brain that the mother and child across the street had gone inside, then met Landry's gaze. "She's gone."

She didn't have to say more because a wail escaped Mary Ellen an instant before she swooned into her brother's arms.

Chapter 4

Landry hadn't shed a single tear or felt a moment's regret for his father's death. He hadn't worried overly much about his mother's whereabouts. But as he clung to Mary Ellen, keeping her limp body from collapsing to the ground, grief rose inside him.

Miss Viola had been like a grandmother to him. She was the only person in his entire life who'd taken a chance on him, who'd stood up to his father for him. She had protected him and Mary Ellen when their own mother wouldn't, had made it possible for both of them to escape the hell their house had become.

"Was it—" He couldn't finish the question. His voice was too husky, his throat too clogged.

"It appears she fell down the stairs."

He began shaking his head before she finished. "She didn't use the stairs—hadn't been up there since she came home from the rehab hospital last year."

Alia nodded as if she already knew that. "We'll know more once the coroner has completed the autopsy."

Mary Ellen stirred, and he glanced down at her, freeing one hand to pull his cell from his pocket. "Can you call my brother-in-law and ask him to come get her?"

Alia took the phone, scrolled through the directory, then moved back down the porch, her voice covering the distance in little more than a murmur.

Landry helped Mary Ellen to the nearest chair, crouching in front of her. Tears seeping from her eyes, she plaintively asked, "What's going on, Landry? First Mama, then the admiral, and now Miss Viola. Why? She never hurt anyone. Everyone loved her."

He noticed she didn't include their father in those sentiments. Jeremiah had hurt everyone, and Landry couldn't think of one person who'd honestly, wholeheartedly loved the bastard. "It was probably an accident," he said, though the words felt like a lie. Maybe it was paranoia, with his life being all disrupted the past day, but there was an icy place inside him that suspected the worst. He continued for Mary Ellen's sake, though. "Maybe her heart..."

Mary Ellen smiled through her tears. "You know she never had a thing wrong with her besides that blasted hip."

He managed his own faint smile. It was true, and Miss Viola had been damned proud of it. No high blood pressure or cholesterol or blood sugar, no weight problems or allergies or senilities, none of the afflictions people her age tended to have. Just a few creaky joints and one blasted hip.

My doctor told me that one in four people die within the first year after breaking their hip, she'd told him not long after her own accident. *I don't plan on being that one.*

She'd made it a little more than a year.

Alia joined them again, offering his phone. His fingers brushed hers when he took it, but the only thing he noticed was that hers were warm, while his felt so damn cold.

"Your husband will be here in a few minutes," she said to Mary Ellen. "Can I get you a glass of water or anything?"

"No, thank you. I'll be fine." Mary Ellen's voice wobbled on the last word. "Who found Miss Viola? Today is Molly's day off."

"I did." Discomfort spread across Alia's face, and she avoided glancing at Landry. "I came to ask her a few more questions."

Come to question Miss Viola without him present, Landry thought with a scowl. *Hoping to get the old lady to let something slip, to trip her into saying something today she wouldn't normally give voice to, most especially with me right there.*

"Oh, my Lord, to fall like that, all alone. That just breaks my heart." His sister raised her watery gaze to Alia. "How long did she lie there? Was she in pain? Did she try to get to the phone? Brett and Mimi—those are her children—they tried to get her to wear one of those emergency call devices, but she was too stubborn. She said when it was her time, it was her time, and she would happily go."

"I really don't know, Mrs. Davison. Once we get some answers, we'll share them with you."

Mary Ellen nodded, satisfied for a moment, then her

eyes widened. "Brett and Mimi... Has anyone told them yet?"

"The police department will notify them if they haven't already."

Landry thought he detected the smallest suggestion of impatience in Alia's voice. She'd come to pump an old lady for gossip, found a suspicious death instead, and then had to break the news to family members. He would bet she didn't get stuck with breaking bad news very often. He would bet it was one of the few jobs she didn't excel at.

A squeal on the street drew their attention that way as Scott parked behind Landry's car. *A few minutes*, Alia had said. An extravagant guess, considering Scott's nerves were twisted nearly as tight as Mary Ellen's. Stunned and pale, he greeted Landry and Alia with troubled looks. Mumbling something about *too much* and *doctor* and *sedatives*, he hustled Mary Ellen into the car, then jumped in himself, backed up into the drive across the street and headed home.

"Do you mind going out back with me and answering some questions?"

Landry gazed at the half dozen or more chairs scattered along the gallery, every one of them with access to the open door and the front windows. Without knowing anything more about the way Miss Viola had died, he knew he didn't want to see her while officers walked around her, talked about her and, eventually, zipped her into a bag and hauled her off.

He went to the back gate, wiggled his fingers inside the heavy growth until he found the key hidden there, then undid the lock. He turned away from the patio and led her back to the twin chairs hidden from sight by the rows of corn.

"Why did she grow such a big garden?" Apparently Special Agent Kingsley preferred to open with the least important of all the questions at her disposal.

"To give away."

"Her family and friends must have been pleased."

"Not to them. Miss Viola figured they could buy their organically grown stuff at their trendy farmers' markets like everyone else. She donated hers to soup kitchens and to markets in lower-income neighborhoods."

She'd done so much more: paid medical bills, made house repairs, provided single mothers with cars to get to their jobs and single fathers with after-school help. She'd bought uniforms to outfit a dozen school classes, stocked preschools with everything, located jobs, provided counseling and made life better.

She'd done enough good to get herself into heaven three or four times over, while there wasn't enough good possible to keep Jeremiah from hell. And if he had in any way contributed to her death, if whatever he'd done that led to his own murder had come back on her…

"Where were you between midnight and three?" Alia asked.

The question was perfunctory, lacking even a fraction of the interest she'd shown when she asked him the same thing with regard to his father. Because she believed he was capable of killing Jeremiah but not Miss Viola?

Score a point for her, because she was right.

"The bar closed at 3:00 a.m. I cleaned up and was in bed by 3:30." He checked the time on his great-grandfather Landry's Patek Philippe. He and Mary Ellen had had an appointment fifteen minutes ago with the funeral director to plan Jeremiah's funeral. Landry hadn't wanted to go at all, and now he would be going alone. What did he know about planning a funeral? He'd be better off trusting the funeral director to make the right choices.

Now it was his turn to ask a question. "You were just here yesterday. Why did you come back this morning?"

Alia crossed her legs. Once again her hair was pulled straight back from her face in a ridiculously tight braid, but she'd traded the drab blue suit for a tan shirt and brown skirt. She still looked all business, but at least the clothes had a little style, and the open-toed shoes with straps around her slender ankles showed off her legs well.

"I thought she was a little too careful with her responses yesterday."

"You thought she was telling you what I wanted her to."

Alia nodded. The sunlight catching in her hair gave it a high sheen. "I thought she might be more comfortable speaking with me about your family if you weren't present."

Tension eased from his shoulders. "You would have been disappointed. Miss Viola was one of the great repositories of information in this town. She observed carefully, asked questions discreetly and shared judiciously. People confided in her because they trusted her. She knew all but never told it."

"She might have made an exception this time to get justice for her dear cousins or vengeance against her hated enemy."

"Hated enemy?" he echoed. "Isn't that a little melodramatic?"

"I asked if she regretted his passing. She said that *not*

regretting it would—quoting here—'be unchristian of me, wouldn't it? I've been a good Christian my entire life. God will forgive me this lapse.'"

It sounded just like Miss Viola. Of course God would forgive her for hating Jeremiah. She'd felt pretty certain that God Himself was none too fond of that particular reptile on His earth.

He envisioned the lower floor of the house, hidden now by cornstalks, and imagined the people working inside: a homicide detective, maybe more, a crime scene team, someone from the coroner's office. A lot of people expending a lot of time in a city where deaths and crimes were always waiting for attention. Turning, he fixed his gaze on Alia. "Do you think she was murdered?"

She pressed her lips together, rubbing off what little lipstick remained there. "That's what we're trying to find out."

"But you have an idea."

Evasively she looked toward the house, as he had, but her gaze followed the lines of empty windows marching in order across the second and third floors before turning back to him. "She told me yesterday that she doesn't go upstairs, just as you said. And yet this morning I found her lying at the foot of the steps, with one of her slippers lying askew halfway up the stairs, leaving the appearance that she fell."

Or was forced up and pushed down again. Carried up and thrown down. The how of it wasn't important to Landry. It was the why. *Why* would anyone hurt Miss Viola?

Alia folded her hands in her lap and changed the subject. "I've known a few people in my life who practically qualified for sainthood, but even they had frenemies."

She gave the made-up word a sardonic twist. "People they were friendly but argued with. What about Miss Viola?"

Landry rubbed the ache in his temple. Too little sleep, too much drama, too much bright sun and loud noises and ugly thoughts. He needed the cool quiet of his bedroom for a few days, at least until Jeremiah had been planted in the family tomb.

"The only person I ever heard say anything bad about her was Jeremiah. They hadn't had any contact with each other since—" He clenched his jaw shut on the words.

"Since you left home."

He refused to answer.

Now Alia was watching him, curiosity in her eyes. "I've known some kids who left at home at fifteen, sixteen. I've investigated a few others. I even considered it a couple times myself, back in the day. But in my experience, it was never such a big deal that family members stopped speaking because of it, especially when it was a well-known fact that the kid was okay. So why are you different? What was special about your leaving home?"

He watched the cornstalks sway in a lazy breeze. Miss Viola had put the chairs back in this corner because, she swore, under the right conditions, the corn grew so fast that a body could actually hear it. He didn't hear anything right now but the heavy cadence of his heart and Alia's even breathing.

"There was nothing special about it. I'd had enough, and I moved out." Miss Viola had helped him rent a tiny apartment in a French Quarter building owned by a friend of hers and had continued to give him money until he was grown. For a runaway, he'd had it damn good.

The only thing special was that at the same time, she'd

coerced Camilla and Jeremiah into sending Mary Ellen to a boarding school in Europe.

"Where was the admiral stationed at the time?"

"He'd just come back here. He'd pulled some strings to be close to his family."

Between the two of them, he and Miss Viola had made the string-pulling all for nothing, and Jeremiah had hated them since. Had it ever bothered him that neither of them had given a damn?

Abruptly Alia gestured to Landry's clothes. "You have an appointment?"

"Funeral home," he said shortly.

"I can accompany you. We can talk on the way."

"I've got nothing else to tell you."

As she stood, she smiled, a professional kind of smile, not insincere, exactly, but not really sincere, either. "Then you shouldn't mind the company."

After checking in with Jimmy, Alia left the Fulsom mansion for the last time with a deep sense of relief. The house she had admired yesterday was cold today, less welcoming, more intimidating. Miss Viola's imprint was everywhere, which made the fact that she was dead more chilling.

The fact that she likely had been murdered…

"Don't you fidget?"

She glanced at Landry. He was sprawled in the driver's seat, his right wrist resting at the top of the steering wheel, with his left arm on the window frame, his fingers tapping a quiet rhythm to music only he heard.

"You prefer your passengers on the hyperactive side?"

"No. But you're awfully still. And quiet."

"Next time I can ask Detective DiBiase to accompany you. He's never still *or* quiet."

Half a block passed before he asked, "How long were you married?"

Alia stiffened, looked at him, out the window, then back at him. It wasn't a deep secret. Pretty much everyone in her life knew, including a fair number of people she'd investigated. The NCIS and local law enforcement communities were close-knit, and word got around.

Still, heat warmed the skin at the base of her throat. "Three years."

"And in that whole time, you didn't try to kill him."

"No." In a softer voice, she added, "Though there were times…"

Landry smiled. It was a really good look on him. Good enough to make a woman spend extra time checking him out. She imagined on a warm evening, when relentless rain had put a dint in the Quarter's usual nightlife, a woman looking for a good time knew she'd found it when she walked into his bar and he welcomed her with that smile.

Further conversation was delayed as he cut across traffic and pulled into the parking lot of what appeared to be another fabulous period mansion. Only the three dozen parking spaces and a discreet sign announcing its name and business gave it away as a funeral home. It was red brick, a bigger-than-life Southern beauty, bright flowers dancing in their beds, Spanish moss trailing from oaks, graceful paths leading from parking lot to doors to small breathtaking gardens.

"Welcome to DeVille and Sons," Landry said drily.

"The Cadillac of funeral services."

He cracked a tiny grin. "Yeah, Mary Ellen says they

take their 'end-of-life transition services' very serious, so don't repeat that inside." He opened the door, slid out and frowned at her over the car roof. "Do you know anything about planning a funeral?"

Alia's brows arched. "My parents are alive and well in San Diego, my maternal grandparents in Chicago and my paternal grandparents in Miami Beach. I've never even been to a funeral. In fact, I was thinking I could wait in the gardens—"

"Yeah, I don't think so." He came around the car, caught her arm and started toward the building.

Letting a man take her arm and guide her anywhere had been unheard of since she was a toddler and learned she'd rather fall on her diapered butt than have her father, or anyone else, holding her up. But her automatic impulse to shrug away from Landry's grip didn't manifest. Not until she'd felt the strength in his fingers, warm, not callused, not smooth, either. Not until she'd identified the tiny tremor that shot through her as something more purely feminine than she'd allowed herself to feel in a very long time.

Not until she'd reminded herself that he was a person of interest in the most important case in her career so far.

And by then, they'd reached the door and he let go anyway.

The air inside was cool enough to raise goose bumps all over her, making her wish for the jacket still sitting in her car's front seat. Thick carpet underneath muffled their footsteps, and heavy perfume from the half dozen large flower arrangements obliterated the interesting scent that was Landry. Soft lights, soft colors, soothing music, leather furniture and upholstered pieces, a *Gone with the Wind*-worthy staircase, pricey artwork that she wasn't entirely sure were reproductions...

"The Cadillac people do well," she whispered as an elegantly dressed silver-haired man approached them from a hallway to the right. How had he known they were here? There'd been no ding from the door, no receptionist sitting politely awaiting customers.

A silent alarm, and probably surveillance cameras for good measure. It was like her office, only in much fancier quarters.

"Mr. Jackson, we're so sorry about your loss. The admiral was a good man, a good friend to the navy as well as New Orleans." The man held Landry's hand exactly the proper length of time, released it just so. "And we just heard about Miss Viola. Such a tragedy."

That done, he turned to Alia. His gaze slid over her badge and weapons without the slightest change in expression. "I'm Matthieu DeVille. And you are?"

Landry answered for her. "A friend of the family."

Surprised by Landry's response, she accepted Mr. DeVille's handshake. His skin was softer than her own. He had a better manicure, too. Did he deal only with the living, or did these hands also help prepare their clients' bodies? She had to restrain a shiver as she quickly let go.

"If you'll follow me, please."

He led them through broad halls, past chapels, offices and casket-display rooms until they finally reached his office. He seated himself behind a mahogany desk, leaving two finely carved matching chairs for Alia and Landry. She didn't want to sit down any more than Landry did, but she did.

She sat quietly, legs crossed, hands clasped and fought the impulse to tap her toes or bounce one foot in the air. She wasn't a fidgeter, she'd told Landry, but energy bubbled and roiled inside her, needing an outlet of some sort. She concentrated on regulating her breathing and on ignoring the fact that somewhere in the building were corpses being cleaned up, dressed up, made up for their last viewing on earth.

She was going to be cremated, she decided on a breath filled with overly sweet flowers.

"What about the admiral's personal information?" Mr. DeVille asked, looking from Landry to her. They had scheduled the service for Friday at the church the Jacksons and the Landrys had attended for more than a century; the interment would be in one of the family vaults; the family would receive mourners at Mary Ellen's house.

"Personal information?" Landry blankly repeated.

"For the obituary. Pertinent dates, education, career highlights, surviving family."

Alia removed her tablet from her purse and, after a quick search, found the admiral's biography online. The page gave great detail to his education and navy career and spared one small paragraph for his family. The way of his life, she thought as she asked for Mr. DeVille's email address.

With a word of thanks, he opened the email on his computer, then printed a copy to go into Jackson's file. He studied the top page a moment, right about where her email address appeared: *@ncis.navy.mil*. His gaze flickered from the page to her, to the badge and weapons he'd noticed earlier but couldn't see now. How many questions was he wishing he could ask? Dozens. Though in his line of work, certainly he would be the soul of discretion.

Once the paperwork was finished, DeVille escorted

them back to the first of the display rooms filled with
caskets. Alia would hazard a guess from all the gleaming
wood and metal, silk and bronze and just pure impression the caskets made that these were the expensive ones.
Jeremiah Jackson had surrounded himself with luxury
in life; why would death be any different?

She walked in, looked at a few—mahogany, ash, teak,
all perfectly fitted and designed as exquisitely as high-
end furniture. None of them bore price tags—*If you have
to ask, you can't afford it*—and all of them struck her
as obscene. The man was dead. Cremate him; donate
any usable organs or bones; give his body to a medical
school; do anything besides spend a fortune getting him
from the coroner's office to the family vault.

DeVille cleared his throat, and she turned to see that
Landry hadn't yet crossed the threshold into the room
and didn't appear likely to anytime soon. He hadn't
wanted to come here in the first place, she would bet,
and damn well hated it without his sister to make the
decisions.

"You knew him," he said, his voice hoarse. "You
know what Mary Ellen would want. You choose."

DeVille couldn't stop the fleeting surprise—and pleasure—that crossed his face, but he tamped it back into
sympathetic concern. "Of course, we can do that, Mr.
Jackson. Don't worry. We'll take care of Jeremiah as if
he were one of our own. But then, he was one of our own,
wasn't he?" From an inside pocket, he produced a piece
of notepaper with a flourish. "Here is a list of things to
be done—meeting with Father Callaghan, choosing the
music, ordering flowers, catering the family meal before
the service. If you or Mary Ellen need help with any of
it, please don't hesitate to call us."

Landry looked at the page a moment before, folding it to fit in his pocket, then walking away toward the exit.

Alia glanced after him, then shrugged. "Sorry. He, uh…"

This time DeVille's smile struck her as sincere. "Don't apologize. People react all kinds of ways to death. You've probably seen that yourself."

Yep, he'd definitely noticed the *ncis* in her email address.

"Landry said you knew the admiral."

"All our lives."

"I'm surprised he didn't make his own arrangements." She intended to email her parents this evening about the wonderful world of preplanned burial services. *It's your eternity. Be happy in it.*

"Don't think I didn't suggest it a time or two. But he intended to live forever. We believed him, too. He was more active than people half his age, still sharp as a tack. He was a good man." DeVille hesitated a moment, then more quietly added, "A tough man."

Tough. Strict. Rigid. Behaviors that could get a man killed.

Before Alia could say anything else, a woman stuck her head out of the nearest office—the only other sign of life they'd seen since they had walked into the building. "Miss Regina's on the phone."

"I have to take this," DeVille said. "Remind Landry that if he needs anything…"

Standing beneath a live oak in the garden, hands in pockets, Landry watched Alia burst out of the funeral home as if the building was too small to contain her natural energy. Her gaze went straight to the car, then swept around until it located him, and she angled in his direction.

Instead of watching her approach, he gazed into the fountain and wondered whose job it was to pick out every leaf, pine needle and acorn every single day of the year. Jeremiah had had his own term for such people—*the others*. In his world, there were people with money, power, social status, and there were *the others*.

Had it bothered him that his only son was just an *other*? God, Landry hoped so. The bastard had likely blamed Camilla for it, though maybe, just once in his life, maybe he had considered that it had been his own doing. When you deliberately broke someone, you had to accept some of the responsibility.

Unless you were Admiral Jeremiah Roy Jackson Junior.

Alia came along the path toward him, fingers linked together as if she was enjoying a midmorning stroll. "You do know you just opened your wallet in there and said, 'Here, take however much you want.'"

He looked up, his brow quirked. "Actually, I opened Scott's wallet. The expenses will be paid once the estate's settled. Scott's covering them until then."

"I take it you, your sister and your mother are the primary heirs."

Landry considered moving the conversation to the bench at the base of the tree, but a growl from his stomach sent him back toward the main path. "Probably just Mary Ellen and our mother. The old man liked the idea of disinheritance."

"So whatever happened between you was unforgivable enough that he would disinherit you."

He only shrugged. It could be easy at times to forget

who she was and just answer, if he hadn't spent most of his years keeping his life to himself. Other kids said, *When Dad and I...* Not him. His best friend from school had thought Jeremiah was dead, had been dead forever. It had puzzled the kid when he found out otherwise, filling him with questions.

"Does the disinheritance possibility bother you?" Alia asked as he opened the passenger door for her.

"Nah, ten million bucks would just make my taxes more difficult." Could he even live with that money knowing where it came from? How much of it would he have to give to charity to cleanse it enough that he could let himself benefit from the rest?

A whole freaking bunch. Jeremiah had worshipped at the altar of everything wrong and sinful in the world.

"It's family money," Alia pointed out as they reached the car. "Not the admiral's. He was just the steward of it for his generation. You're as entitled to it as your sister is."

"Except she didn't cut him out of the last half of her life. She was a dutiful daughter—visited him regularly, called him Daddy, walked down the aisle on his arm when she married, included him in every part of the girls' lives." He truly didn't understand any of that. Mary Ellen had had as much reason to hate him as Landry, but instead she'd *welcomed* him into her life. She'd done a lot of forgiving and a whole lot of forgetting.

Landry never forgot a thing.

"I'm going to lunch," he announced as they settled in the car. "You interested in some good food, or does duty call your name?"

He'd swear her ears pricked at the mention of food. "No, I've got to meet Jim—What kind of food?"

"You name it, Huong can make it."

"Huong?" A glance showed her interest was definitely piqued. "What's the name of the place?"

"Mama's Table. Huong took it over when her mama got too old, but Mama Trahn still helps with lunch."

"Sounds really good. But, no, I do have to meet Detective DiBiase."

"What, doesn't he eat?"

"Not like he means it," she muttered.

When they reached Miss Viola's house, the ambulance was gone, along with the coroner's people, and the only vehicles left were official. He was grateful. He didn't know Miss Viola's kids nearly as well as Mary Ellen did. About all he would have to discuss with them was the methods of their parents' murders.

Thirty-plus stab wounds beat a shove down the stairs any day.

Alia unbuckled her seat belt and gave him a narrow-eyed look. "Mama's Table, huh?"

"At the far end of Decatur. Don't let the outside fool you."

With a nod, she got out of the car and climbed the steps to the gallery. She really had great legs, he thought again, and taking down that braid would be like unraveling a puzzle of silk strands that would tangle around his fingers before sliding free.

Him taking down her braid wasn't gonna happen, but he wouldn't be a man if he didn't think about it.

Landry shifted into Reverse, but just sat there a moment. He would likely never come back to Miss Viola's house. It had always been a haven for him, a place his mother had brought him and Mary Ellen for family time out when Jeremiah was out of town, the place he'd run to for escape when Jeremiah was home. He'd never been close to his grandmothers, but it had never mattered because he'd had a cousin who was better than all the grandmothers in the world combined. He'd loved Miss Viola, and she'd loved him back.

Now he didn't have anyone who truly understood…

Grimly he swiped one hand across his eyes, then backed out of the driveway. He had every intention of visiting Mama's Table, as he'd told Alia, but he had to make one stop first.

Mary Ellen lay on the chaise in the sunroom, a pillow tucked beneath her cheek, its lace edging obscuring part of the writing on her nightshirt: *Best Mom Ever*. Her makeup had been cried off, the color washed out of her face. She was nibbling on a fingertip and looking sad and heartbroken and lost, even more so than when he'd left her to live alone with their ineffectual mother and their lousy father.

She smiled wanly. "Did you get everything taken care of?"

"Sort of. Mr. DeVille's doing it all."

"Oh, Aunt Louisianne will hate that. She's held the honor for most outrageous funeral for Uncle Orland for twenty years. Mr. DeVille will surely top that for Daddy's service."

Landry vaguely remembered Uncle Orland's passage, drawing a smile. "How do you top a spectacle? Harp-playing cats? Flying chimps swooping in to carry the casket away?"

Mary Ellen tried to keep her expression somber, but a tiny smile worked free. "Daddy did like a spectacle—as long as you, Mama and I weren't involved." When Landry pulled a stool closer and sat, she grasped his hand. "I'm so sorry I let you down today, Landry. Finding out about Miss Viola, I just couldn't—I'm sorry you had to go to the funeral home alone."

"I didn't go alone. Special Agent Kingsley went with me."

Mary Ellen's brows arched with surprise. "I guess that's part of the navy's service to the grieving family."

Only if the family member is a person of interest in the murder. Mary Ellen was so naive, so convinced of the natural goodness in everyone, that it probably hadn't occurred to her yet that she and Landry were almost definitely people of interest.

Her fingers tightened on his hand, and shadows darkened her eyes. "Why would anyone hurt Miss Viola? She was the sweetest person in the world and would have given that precious ruby off her finger to help someone in need. God, Landry, it's like someone has it in for our family. First Mama goes off to God knows where, then Daddy dies, and then Miss Viola—I don't understand what's going on!"

She drew a sobbing breath and smiled through her tears. "Bad things come in threes, they say, so the Jackson family has officially had its three. I hereby declare that nothing else will happen to us."

Landry hoped like hell she was right.

But deep down inside, he doubted it.

Chapter 5

"I swear, Jeremiah Jackson and Viola Fulsom had enough family, friends and acquaintances to fill a good-sized book."

In the process of tearing open a package of vending-machine cookies, Alia glanced across the scarred conference room table at Jimmy. Though her ex had a tendency to exaggerate, this time he'd stated God's honest truth. The Jackson and Landry families had taken to heart the advice to go forth and multiply. Add in their social, political and charitable contacts, as well as the admiral's navy associates, and she and Jimmy had more names than they and their fellow detectives/special agents could interview in a year's time.

Jimmy ran a hand through his hair. "You think the murders are connected?"

"You think they're coincidence?"

"Stranger things have happened."

"Yeah, like me marrying you."

He grinned. "Like you divorcing me."

"Like me not killing you."

"Anyone ever tell you that holding a grudge is bad for your health?"

Not nearly as bad as sleeping around should have been for his. The first time, when she'd heard the news through the law enforcement grapevine, she'd been furious as hell. By the last time, when she'd actually walked in on him with his girlfriend of the week, she hadn't felt anything. Their marriage had ended in the sixty seconds it had taken her brain to process the scene, and her heart had been safe ever since.

There was a part of her that wouldn't mind walking on the wild side. Just a little.

But, damn, why did the first image that popped into her mind at that longing have to be Landry Jackson?

Leaning back in his chair, Jimmy fixed his gaze on the ceiling. "What do you think of the son?"

She blinked, caught off guard that Jimmy had spoken of Landry just seconds after she'd envisioned being wild and reckless and him. Clearing her throat, she said, "Landry?"

What she thought of him was probably what every other woman did: damn, he was gorgeous. Those eyes, that hair, the body, the brooding bad-boy aura... His smile was none too shabby, either.

But every other woman could appreciate him up close and personal. Alia couldn't.

With a twinge of regret, she pushed the personal stuff to the back of her mind and focused on the conversation.

"Yeah, Landry," Jimmy said, oblivious. "He was estranged from his parents. He stands to inherit a boat-load of money."

Money was always such a good motive for murder, hence the standard question: who profited from the victim's death? In this case, though, she didn't believe Jackson's murder involved money at all. "As far as he knows, he's out of the will, and he doesn't seem to care."

"You believe him?"

She bit a cookie in half and considered it while chewing. "You've seen his financials. He lives within his means. He's never been arrested, nothing to suggest a problem with drinking, drugs, gambling or women." And he'd sounded believable. Sure, she'd met people who could lie with utter sincerity—Jimmy was a prime example—but she would bet a dozen beignets that Landry wasn't one of them.

"Yeah. I believed him. Besides, his alibi checked out. He was playing poker until nearly six." She popped another cookie into her mouth.

"Okay, so he's off the suspect list."

Alia leaned forward and twisted his laptop around so she could see what he'd typed. She snorted. "When did we take Mary Ellen Davison off the suspect list?"

"Come on, look at her."

"Look at what? Her big brown eyes brimming with tears? Her Cupid's bow mouth? Her sweet, sad smile? The neon lights around her flashing *damsel in distress*?"

"She's the original steel magnolia. She's not gonna stab someone thirty-some times."

Slumping back in her chair, Alia pretended to thump her forehead with her palm. "The *steel* part of *steel magnolia* refers to strength, doofus."

He wasn't the least bit fazed by his mistake or her

insult. "No matter what it means, Mary Ellen Davison didn't kill her daddy or the old lady. She'd be more likely to love someone to death."

He was right about that, Alia conceded. Mary Ellen was delicate, the kind of feminine flower who used to make her feel too tall, too thin, too flat chested, too *un*-feminine. Ah, she remembered well the teenage days when she was first getting into boys, when so many of them were into girlie girls like Mary Ellen.

What kind of woman was Landry into?

The kind that didn't wear a badge or credentials and carry a gun, she thought as she took her turn to study the ceiling. Probably someone as impressive as he was, with a great face, great body, though probably not as fragile as his sister. Like Jimmy, Landry probably didn't favor a particular type—redhead, brunette, blonde; white, black, Latina, Asian; working girl or career woman. Pretty, hot-blooded, cooking skills a plus but not required.

She washed down the last cookie with half a can of pop, then asked, "Aren't you ready for lunch yet?"

"Holy hell, sweet pea, it's barely 12:15. Where do you put all those calories? If I ate like you do, I'd be too big to fit through the door."

"That's because you're lazy. I heard there's a really good restaurant near here called Mama's Table. You been there?"

"I don't like Vietnamese food, remember?"

She smirked as she stood again, swinging the strap of her bag over one shoulder. "Oh, Jimmy, your ego would shrivel if you knew how much I've forgotten about you." It wasn't true, but he didn't know it. She remembered the first time they'd gone to visit her parents, the first time they'd visited her mother's parents. The way he'd carried on, a reasonable person would have been forgiven for thinking he was going to starve to death after his first taste of *pho ga*, a savory chicken and noodle soup, *bò luc lac* and *mi xao don*. He'd hated lemongrass and cilantro and *nuoc mam*, three of her favorite food items in the world.

Landry apparently had a finer appreciation for her culture's food.

When they walked out of the building, she automatically turned right, and Jimmy followed her. She wouldn't force him to eat something he didn't like, so she headed for a little Cajun place they'd frequented in their years together.

"How are your mom and dad?" he asked, holding the restaurant door for her.

"They're fine. Mom still hates you."

"Good to know."

"I talked to Dad last night. He knew Jackson."

Jimmy nodded absently, checking out the hostess who led them to a table. "Anything useful to add?"

"Nothing we haven't already heard." She didn't bother with the menu the petite blonde set in front of her but looked around for the waitperson instead. Quint, a thin, young redhead and the best waiter in five square blocks, signaled one minute with his finger when he saw her, delivered drinks to another table, then swooped over to their table.

"Kingsley and DiBiase, my favorite cops." His accent was pure Southern drawl, his blue eyes shifting from her to Jimmy. "Aw, don't tell me you two are back together."

"Not in this lifetime," she replied.

His smile spread as he gave Jimmy an appreciative look. It made her ex's cheeks turn as red as Quint's hair.

Alia ordered her usual—a shrimp cocktail, a basket of warm bread and jambalaya, along with sweet tea—and Jimmy ordered a shrimp po'boy and bottled water.

"I talked to more people wearing khaki yesterday than I can count," Jimmy said once Quint left to get their drinks. His reference was to the standard uniform worn by senior enlisted navy personnel and officers. She had interviewed plenty of sailors in her career; she'd been happy to let him have a run at them. "Nobody had anything interesting to say. He was a good officer, he was big on discipline and order, so on and so on. Funny thing, though—none of them knew the first thing about his family. Weren't even sure he had one."

"My dad never met Jackson's wife, knew he had a daughter, didn't have a clue there was a son."

"You find out what caused the split between them?"

"Nope." She tore apart a piece of still-warm rye bread, breathing deeply of its aroma. "Miss Viola knew, but she didn't tell me anything he didn't want me to know." After a pause to butter the bread, she added, "Landry said he wished he'd killed Jeremiah."

The comment made no more impact on Jimmy than it had on her. "That's one of the problems with homicide. A lot of people who get murdered tend to do something to deserve it. We just have to find out what that was."

And why Miss Viola had to die, too.

Friday promised to be the hottest day so far this year. Given a choice, Landry wouldn't leave this block. He would get a mess of shrimp from the restaurant across the street, pick up a newspaper and a tall glass of iced tea, settle into a chair in the courtyard near the fountain and let the lazy breezes and the sharp-edged rays of the sun lull him into a stupor.

But he didn't have a choice.

Facing the mirror over the bureau, he tried one last time to knot the tie draped around his neck without any more success than the first three times. He swore, thought how Jeremiah would react to his inability to tie a simple knot and smiled tautly.

The light gray suit was uncomfortable. He had no use for dressy clothes, so he'd bought it just for this occasion. The dress shirt had a crisp, freshly pressed smell to it, and the shoes, also new, made him wish for sandals. There was a reason he lived in jeans, cargo shorts and T-shirts or aloha shirts. They suited him, didn't choke him and didn't remind him in the least of the life he'd escaped.

Yet in the end, the bastard had managed to drag him back into it.

Leaving the tie dangling, he scooped up his keys and cell and left the apartment. The family—extended to include a few aunts, uncles and cousins—were meeting at Mary Ellen and Scott's, where the family cars would pick them up for delivery to the church. With all the lying that would be going on, he hoped they made it through the service without God striking someone dead.

By the time he reached the Davison house, his nerves were humming. He had to park halfway down the block and walk back, steeling himself for seeing relatives he hardly knew anymore. But there were trade-offs, and they leaped into his arms the minute Geneva let him in the door, getting his attention while he spared no more than a glance for the somber group in the drawing room.

"Uncle Landry!" seven-year-old Mariela squealed.

Immediately nine-year-old Faith shushed her. "We're s'posed to be quiet!"

Mariela scowled at her. "You're not the boss."

"I am, too. The bigger kid is always the boss of the little one. Isn't that right, Uncle Landry?"

He settled a girl on each hip, their dresses—dark green for Mariela, dark red for Faith—vivid against his gray suit. "Sorry, sweetie. That's not always the case." Ducking his head, he whispered conspiratorially, "I'm bigger than your mom, and I can't boss her around at all."

Mariela stuck her tongue out at Faith, who retaliated with a pinch. Though they looked like pint-size versions of their mother with brown hair, dark eyes and porcelain skin, they'd been known to indulge in more than a few brawls, like their uncle. The thought made him smile.

"Can I wear your scarf?" Mariela pulled his tie free of his collar and wrapped it around her neck. "Do I look pretty?"

"Gorgeous. But I'm afraid I've got to wear it. In fact, I need to find your mom so she can help me put it on."

With a roll of her eyes, Mariela wrapped it twice around his neck, tucked the loose ends into his collar, then cupped her little hands to his face. "Now *you* look gorgeous."

Faith gave a long-suffering sigh. "Mama's in the kitchen."

He let them slide to the floor and strode down the hall to the last doorway before the sunroom. The caterers were at work, covering every surface in the large kitchen with trays, bowls and pans of food. They hurried about, avoiding collisions practically every time they turned around, intent on their work, paying no attention to Mary Ellen, seated at the small table out of the way, a glass of iced water in front of her.

"Hey." Landry nudged her as he pulled out a chair to join her. "You okay?"

Though she gave him a smile, her face was as pale as the starched napkins stacked two feet high on the counter behind her. The sadness in her eyes wrenched at him, reminding him *why* he'd had no choice in coming today. "I'm okay. Lord, can you believe we have to do this again tomorrow for Miss Viola?"

He nodded grimly. He'd got a call from Brett Fulsom yesterday.

Her voice dropped to a quavery whisper. "I wonder where Mama is. I wonder if she knows...."

Landry wondered if she knew, was she celebrating? Deeply relieved? Or was it possible she might/could/did miss the man they were well rid of?

"Why would she disappear like that? She loved Daddy. He loved her. With his retirement coming up, they were going to have time for each other, to travel and just enjoy each other." Mary Ellen's breath caught in a hiccup. "Scott thinks she left him, but he's wrong. Mama would never do that...would she?"

This would be the perfect moment for some nearly forgotten family member to come into the room or for one of the catering people to drop a load of glassware. He looked around for a distraction, but no one wanted attention, not even his nieces, who had mastered the art of interruption before the end of the days they were born.

Then Mary Ellen's cell phone chirped, and he stood with a great rush of relief. He caught her attention, waved, and she wiggled her index finger, something she'd started when a pacifier had still been one of the most important things in her world.

Back in the hallway, he listened to the voices from the front of the house, an even mix of men and women, from places all around the country but each of them sounding as if they'd been born and raised on the bayou. You could take the family out of the South, but it just reclaimed them the instant they set foot back on Louisiana soil. He didn't dislike most of them. They were like any other family—some friendly, some not, some barely tolerable.

He just didn't want to interact with them.

A left turn took him through the sunroom, then he headed outside. He didn't stay in the back—too many windows offering full views—but circled the house and found a quiet place on the front veranda, on the opposite side from the room the Jacksons and Landrys occupied. The seldom-used steps creaked under his weight, but none of the suits gathered around the door seemed to notice him.

Sliding out of his jacket, he hung it on the back of the nearest wrought iron chair. Before he'd managed to return to the railing to gaze off down the street, a dry voice spoke.

"The porch furniture is cleaner than the tables and chairs inside my house."

Alia Kingsley stood six feet away. Her hair was neatly contained on the back of her head, leaving her neck bare to catch the occasional breeze, but that was the only concession she'd made to the heat. She wore pants and a jacket in a delicate shade of gray with a white shirt. Her shoes were gray, too, ugly, with a low heel. Even her jewelry was subdued: a sterling watch on her left wrist, a sterling disk with a white pearl on a chain around her neck.

"Yours would be spotless, too, if you had staff."

She came a few steps closer, into the shade cast by a nearby tree. "We had staff a few times when I was growing up, thanks to my father's job. My mother hated it. I wouldn't mind a little part-time help myself." She removed her sunglasses and dangled them by the earpieces. "We look like we shopped at the same store."

He gave her another once-over, not noticing the clothes so much as the way they fit her. The shirt clung to her breasts, lying snug against her midriff, and the pants hugged her flat belly. The fabric flared with the curve of her hips before falling in a long, straight expanse over muscled thighs and lean calves to partially cover the ugly shoes. "Nah. They didn't have anything in my store that would do you justice."

But that was a lie. The shirt he was wearing would look damn good on her, especially if she had nothing else on. The stark white would enhance the olive shade of her skin, and with enough buttons left undone, the shirt would reveal the long line of her throat, the curve of her breasts, the hollow between them.

He drew a breath to clear the thoughts from his mind. All he needed now was to imagine her with her hair down, tumbling loose around her shoulders, and he'd have to put his jacket back on. It was too damn hot for that.

"What does your father do?"

She blinked, apparently needing a moment to remember that she'd mentioned her father's job. "He's retired now."

"What did he do before he retired?"

She did a cute little thing with her mouth, kind of pursing it, before looking away, then finally back. "He was in the navy. He was a rear admiral."

Landry couldn't say why that surprised him, maybe because people tended to remark on things they shared in common with someone else. And there had to be restrictions on how many admirals the navy had at any given time. A person didn't run into those admirals' grown children every day.

But he hadn't *run into* Alia. She was trying to find out who killed Jeremiah, whether Landry was the guilty party. Hardly the situation to say, *Hey, your father's an admiral? Guess what? So is mine.*

"The same as Jeremiah?" he asked.

"Not entirely. My father retired a rear admiral, lower half—a one-star admiral. Your father was upper half with two stars."

He smiled thinly. What were the odds that an admiral's daughter would be considering another admiral's son a possible murderer? "So you went through the whole navy brat experience."

She shrugged. "Like you, my father didn't tolerate brattiness, but I did get to do all the moving around. The upside is I can adapt to anything. The downside is I don't have that roots-heart-and-home attachment anywhere."

For years Landry had thought that kind of detachment sounded pretty damn appealing, but he never could have abandoned Mary Ellen completely or cut off contact with Miss Viola. He had to admit, he would miss New Orleans, too—the people, the music, the food, the life, the history, the strength, even the weather. And, yeah, that roots-heart-and-home thing.

"Do You Know What It Means to Miss New Orleans?" Louis Armstrong had sung. Landry didn't know personally because every time he'd gone away, he'd always come back a week or two later. More than that, he didn't want to know. He didn't have a whole lot in his life, thanks to Jeremiah.

And he wasn't about to give up anything he did have.

She gestured to his throat. "Have I missed the new trend in neckwear?"

He looked down, from his perspective, seeing only bits of the "scarf" Mariela had wrapped around him, and smiled. "Apparently, my seven-year-old niece is no more knowledgeable about tying ties than I am."

"May I?" After his nod, she caught the end of the tie, pulled it free and draped it around her own neck. "I only know how to do it when I'm wearing it. Mom has pretied Dad's ties for him their whole marriage. I was her backup for emergencies when she was out of town."

He watched as her thin fingers pulled fabric here, slid it through there, tugged it back over here. The black-silver-and-red-striped pattern went with her clothes as well as his own, and there was something about a woman in a tie pulled loose, loose…

"Here you go." She tugged the tie over her head, stepped closer and lowered it over his head. It took her seconds to straighten, snug, slide, and then she stepped away again.

But he still smelled her. No longer than the tie had been around her neck, no more than it had touched her bare skin, it had picked up traces of her perfume, rich and sexy and intimate.

He hoped it stayed with him through the rest of the day.

* * *

By two thirty-seven that afternoon, Alia was officially pooped. First, it was about a hundred and ninety degrees outside, and the accompanying humidity hovered somewhere around "that's impossible." Second, even low heels that weren't supposed to torture her feet did torture them after three hours constantly moving at the Davison home, the church and the cemetery. Third, dehydration had kicked in because she got minimal bathroom breaks, which prevented her from drinking anywhere near the amount of water she needed to stave off the heat and sweat.

"Thank God it's almost over." Jimmy swiped a handkerchief across his forehead before returning it to his pocket. He'd just returned from checking in with everybody around the perimeter of the cemetery.

Alia hadn't counted how many NCIS agents and police officers were there. The admirals who'd traveled in from various commands, their white dress uniforms a splendid contrast to the many dark outfits, had brought their own security details with them. But those agents' focus was on protecting their own flag officer, not assisting in the surveillance.

Thanks to digital photography, Alia and Jimmy would have snapshots of every single person in attendance, of who was talking to whom, who prayed fervently and who didn't pray at all, who seemed particularly grief-stricken, resigned, sad or, more importantly, unconcerned or even satisfied.

Odds were good they would get a shot of the killer. The investigative team just had to recognize it.

Though the casket had been open at the church—the admiral visible from the middle up, his expression stern, his dress white coat covered with row after row of medals—there had been no reception line. After the final prayer, the casket had been secured, and the pall-bearers, half navy, half civilian, had carried the casket outside and to the hearse.

So the mourners had formed a ragged reception line here in the cemetery, near the vehicles, with live oaks for shade, a good distance from the family crypts. Endless handshakes, hugs, words of regret. Did it mean anything to them? Alia wondered. Mary Ellen seemed the type to find comfort in so many people saying good things about her father. Landry looked like walking home barefoot on sunbaked pavement sounded more enticing than hearing a second's more praise about Jeremiah.

"As soon as the others leave, the cemetery work-ers will open the crypt." Jimmy gestured toward the structure twenty feet away that reminded her of a small marble temple with elaborate carvings on the outside. "They'll slide him inside, then seal it up until the next family member croaks. If it's less than a year and a day, the next one will have to go into another crypt. That's why so many families have more than one."

Alia blocked a bead of sweat before it reached the cor-ner of her eye, then wrinkled her nose in a sniff. "The flowers are going bad."

Jimmy laughed. "Haven't you ever smelled decomp? Bodies stink, sweet pea, and nothing out here seals to-tally airtight. A little stench escapes in all cemeteries."

"I try not to hang out in cemeteries," she retorted.

With the number of mourners dwindling, the ceme-tery workers who would finish the burial moved to the Jackson crypt, one carrying a wide broom with a long handle, just like the one her dad used for sweeping out his garage. It brought her a shudder.

While they went to work, she deliberately shifted her attention to the small group of people still talking under the trees. Mary Ellen and Scott, their daughters' hands gripped between them. Two older couples, husbands and wives: Miss Viola's children and their spouses, Jimmy had said. Landry, a few feet off to the side, his back to her, hands in his pockets, looking at something she couldn't identify.

She'd watched him off and on through the service, as circumstances allowed. A lot of mourners had greeted him with hugs and kisses on his cheek—female mourners, most old enough to be his parents' friends, the others young enough to be the friends' daughters, girls he had grown up with. Everyone from the navy side of the house had shaken hands with him, but at least some of the civilians in outrageously expensive custom suits—Jeremiah's friends, best bet—had hardly acknowledged that he was there.

Interesting.

Hot, tired, anxious to get out of the sun, she was thinking an early dinner would be nice, comfort food that she could take home, curl up on her couch and make happy with, when the sky darkened and a breeze stirred her clothes. It was damp and smelled of rain, sweet scents that teased heartlessly through the summer days, occasionally delivering, just as often scudding away without spilling more than a few drops. A thunderstorm sounded so appealing—would make her comfort food that much more comforting and be the perfect ending to this sucky day.

The next gust of breeze was harder, flapping the open

edges of her jacket back enough to reveal her badge, pistol and Taser. It pulled a few strands of hair loose from its chignon and whipped her bangs to the side.

A few creaks and low conversation came from the area of the crypt. Alia stayed back far enough to get the general idea—there were some sort of fastenings holding the front plate to the marble that they had to undo—but she had no desire to match the imaginings in her head with what a real crypt looked like inside. She gazed at the family, then at the rows of tombs across the grass, some built of brick, some of concrete, most of marble, and she wondered how a cemetery had grown to encompass so much land in a neighborhood where small lots sold for six figures. Wealthy people, wanting the best address in life, apparently needed it in death, as well.

"Another minute," Jimmy said, and without thinking, she moved her gaze back to the crypt. The front panel was loose at the top, but the workers were having trouble with the bottom right corner. After a moment, one of the men jerked it to the sound of tearing fabric. They lifted it out of place, then it clattered to the ground, banging marble on the way down.

The two men spoke at the same time, one muttering, "Holy Mother of God!" while the other shrieked a profane version of the same words. Alia remained frozen for an instant, then caught up to Jimmy's long strides. He was speaking into his radio, calling the remaining team members to the crypt.

Abruptly he stopped, and she automatically sidestepped before pulling up short herself.

A form lay at the bottom of the crypt, dragged halfway out by the front that had snagged on fabric. It was curled into the fetal position and looked—God help her, she couldn't let herself focus on how it looked unless she wanted grotesque nightmares for the rest of her life. Holding her hand to her nose and mouth, she focused on the clothing: shades of pink and white, a jacket, a solid pink skirt. The shoes that no longer fit the decaying feet were pink, too, finely made, Louboutin, she thought. Alia's mother's only vice, her father often said, was those pricy red-soled shoes she loved so much.

"I guess the mystery regarding Camilla Jackson's whereabouts is solved." Jimmy sounded queasy, grim. He gestured the cemetery workers to wait near a crypt off in the distance, then said sourly, "Landry and his brother-in-law are on their way over here. I'll take care of this. You keep them away."

"I owe you, Jimmy." She took long strides, happy to find the air quality clearing significantly the farther she went. Catching Landry's arm, then Scott's with enough strength to turn them around, she said, "You can't go over there. In fact, it's best if you guys go home now." Miss Viola's family, she saw, were driving away without a clue that something had happened. Only Mary Ellen and the two girls waited next to the family car while the driver sat on a bench thirty feet away.

"What's going on?" Landry demanded, trying to pull free of her, twisting to look over his shoulder. She didn't let go, didn't slow her steps but continued to force them along with her. "What happened?"

At last, he dug in his heels, turning around, blocking her way with his body, making her stop or plow into him. His eyes dark and stormy, he stared at her, silently demanding an answer. She gave it quietly.

"It appears we've found your mother."

Chapter 6

Landry stared at her, the words echoing in his head, needing a minute to grasp their meaning. He looked at the crypt, at the bundle lying half in, half out. It didn't belong there, some part of his rational brain thought. When a crypt was opened, the remains of the last person buried were swept to the back, into a sort of well. There shouldn't be anything that close to the door, close enough to fall out.

Then that same part of his brain noticed the blond hair and the pink material—clothing—and remembered that his mother loved pink before it shut down. Blankness spread through him. He couldn't think, couldn't feel, couldn't shrug off Alia's hold and move closer.

It appears we've found your mother.

His stomach roiled, bile rising into his throat. He jerked his gaze back to Alia, searching her face for some sign that he'd misunderstood her words, but her features were solemn, sympathetic.

It appears we've found your mother.

Beside him, Scott murmured something—*Oh, dear God*—then a delicate hand gripped Landry's left arm. Not Alia's. He could still feel it, the pressure of her fingers, the warmth of her touch, on his right arm. He looked at Mary Ellen, whose pale face was marked with five days of heartbreaking grief, whose eyes were so wide that they looked as if they might pop right out of her head.

"Landry, she said— What about Mama? What did she—" Her gaze slid from him to Alia, then to the activity at the crypt. Other cops had joined DiBiase there, blocking the body from sight. But Mary Ellen didn't need to see more. Her fingers bit into his arm, tears welled in her eyes and an unholy scream echoed off the nearest tombs, scraping his skin raw, making him wince and, for an instant, try to move away.

The wail ended abruptly as Mary Ellen sagged to the ground. Landry grabbed her right arm, Scott her left. Landry swung her into his arms—she hardly weighed more than the girls—and started toward the car. As they drew close, the driver hustled over to open the rear door. Faith and Mariela were crying, Scott clutching Mary Ellen's limp hand, and the sky chose that moment to let the rain fall down.

After settling his sister on the wide rear seat, he straightened. "Take her to the hospital," he said quietly to Scott. She'd been taking sedatives all week; he was afraid this was one shock too many for those to manage.

"What about you and the girls?" Scott asked, even as he slid into the car.

"We'll get a ride home."

"My parents can take care of them. I'll call as soon as…"

Landry nodded, then lifted the girls into his arms, their thin little arms clenching his neck tightly. They watched solemnly as the limo pulled away.

"What's wrong with Mama?" Faith whispered.

"She's just sad and tired. She'll be fine after she's rested awhile." He hoped she was fine. She'd never been the strongest person around…but she'd survived hell before. This time she had her girls and Scott to help her.

Wearily he looked at Alia. "Can someone give us a ride?"

"I will. My car's the gray one right there." She beeped open the doors on a midsize sedan down the block. "Just give me a minute."

He took the girls to the car, fastening their seat belts, giving them reassuring smiles. "Everything's gonna be all right," he said, forcing a smile. "Your mama and daddy will be home as soon as possible, and Nana and Papa are at the house waiting for you." The elder Davisons had driven down from Baton Rouge for the funeral. They were as well entrenched in Baton Rouge society as the Jacksons were in New Orleans, but that was where the similarities ended. Mr. and Mrs. Davison were honorable, loving, decent people, who treasured their family and most other people.

"Will they take us for ice cream after dinner if we've been good?" Mariela's voice trembled, and a fat tear was caught in her long lashes.

Landry brushed away the tear. "Don't they always take you for ice cream?"

"Yep, except once when I punched Faith and she

looked like a purple-eyed monster. They took her but made me stay home with Mama, and they didn't bring me nothing, neither."

Landry managed a grin. "Did you learn your lesson about punching people colors they aren't supposed to be?"

"Yeah." She didn't sound particularly convincing. After a moment, she added in a whisper, "Mama turned white. She looked like a ghost."

Or as if she'd seen one.

He responded absently, then closed the door and waited near the front of the car. The trees that lined the street provided protection from the rain; only the occasional drop made it through to splatter him. Not so for the detectives and NCIS agents out in the open of the cemetery. They looked as if they'd had to swim upriver in the Mississippi to get to the tombs. They would be there awhile, gathering whatever evidence remained from the taking of Camilla's life and stuffing her body into a mostly airtight chamber, and they'd pulled out tarps and slickers to protect both them and the crime scene.

Crime scene. First the site of his father's death, now that of his mother's.

Despite her suit—gray seemed to be the color of the day—it was easy to pick out Alia. There were other women, but she was the tallest, the leanest, and she held herself with the most confidence. After a moment, she finished her conversation with DiBiase, then jogged to the car, her heels and the rapidly softening ground providing no obstacle. He suspected she was the sort of woman who could run in sky-high heels—or barefoot across glass—if the situation required it.

Raindrops glistened in her hair and on her face as she

looked at him over the roof of the car, waiting for his questions, but he had only one.

"Are you sure?"

She didn't dodge his gaze, didn't try to put him off. "As sure as we can be without the coroner signing off on it."

Of course they were sure. Camilla was missing, and there was an extra body in the Jackson crypt that fitted her description. Who else could it be?

As the leaves overhead grew more sodden, more rain slipped through. He ignored it, though, staring at Alia, aware of the activity in the distance but unwilling to break his gaze and look that way. "I thought…I thought maybe she'd finally found the courage to leave Jeremiah, or that the old man had committed her somewhere for her drinking. But I never thought…"

…that someone had hated her enough to want her dead. Had despised her enough to leave her body inside the family crypt—

A chill passed through him, knotting in his gut. What if she hadn't been dead when she was put inside? Dear God, what if she had been buried alive? She'd apparently been huddled next to the door. Banging on it? Screaming for help? Trying to claw her way free? Knowing she was going to die, suffering from dehydration, sweltering in the heat and humidity, horrified by what was happening with no way to prevent it or hasten it.

His stomach heaved, and he clamped one hand over his mouth.

Wishing the numbness would return, Landry got into the car. Alia did the same, starting the engine, buckling her seat belt. It took only a few minutes to reach Mary Ellen and Scott's house, where she took advantage of an empty space in the driveway. Guests were visible through the open windows and gathered in small groups on the veranda. No doubt they had wondered what had taken so long for the immediate family to return, and now, seeing only him and the girls, they began stepping outside, staring, speaking in low voices to one another. The only face he was happy to see was Miss Geneva's. As he freed the girls from the backseat, he instructed them to go straight to the housekeeper and tell her he'd talk to her in a minute.

Mariela and Faith knew when to press their luck. Ordinarily, they would have stopped at each group of people who called their names, but this time they did exactly as he requested, not talking to anyone until they reached Geneva.

Landry walked around to the driver's door, and Alia rolled down the window. There were about a dozen things he could say, but not one of them could make its way past the shock keeping him stiff and cold. He settled on the easiest. "Thanks for the ride."

"You're welcome. Let me know how Mary Ellen is." She offered him a business card, identical to the one he'd left in the backyard on Monday, and their fingers touched when he took it. It was the same contact he made every day, passing drinks to customers, taking credit cards, returning change, impersonal, over and done with in seconds.

Except this time. It felt anything but impersonal: sympathetic, reassuring, just plain…nice. He looked at the cell number, an easy one to recall, and slid it into his coat pocket.

"When you find out something about Camilla…"

"I'll let you know."

The coroner could tell them a few interesting facts—how Camilla died, when—but would he be able to answer the important stuff, like how she had wound up inside a sealed tomb? Had she gone willingly with the person who locked her inside or been forced by someone armed, someone dangerous? Had she been conscious and alert or drugged only to awaken alone in the dark? Would the coroner have an explanation for what kind of sick person chose a nightmare like this to kill?

Someone called his name from the steps—a cousin on the Landry side of the family, he thought—and he glanced that way before looking back at Alia. He didn't have anything else to say, though. She smiled faintly, waited for him to step back, then pulled out of the driveway.

Hands in his pockets, he climbed the porch steps where all the little knots of people were consolidating into one large crowd. Ignoring their looks, he wrapped his arm around Geneva's shoulders and walked inside with her and the girls, located Scott's parents and went onto the sunporch to break the news.

Nothing spoke to Alia's soul like the blues on a rainy New Orleans evening.

She stood just inside the doors of Blue Orleans, listening to the mournful wail of a solitary saxophone, its notes high and clear, sending a wave of melancholy and pleasure and pure emotion through to her bones.

The bar was crowded, every table occupied, customers three-deep at the bar. Given the rain that flowed in small rivers down the street, she would bet most of the customers were tourists, unwilling to let a little bad weather interfere with their limited time in the Big Easy.

Umbrellas lay scattered beneath tables, and cheap pon-chos dangled from chair backs, their advertising visible only in folds. Raucous laughter echoed off the high ceil-ing, bounced off the brick walls and drifted out the four sets of open double doors, the best kind of advertising: *fun being had here.*

According to her notes, Landry had an apartment in the building, somewhere through the locked gate around to the right. She could have called him—could have waited until working hours on Monday—but she'd been in a mood to get out, to remind herself that the city was still filled with polite, funny, rude, arrogant, living peo-ple, that not everything right now was about death.

She was about to shuck her slicker and head for the bar when movement in the corner to her left caught her attention. A waitress stood at the table, her lime-green T-shirt practically glowing in the dim light, a tray in one hand, the other on her hip, but she didn't interest Alia. Her customer did.

It was easier to step outside again, one large step onto the battered sidewalk, then stride to the last set of doors propped open for fresh and cooling air. She took the overhigh step up again, then slid into the nearest chair, pulled her arms from the waterproof jacket and wel-comed the breeze washing over her skin.

Landry looked up at her, his eyes fatigued, beard stubble dark on his jaw. He looked much the same as the first time she'd seen him, motionless and alert in his sister's sunroom, wearing an aloha shirt and shorts, this time with much-abused tennis shoes. Except for his face. Weariness was etched in deep lines alongside his mouth and at the corners of his eyes, and his lips were set in so thin a line that they practically disappeared. She couldn't tell if he was happy, annoyed or unconcerned to see her here.

"How is Mary Ellen?" she asked.

"Sedated. The hospital's keeping her for a couple of days." His voice was little more than a rasp. Had he talked too much, explaining the surprises of the funeral to too many people? Or had that rawness come from tears? He may have hated his father, but there'd been softer emotions between him and Camilla. It wouldn't surprise anyone to find he'd shed tears for her.

She waited a moment as a group of young women splashed by loudly on the sidewalk, shrieking, their accents nasal and hard on the ear. When they were out of earshot, she asked, "How are you?"

"I've been better." He shrugged. "I've been worse, too."

The waitress held up a beer bottle as she passed, but Alia shook her head and asked for water.

What qualified for worse? she wondered as the woman brought a local brand of water. What was worse than your father's violent murder, your surrogate grandmother's killing and the discovery of your mother's gruesome death all in five days? She wasn't sure she wanted to know. She didn't need those thoughts in her head.

Landry was drinking but not bothering with a glass. A bottle of tequila, the good stuff, sat in the middle of the table, and he lifted it to take a cautious swallow. Nearly half of the bottle was gone, but she couldn't see its effects on him. No slurring, no shakes, no hysterics.

As he set it down, his fingers gave the etched bottle a lingering caress. "The people I work with don't waste their money on flowers. They let aged liquor do their speaking for them."

"Good people. I'm not sure the ones I work with have ever bought me more than a Coke."

"That's because your people are out to save the world, not meet its sinners halfway." He paused, his lean fingers twined around the base of the tequila bottle. "Have you heard anything from the coroner?"

"Jimmy just called." He'd offered to break the news to Landry, but Alia had volunteered. Her house was near; she needed to get out. Jimmy had scoffed, not impressed by either reason. *He's not half as handsome as I am, and I'm not wearing a hands-off sign. Playing with me won't get a slap on the wrist in your jacket for inappropriate conduct.*

But her ex had made his argument and left it at that. Rules weren't sacred to Jimmy but were more like suggestions. In his world, the good guys took advantage of the rules that helped them get what they needed and ignored the ones that didn't. It was one reason he'd had such a good solve rate in his career.

Alia drew a deep breath and locked gazes with Landry. "DNA will take a while, but the dental records are a match. The body was definitely your mother's."

The color didn't drain from his face. The only color he'd got back after they'd spoken at the cemetery was the flush in his cheeks that came from the liquor. Something appeared in his eyes, though—shock, sick to his soul, unable to grasp the insanity that would make a person do this thing to another person.

"How long had she been…?"

"Best guess is three to four weeks."

"So she didn't take off to visit relatives like the old man claimed. She was dead the whole time he was lying about her."

"Very likely."

Alia and Jimmy had debated it earlier. What had Jackson known and when had he known it? Had he been the one to kill Camilla? Had he discovered that she was having an affair and intended to leave him? Had he killed her, then disposed of her body where she would be trapped with the Jacksons forever? Or had she refused to leave her husband, so her lover had entombed her in the family crypt?

"Was she—?"

Alia could guess the question from the reluctance suddenly radiating from him and the certainty, sharp and electric, that he didn't want to know, but she figured he had to ask. No matter how he hated it, how totally comfortably he could live the rest of his life without hearing the answer, he forced the words out.

"Was she alive when she was put there?" The last few words stuck in his throat, and he swallowed hard, as if they'd created a huge blockage nothing more than air could get around.

She answered, her voice only a little louder than the rain plopping outside the door. "Yes." *Please don't ask how we know,* she prayed. *Please don't make me tell you that her fingernails were broken and bloodied from trying to claw her way out.* She didn't want those nightmares in her head, and she damn sure didn't want to put them in his.

His mouth fixed again in a narrow line, he stood, his chair scraping loudly, handed the tequila off to the waitress and headed out the door. Alia swung her jacket on as she followed. Instead of turning left, toward the entrance to his apartment, he went right, and she matched pace with him, grateful she'd chosen sturdy sandals that would dry in an hour, with thick straps that kept them from slipping and sliding on her feet.

Halfway down the block, he glanced at her. Rain dripped from his hair, forcing it flat against his head, catching on his lashes, leaving him to squint to bring her into focus. "So this is the career you've chosen for yourself."

She pushed her hands into her pockets, the bulges of her badge, her weapon and her Taser pressing back comfortably. If not for those items, she'd be in shirtsleeves, like him, and enjoying the rain more. "The job's not all about making notifications."

"Or seeing dead bodies. Or interviewing people who do awful things to other people because they can. But that's a lot of it."

She gave him the answer that, right out of college, she had given her mother. "As long as there are criminals in the world, there's got to be someone to catch them."

And he responded with her mother's retort. "Why does that someone have to be you?"

Smiling thinly, she swiped a stream of water from her face. "I love my job. It gives me a sense of satisfaction. I know I do something that matters."

"It doesn't give you nightmares?"

"On occasion. But so does late-night TV."

"Do you ever turn it off?"

They stopped at a corner to let a cab pass. The rain formed halos around the streetlights ahead, muted the music and conversation coming through open doors and turned the few people other than tourists on the street into huddling, hustling figures, keeping to the building sides in an effort to minimize the soaking. Even the tourists hurried, dashing and laughing from one bar to the next. Only she and Landry took their time.

"I have a life outside of work," she said evenly.

"Though present circumstances might argue the opposite. Your day should have ended three or four hours ago, and yet here you are."

It was the perfect statement to ignore. That was her intention, but all on its own, her mouth opened and words she shouldn't be thinking, much less speaking aloud, found their way out. "Work was just the excuse. I wondered how you were doing."

He looked at her—just that—and heat began rising from deep inside. If she were in the habit of lying to herself, she would have said it was due to the slicker, too heavy and too waterproof for a warm wet night. But she didn't lie to herself. Though the slicker was uncomfortable, it wasn't responsible for her increasing temperature.

After a long time, he looked away, as physical a feeling as removing his hand from hers would have been, and they began walking again. "It's been a tough five days." He gazed ahead as if the drenched scene bore watching.

Recalling his words in the bar—*I've been better. I've been worse, too*—she said, "Please don't say you've had worse."

The bit of his mouth she could see curved up in a sardonic smile. "No, of course not. What could be worse?"

Scowling, she bumped her shoulder against his. "Now I know you're lying, and I'll have to wonder—"

"Don't." His voice was barely audible, his gaze narrowed, his mouth thinned again. It was the last he spoke for more than a block.

Lies and secrets. A hell of a legacy for Jeremiah and

Camilla Jackson to have left their children, compared to Alia's own parents, who'd wanted nothing more than for her to be happy, healthy and loved. If she were an overly emotional person, the difference would make her misty-eyed. She would hurt for the children Landry and Mary Ellen had been, for the people they had become, for the people they would be once all this ugliness was sorted out.

In an effort to lighten the mood, she said, "Your nieces are cute."

That earned her more of a smile, lacking the sardonic curl. "They're angels when they want to be."

"How often is that?"

"Not as often as it should be. They hate to upset their mother, but sometimes the opportunity to be bad is just too good to pass up."

"Hell, I'm thirty, and I still occasionally find myself in those situations. My theory is you have to be bad once in a while to appreciate the good."

He gave her a sidelong look. "What does Special Agent/Admiral's Daughter Kingsley do to appreciate the good?"

The fact that no answer popped instantly into her mind made her mouth quirk. Obviously, she was never really bad, or she wouldn't have to think to find a response. She shrugged. "Once a month, my friends and I go out and put the loud, tipsy, flingy tourists to shame." Except that her last fling had been so long ago, she couldn't have remembered it even if she hadn't been tipsy at the time, though she did have this vague recollection of fumbling in the dark to step into indecently high heels, having to balance herself against a hotel room door and spending the time it took her to escape the hotel trying to remember if her car was nearby or at home.

Now, it was mostly her responsibility to get all her friends back home again when the evening was over.

"Wow," he said, unimpressed. "You're going to hell for that."

She laughed. "Okay, so I'm not wild, wicked or reckless."

"Being wild, wicked and reckless is overrated anyway."

"Spoken from experience?"

Landry had had a lot of experiences, including some he'd rather never think about again. Thanks to *those* experiences, he'd also missed out on others that he was pretty sure would surprise Alia. "You think I'm wild, wicked or reckless because I tend bar on Bourbon Street?"

"No. Because you look like every woman's fantasy of the quintessential bad boy."

Did *every woman* include her? he wondered, because he had to admit, he wouldn't mind being her fantasy, at least for a while. "Sorry to disappoint you, but I'm not wild or wicked or reckless. I didn't have much choice about being responsible, not if I wanted to stay off the streets." Miss Viola had helped him financially in the beginning and would have continued to do so much longer, but he'd wanted independence. He'd wanted to prove to himself and to Jeremiah, even if the old man never actually knew, that he could take care of himself, that he didn't need anybody.

At the end of the block, they turned right, heading toward the Mississippi River a few streets ahead. There were fewer people, less traffic, more homes than businesses and no signs of life besides the television blaring from an open window and a cat picking its way along the top of an eight-foot-high cinder-block wall, tail curled over its back, unmindful of the rain. A sideways look showed Alia keeping a wary gaze on it until they passed the property.

"Don't like cats?" He kept his grin from fully forming but couldn't stop the amusement audible in his voice.

"Don't trust them." Her own tone was suspicious. "They always seem to be plotting something."

"Our neighbors had one when Mary Ellen and I were kids." Its name was Ginger, and he hadn't thought about it in at least fifteen years. "It used to come through the bars of the wrought iron fence and use the flower beds as a litter box. It drove the gardener crazy."

Mention of the gardener made him think of Constance Marks. He was ashamed to admit that he hadn't spared any thought for the others who had died along with the admiral. He'd never met Jeremiah's housekeeper and had run into Constance only a time or two on visits to Miss Viola's. She'd been pleasant, friendly and happy with her work…and she'd died because of Jeremiah. As if he hadn't ruined enough lives already.

Alia must have gotten distracted by the same thing because her next question was on that subject. "I can't remember if I've asked… Did you know Constance Marks?"

Delaying, he made a show of checking his watch. "I was wondering how long it would be until you got back to the case."

"No, you weren't." When he merely lifted one brow in question, she scowled. Would she be flattered if he told her she looked cute when she did that: forehead wrinkled, mouth thinned, eyelashes glistening with rain-drops? Probably not. He suspected she wanted to be per-ceived as tough and capable and kick-ass. Hell, as far as he'd seen, she *was* tough and capable and kick-ass.

"Okay," she challenged. "How long was it?"

"Uh…sorry, I don't do math in my head."

"You can't answer because you didn't get a starting time." Giving him a chastising look, she waited a beat, then asked, "So, did you? Know Constance, I mean."

Landry sighed. "Never to say more than hi-how-are-you. She was picking up new clients and working long hours. Miss Viola regretted that Constance didn't have time to chat much anymore. Have you talked to her fam-ily and friends?"

"No, but some of our team have. She was single, loved her work and being her own boss. She dated but never exclusively. She could be a bitch at times but had a knack for dealing with difficult people. Her career goals were princess or lawn service entrepreneur, her brother said, but since there weren't many princes seeking wives, she'd opted for the lawn service. Her five-year plan in-cluded franchises within the state; in ten years, she in-tended to have them everywhere."

But then she'd been in the wrong place at the wrong time. End of hopes and goals and plans.

"Is it possible your mother could have been having an affair?" Of course once the subject had been reopened, Alia had thought of another question. No matter what she said about having a life outside of work, he'd bet this was the norm for her: focusing intently on the mystery in front of her, searching and probing until she resolved it.

Music drifting on the sodden air drew his gaze to a restaurant half a block down the street on Decatur. The blues guitar came from there, the band set up under-neath the canopy that sheltered the restaurant's patio dining area.

"I'm hungry," he said and realized it was true. Though there had been enough food at Mary Ellen's to feed half the city, he'd got out of there as quickly as he could, with-out tasting even one oyster on the half shell. "Are you?"

"I can always eat."

They stopped, waiting for the light to turn green, and crossed the street, then he steered Alia toward the music as he finally responded to her question. "I wonder what it's like to have a normal family, where you don't get asked questions like, 'Who would want your father dead?' or 'Was your mother sleeping with anyone other than your father?'"

"Sorry."

She probably was, he acknowledged. But she had a job to do, and he'd already seen that she didn't shy away from the tough parts.

They reached the brighter lights of the restaurant and within minutes were seated at a table on the patio as the band launched into an old Bobby Bland tune. There was a slight slope to the bricks that made up the patio, not even noticeable if not for thin streams of rain running toward the curb.

He ordered a shrimp po' boy and beer; she got a shrimp cocktail, oysters and tea, and finally he returned to her question. "You're asking a pretty personal thing about someone I only see—" Pain sliced through him, and he corrected himself. "Someone I only saw twice a year for a few hours. Anything's possible. I'd like to think maybe she was, just to have the satisfaction of knowing she'd betrayed the old man. It would be nice to believe that, at least for a while, she'd had some guy in her life who actually gave a damn about her. But anything I say would only be a guess. I have no more idea about Camilla's faithfulness than I'd have about yours when you were married."

There was an extra napkin on the table. She used it to pat her face, then combed back her hair so it dripped down her back. "I had to be faithful enough for both Jimmy and me. Who would your mother have confided in?"

It took a moment for her first statement to sink in, thrown out there so casually as if it was something everyone knew or was so insignificant that she didn't care who knew it. "Wait. Say that again?"

She pulled off her slicker, exposing her long bare arms, lacking the impressive muscles of her legs but none too shabby, either. Once she hung the jacket over the back of her chair, she tugged her tank top down, paying particular attention to the part covering the weapons he'd grown accustomed to, and then her dark gaze locked with his. "Your response indicates that you heard it perfectly well the first time."

"And you let him live?"

She smiled. "Divorce was a lot easier than going to prison."

What had been going through DiBiase's mind, having a woman like this to go home to and looking elsewhere? The guy was crazy. But she seemed all right with it, now, at least. There wasn't any hurt in her expression, no anger or regret. No leftover love, no broken heart. He'd been a fool, but she'd moved on.

Did DiBiase have regrets? When he looked at her,

worked a case with her, shared a meal with her, did he wish they were still together?

The waitress set their food in front of them, and Alia removed the silverware from her napkin before shaking out the linen and laying it across her lap. Wasting no time, she peeled a jumbo shrimp, coated it liberally with cocktail sauce and took a bite before closing her eyes and sighing. "Mmm. Ketchup, of course. Worcestershire sauce, hot sauce, horseradish and…" She dipped the shrimp again, took another bite, her brow wrinkling. "There's something else…"

Landry leaned across to pick up the glass. One sniff, and he answered for her. "Gin." At her glance, he shrugged. "When you spend eight to ten hours a day pouring booze, you get familiar with the smells."

They both fell silent, switching their attention to their food. It had taken only a few bites of po' boy to settle the pangs in his stomach, but he forced a few more. It had been a tough few days, he'd told Alia earlier, but the truth was, the bad days, they were still coming, with Miss Viola's funeral scheduled for tomorrow and, soon as the coroner released Camilla's body, hers to arrange and get through.

Seemed like a hell of a good time to take a vacation. Someplace tropical, maybe, with salt-rimmed margaritas, good food and fine-sand beaches, lying in a hammock and letting the pounding waves lull him into a state where nothing mattered but that minute, that drink, that nap, that meal.

He was feeling a little lulled right now: the hammock turning into a chair, the margarita looking and tasting more like a beer, rain pounding instead of waves, good food and definitely good company.

Alia had finished the shrimp and was squeezing lemon over the oysters, nestled in their shells on a bed of ice. Apparently having taken the edge off her hunger, she dried her hands fastidiously on her napkin, then fixed her gaze on him. "Want an oyster?"

"No, thanks."

She didn't miss a beat. "We were talking about who Camilla would have told about an affair."

"It never would have been me or Mary Ellen. You'd do better asking her who Camilla's friends were once she's feeling better."

"Maybe Miss Viola?"

He appreciated the chance to smile, however ruefully. "Oh, hell, no. Miss Viola didn't tolerate adulterers. Her father ran around on her mother every chance he got, and the word *discreetly* wasn't in his vocabulary. Her mother just shrugged and said that's the way men are. He topped it all off by dying in a hotel room with a prostitute half his age." He shook his head, remembering when the old lady had told him the story. She'd meant it as a teachable moment, but he'd been old enough to figure out fidelity, commitment and honor on his own. "Much as she despised Jeremiah, Miss Viola never would have forgiven Camilla for breaking her marriage vows."

Alia sprinkled a tiny bit of salt, no more than five or six grains, on an oyster, lifted the shell and tilted it into her mouth. The look on her face was one of sheer pleasure. Food, it seemed, made her very happy.

He liked a woman who appreciated the simple things in life.

Swiping her mouth with a napkin, she took a drink, then frowned. "Well, that rules out that theory. We thought Camilla might have been killed by a spurned lover, who then killed the admiral for standing in the way of his happiness, and because Miss Viola was aware of the affair, he had to silence her, as well. But if Miss Viola didn't know…"

Then why was she killed? Landry supposed it was possible that there could have been two murderers, two motives, but he didn't buy it for a moment. Jeremiah's and Miss Viola's deaths had to be connected. They'd lived in the same city, the same neighborhood, known the same people, had gone to the same parties, had the same kind of influence. But the only connection of any substance between them was Camilla, Mary Ellen and the girls and, more distantly, Landry. No reason there for murder.

"Could have been a family dispute of some sort," Alia said in a dubious voice that suggested she was thinking aloud rather than putting forth a real theory.

"Except they weren't family."

"Yeah, there is that." She turned her chair to face him, then drew her feet into the seat. To go with the white tank, she wore denim shorts, snug-fitting and showing a lot of shapely brown leg, and sandals. She looked younger than he felt, energy humming just below the surface but lacking any nervous habits to dispel any of it. She was still and thoughtful and prettier than he'd thought the first time he'd seen her.

…You look like every woman's fantasy of the quintessential bad boy.

If the opportunity to be bad—with her—presented itself, he just might have to take it. She was a pretty damn good fantasy, too.

With a one-track mind.

"Your mother's death was awful," she began again.

"Your father's was vicious. There was no effort to make them look like anything but what they were—the acts of a very angry person. Miss Viola's, though, was meant to look like an accident. It could have so easily slipped past us."

"So what does that mean?" Landry was aware there were various successful television series, to say nothing of countless books and websites, dealing with crimes and investigations, but he'd had enough ugliness in his life. He wasn't particularly interested in the medical, legal, technical or psychological aspects of law and order.

"The obvious, of course—that the killer was more pissed off with Jeremiah and Camilla than with Miss Viola. He felt more…well, not kindly but less angry with her." Her lips pursed, pretty and pink though any lipstick she'd put on had long since worn off. "It just doesn't seem her and Jeremiah's paths crossed very often, not recently and certainly not in a way that would lead to their deaths."

For a time she focused on the band, keeping time with the music with her entire body. He wondered if she'd ever studied ballet or gymnastics, if she liked to dance, not just to hook up with some guy in a club but because the music touched her, drew the movement from her.

There was room between the tables. What if he helped her to her feet, pushed their chairs aside and took her in his arms? Would she remember too quickly that she was investigating three crimes and that he was an unwilling subject caught in the aftermath? Or would she shut off the questions and the theories and striving to solve the puzzle and just dance with him?

There was only one way to find out, but he didn't do it—didn't pull her from the chair, wrap his arms around her, draw her near and wait for her response. Maybe sometime he would, if he saw her again on a night like tonight. Maybe when the murders weren't between them.

When he'd finally brought his own secrets out of the dark.

Chapter 7

Saturday was the kind of day that, no matter where she lived, would always make Alia think of New Orleans: the sun burning hot in a sky of thin, pale blue, the air so muggy that it shimmered and danced, blinding the eye when it happened upon a shiny surface. It was the sort of day for sitting on a broad shaded porch, paddle fan turning overhead, a pitcher of iced tea sweating on the table, wicker creaking, cushions shifting, bees buzzing in the flowers nearby. Laziness would float on the air, along with Eric Clapton, B. B. King or Louis Armstrong himself, while kids played in sprinklers and dogs hunkered in the cool damp earth beneath an azalea bush.

It was a day only a true Southerner could enjoy, a day for making outsiders think about returning to wherever they came from.

A day for laying to rest a woman who had thrived through thousands of such days.

Alia stood in the shade of a tree she didn't recognize—much to her mother's dismay when it came weeding time in the garden, she'd never been interested in flora and fauna—and watched as mourners filed from the church. Some stood and talked, some left and others went to their cars, starting the engines, rolling down windows and turning the air-conditioning to high while they waited for the procession to the cemetery to begin. She'd seen a lot of the same faces yesterday, genuine regret replacing yesterday's curiosity and obligation. No doubt, Miss Viola was a much easier person to mourn than Jeremiah.

Landry's gaze sought hers as he came out of the church and started down the wide brick steps. She'd seen him arrive, alone, looking as if he'd rather be anywhere else in the world. Miss Viola's daughter had greeted him at the door with a hug and an affectionate squeeze on the arm before walking inside with him. Lucky for Landry, she seemed well aware of her mother's fondness for him and his for her.

He came to stand beside her, hands in his pockets. He was dressed more casually than yesterday, in dark gray trousers and a dress shirt of a paler shade. Gray was such an inoffensive color, somber, suitable for everyone, but with the shirt collar undone and the sleeves rolled halfway up his forearms, he still pulled off an effortless sense of elegance and grace.

"Are you allowed to speak to the suspects while you're surveilling them?" he asked, gazing at the mourners instead of her.

Following his lead, she kept her own gaze directed elsewhere. "Only when I interrogate them."

He remained silent for so long that she slanted a look his way. "That was meant to be humorous."

"You have an odd sense of humor."

"I work with dead people and the criminals who made them that way." Almost immediately, she winced. "I shouldn't be flippant."

His shoulders shifted in the slightest of accepting shrugs. "If you can't laugh, you have to drink until you cry."

A moment passed, fewer people trailing out of the church. She, Jimmy and the rest of the squad would be studying their photographs later, looking for a person who might have pushed a frail eighty-one-year-old lady down the stairs. Landry was right. If she couldn't laugh, booze would be a tempting alternative.

"How is your sister?"

"The doctor released her today. She wanted to come, but…" His tone turned dark, laced with pain. "She couldn't stop shaking long enough to get dressed. Scott said the doctor sent a medicine cabinet full of sedatives, sleeping pills and antianxiety drugs with her."

Like Miss Viola—even more than Miss Viola—Mary Ellen was frail. Given the past week, even the strongest woman Alia knew would have taken to her bed with a handful of pills.

"I'm really sorry about Miss Viola," she said at last.

Finally he looked at her. Shadows smudged across his cheeks, making his eyes seem even darker, and lines etched outward from the corners of his eyes and his mouth. "Thank you."

"Are you going to the cemetery?"

"Are there any other missing people who might fall out of the crypt when they open it?"

"None that I know of. We'll cross our fingers." She raised her left hand, showing her index and middle fingers twined together.

Again, silence settled between them, but it was comfortable, not the kind she felt the urge to fill with chatter. A good thing, since she'd never had much talent for chatter.

Finally the church doors were propped open wide, and the funeral director led six young men bearing the casket down the steps and to the hearse. Jimmy had identified them before the service: three grandsons and three grandsons-in-law. They carried out this last task they could do for the old lady stoically, though tears streaked silently down the face of the youngest.

"I've never had to bury anyone I loved," she murmured.

"Not even a dog?"

"The only pet we ever had is my mother's Chihuahua. He's too mean to die. Every time I see him, he snaps and snarls like I'm some stray trying to steal the juicy T-bone he's got his eye on."

Unexpectedly, Landry grinned. "Aw, come on, admit it—you'd steal a T-bone from him if he had one, wouldn't you?"

She allowed a slow smile in response. "On the eighth day, God created steak, cooked it rare and it was good."

"Eat it raw, baby," he murmured with a chuckle.

From the far side of the church doors, Jimmy signaled, and she nodded. "Time to move out." She would bring up the rear of the procession today, giving her a little more time in the air-conditioned comfort of her vehicle, time to rejuvenate before getting out into the heat to wilt all over again.

She and Landry headed in different directions. The inside of her car was a pretty good approximation of hell itself, at least until she'd lowered all four windows and turned the AC on arctic blast. The breeze lifted damp tendrils of hair from her forehead and stirred the heavier braided strands on her neck. She'd worn a skirt today, linen in the same shade of khaki as the navy uniforms she saw at work every day, with a matching jacket and a sleeveless white blouse. She'd thought bare legs would be a little cooler, but that didn't seem to be the case.

After the last car had joined the procession, she pulled into line, followed only by the police escort bringing up the rear. There were enough cars that she imagined the first had arrived at the cemetery by the time she'd left the church. Lucky for her, she didn't have to worry about parking violations, or she would have been hiking five or six blocks back to the cemetery. Instead, she double-parked beside Jimmy's car, leaving just enough room for traffic to go around, and went in search of him.

She found him walking the southeast side of the graveyard. His face was flushed, his hair sticking to his forehead, his sunglasses pressing into the bridge of his nose. Fortunately, *hot and sweaty* was a good look for him. In the few moments it took her to catch up to him, she'd noticed a number of women, one from her own office, watching him with great appreciation.

Only Jimmy could hook up in the middle of a funeral. She shook her head with vague amusement.

"You look pretty, sweet pea," he drawled. "How 'bout you and I go out for a little dinner and dancing when this mess is over?"

Only Jimmy would ask for a date in the middle of a funeral.

"Nice turnout."

"Better than Jackson's." Jimmy laughed. "These folks are giving their funeral best a workout. They'll be back out here in a few days for Camilla's burial. Definitely no open casket for that one."

Alia's jaw tightened. What she'd seen of Camilla Jackson yesterday had topped her list of freakiest things ever and, please, God, would never be outdone.

"Does the coroner have a cause of death on Camilla?" she asked, wiggling her shoulders to loosen her sweat-soaked shirt from her back.

"It would be easier to figure out if he'd gotten the body before it turned to soup." Jimmy raised one hand to ward off a chastisement. "His words, not mine. Probably all he'll be able to offer on cause of death is an educated guess. Dehydration, maybe."

"Maybe she was literally scared to death." Alia rather liked small spaces herself, but finding herself in a crypt would certainly stop her heart.

"How's the daughter?"

"Out of the hospital and medicated out of her senses."

"How's the son?"

There was a slyness to his tone that made her turn her narrowed gaze on Jimmy. His features were almost expressionless, but there was a hint, just a hint, of a grin trying to break free. Haughtily, she said, "He's coping."

The grin succeeded. "You appear to be helping him with that." When she didn't respond, he went on. "Word is, you two took a long walk in the rain, then had dinner last night."

"You have him under surveillance?" The fine hairs on the back of her neck bristled. That was something she should have expected—and not a decision left to Jimmy alone. He wasn't the primary on the case; they shared those responsibilities. He should have discussed—

"Nah. I was going down to see Nina before she went to work and saw you at the restaurant. You both looked like you got dunked in the Mississippi, so I made a guess about the walk." He leered at her, but it was hard to take offense at it, what with him being Jimmy. "Besides, I remember that you used to like walking in the rain."

Alia forced a deep, calming breath. "I told him a positive ID had been made on Camilla and checked on Mary Ellen."

"So it was just business."

"Yeah." She breathed again. "Pretty much. Mostly." Something akin to relief at acknowledging her attraction to Landry seeped through her, easing the taut muscles in her neck. It wasn't really something she could discuss with either of her parents or anyone she worked with, and her ex excelled at keeping confidences, even though he was constitutionally incapable of fidelity. Maybe *because* he was constitutionally incapable of fidelity.

"You gone and gotten interested in some guy who isn't me?" He gave her a wounded look. "You're heartless, you know that? How we ever gonna work things out if you're seeing someone else?"

She met his gaze, hers level and unimpressed. "Jimmy, if we ever work things out, do me a favor and shoot me." Before he could respond, she changed the subject. "Who is Nina? Your girlfriend of the week?"

"Aw, we've been together way longer than that. At least two weeks." As they passed one of his fellow detectives, he nodded to the man, shoved his hands into his pockets, then slanted a look at her. "She's a nice woman. You'd like her."

"Really," she said drolly. "Because I don't remember liking *any* of your girlfriends when we were married. Where did you meet her?"

"Where she works. Down on Bourbon Street."

His face turned a deeper shade of crimson, the change having nothing to do with the heat, and it made Alia choke back a laugh. "You're dating a stripper, aren't you?" God, he was so predictable. "On second thought, if we ever work things out…" She gave him the same sort of sly look he'd passed her way earlier.

"I'll just shoot myself."

God love Saturday nights, it didn't matter how hot, humid, chilly or dreary they were, people still flooded the Quarter in general and Blue Orleans in particular. Landry had this one off, though, so he wasn't behind the bar, filling orders, visiting with friends or engaging in a little harmless flirtation with pretty tourists. He didn't feel like staying in the apartment, either, watching crap on TV and listening to the drone of the window air conditioner, so he'd headed out soon after the sun went down, aimlessly wandering the streets.

Now he was seated on the steps across from Jackson Square, listening to a lone saxophone down the street, punctuated by an occasional ship's whistle from the river. People thronged the sidewalks, drifting from restaurant to bar and out again, lining up for carriage rides, laughing, letting the good times roll. That was what New Orleans was known for, right? *Laissez les bons temps rouler.*

Miss Viola had been a good one for celebrating. She'd ridden Mardi Gras floats, dined at the finest restaurants and danced in the streets. Now she was gone. He'd seen her in her casket, had listened to the prayers said for her eternal soul, had watched her children and grandchildren cry, and still none of it seemed real. She'd been in his life forever, the one person he could always count on, and it was too damn wrong that he would never see her again.

"Hey."

It took him a moment to realize the voice was addressing him. He shifted his gaze from the Saint Louis Cathedral on the far side of the square to the woman—no, girl—standing a few steps down from the one he sat on. She was blond, slight, smiling at him the way the Kingsley family's Chihuahua likely eyed the T-bones Alia had talked about. He nodded in greeting, hoping she would go away, knowing she would…eventually.

The girl cast a look over her shoulder, and he followed her glance to the three girls watching a few yards away, all of them blond and slight and enjoying their night in the Big Easy. They were dressed for the weather and for fun, their four dresses combined falling short of enough fabric to make a decent tablecloth.

Not that he had anything against skimpy.

The nearest blonde smiled again, and the tiny stud in her nose flashed in the light. "My friends and I thought you looked lonely."

"You did, huh."

"We did." She tugged her tight blue dress down an inch or so before seating herself on the warm concrete beside him. Expensive perfume and cheap beer caught on the air for a moment, too much of both. "We thought you might like a little company."

He gave her a long look. If she and her friends showed up in his bar, he'd definitely card them and, depending on the quality of their fake IDs, probably wouldn't serve them. Obviously, not all bartenders had his high standards, he thought sardonically. "I appreciate the invitation, but—"

A flash of long legs in killer heels caught his attention. The newcomer stopped a few feet from the other girls and said in her dry, steady voice, "Whoa, catch and release, Landry."

Slowly he looked upward over lean calves, muscular thighs and a white dress as short and snug as any of the girls' to Alia's face, her smug smile, her black hair done up in some style that bared her neck. Oh, hell, yeah, he appreciated skimpy, even more on a woman who did it such justice.

"What does that mean?" The girl beside him didn't sound as if she was smiling anymore, a fact confirmed by a glance that showed her brows drawn together into a pouty frown.

Sure she wouldn't appreciate being compared to an undersized fish tossed back into the water, Landry shrugged. "Like I said, I appreciate the invitation, but..."

Scowling, the blonde stood, tossed her long curls, flounced down the steps and took off across the street with her friends.

Alia watched them. "They're too young to be allowed in public without a chaperone." Then she looked back at him. "I hope your tastes don't run that young. They'll get you in trouble."

"My tastes didn't run that young when I *was* that young." He let his gaze slide down again. "So you do have something other than ugly shoes in your closet."

"You try running around in heels all day. You'd prefer ugly shoes, too." She grimaced. "My feet are killing me. I intend to take them off as soon as I get to my car."

"An early end for a date, isn't it?"

"My friend got a babysitter at the last minute, so we had dinner at a new place over there." She waved off past Jax Brewery. "Unfortunately, Mom with a seven-month-old doesn't stay out late."

He didn't allow himself to consider that bit of relief he felt at hearing she hadn't dressed like that for a particular man. It wasn't his business who she dated or if she dated. "The dress is a nice change from the suits."

She glanced down at herself, then smiled. "Yeah, I like dressing up from time to time. I look pretty damn good."

Amen.

Gesturing to the foot traffic around them with her small white purse, she said, "Best free entertainment around, isn't it? The last time my parents visited, their favorite pastime was people-watching. Mom critiqued their outfits, Dad their behavior." She gave a soft regretful sigh. "If I'd ever left the house wearing dresses like your young friends', he would have sent the MPs after me—and trust me, there's not much more embarrassing to a teenage girl than being escorted from a party by MPs."

"You mean dresses like the one you're wearing?"

"Yes, but I'm thirty now, and Dad's retired. He doesn't get a say, and the MPs are no longer an option. Mom's only complaint, on the other hand, would be that I'm six inches taller than her so she couldn't wear it." She shifted her weight side to side, looked away, back, then asked, "You want a drink?"

Landry gave it a thought or two, though there was no question what his answer would be. He worked at a bar; he lived above it. Drinks were never hard to come by. But drinks with Alia… Even if he didn't have a taste for alcohol tonight, the company was worth his time.

"Sure." Pushing to his feet, he dusted his cargo shorts, then took the few steps to the sidewalk. "Where?"

"I—" Another shifting of feet in killer heels, another look away, then back. "I know a quiet place. My car is in the lot back here."

They were surrounded by bars, and she chose one not in walking distance. Again, not that he minded.

They moved in silence from concrete to gravel to pavement, then she stopped beside her gunmetal gray car, the same one that had been parked in Miss Viola's driveway on Tuesday. She beeped the doors open, then slid easily into the driver's seat. As he settled opposite her, true to her word, she slipped the heels off and tossed them into the back.

"I know women are supposed to have a great appreciation for heels," she said, bending forward to ruefully rub first one foot, then the other. "Mom has never worn anything else my whole life, but damn, I don't have that kind of pain threshold."

He watched the silky dress stretch and tighten across her shoulders, gleaming in the thin light of the streetlamps to contrast against the dark expanse of her bare arms. The sight was enough to form a lump in his throat that made him swallow hard. "You know, stores are filled with shoes that are flat or have a low heel that aren't ugly." He sounded strained, hoarse.

"Pardon me if I don't take footwear advice from the man wearing the rattiest pair of sandals I've seen in a long time." Leaning back, she fastened the seat belt— another enticing sight where the belt crossed between her breasts, then across her flat abdomen from hip to narrow hip.

In need of a breath, he took it and wound up snorting. "They're nowhere near the rattiest. I've got way rattier ones at home."

Her smile flashed as she backed out of the parking space. In a moment they were on Decatur, passing Jackson Square, heading toward the market. The restaurant they'd eaten at last night appeared, then flashed past, and the street got quieter, the sidewalks emptier, the streetlights fewer and farther between.

When she slowed, then turned onto a narrow street, he blinked. "You hang out on Serenity Street?" The neighborhood was small, only three main streets plus one two blocks long that connected them. The original houses had been stately, smaller versions of the Garden District homes—Greek Revivals, Creole cottages, Queen Anne Victorians—but as the crime rate went up, the families moved out and gangs moved in. Fifteen years ago, paramedics had required backup from the police before they would answer a call here. Ten years ago, the cops had required their own backup before coming in.

She pulled to the curb in front of an apparently abandoned house and shut off the engine. "Actually, I live on Trinity. About a half block down. It's not a bad place."

"Uh-huh. Miss Viola used to own a rental house at the end of Serenity Street. She wanted to check on it one day, so I came with her. We couldn't go any farther than this because some guy had gotten shot next door to her house because the beer he'd given his buddy wasn't cold enough." Landry got out when she did, looking around while she fumbled for her shoes, then circled the car to join him. "I don't suppose you're armed."

She gave him a dry look, arms held out from her body. "Do I look like I'm concealing a weapon here?"

Yeah, foolish question. But a man could do worse than an invitation to closely inspect a beautiful woman's body—visually, at least. He couldn't do much better than an invitation to repeat it physically.

Music and laughter came from down the street, and they headed in that direction. The sounds weren't from the bar Alia turned into, though—O'Shea's on the right side of the block—but originated in the yard of the house on the left side, where a dozen or so adults sat under tall oaks and an equal number of kids ran wild around them, ranging in age from barely toddling to watchful teenagers.

On his one trip to Serenity Street, he hadn't seen a single kid. Their parents didn't allow them to play outside, Miss Viola had told him, a sorry state from back in the day when it had been a real family neighborhood.

A half dozen whistles and appreciative calls greeted Alia as she made her way between tables in O'Shea's. She acknowledged them with a wave before claiming a table near a set of open French doors. Landry wondered about her choice when he glanced at the tall shutters that protected the glass from weather and saw what looked like a half dozen bullet holes in the much-painted wood.

But hell, why would he pay attention to bullet holes when he had Alia to look at?

The waitress, a college student who lived on Divinity Street, made Alia stand and turn so she could get a good look at the dress before switching her attention to Landry, in cargo shorts and snug-fitting T-shirt that said Welcome to New Orleans. Now Go Home. "Okay, guys, either one of you is way overdressed or the other is seriously underdressed," she commented in a drawl. "You need to coordinate your wardrobes better next time you go out."

Alia didn't correct her mistaken impression that they were on a date. She did spend a moment, though, thinking about a *next time*. She'd seen Landry dressed up and thought they'd make a damn good-looking couple. He'd seen her dressed down and didn't seem to mind. They'd still be damn good-looking. Besides, it was the *couple* part that made her heart go pitter-patter.

It had been a long time since that happened.

"Rum and Coke for you, Alia?" Tish asked, waiting for her nod before turning to Landry. "What about you, sweetie?"

He looked amused by the endearment and the motherly way she said it when she was at least eight or ten years younger than him. "Just a Coke."

As Tish left the table, Alia gazed out the door at the market they'd passed on the corner. Just the fact that the neighborhood had a market to provide its residents access to fresh and affordable food was a huge improvement, but the shutters bolted across the front, all the way from one brick wall to another, were a sign that not everything was changed. Like every part of every city, there were still problems.

Alia just might be facing a problem of her own. She shouldn't be here with Landry—should have kept walking back there in the Quarter, shouldn't have asked him to have a drink and damn sure shouldn't have brought him here, into her neighborhood. If he weren't a murder victim's son, if she weren't assigned to the case, no one would think twice about their sharing a purely social evening out. But he *was* a victim's son, and she *was* assigned to the case. Their spending time together could be construed as unprofessional—she was fairly certain her boss would think so—and Alia never did *anything* that even hinted at unprofessional.

Maybe she should. Maybe, just once, she could do what she wanted instead of what she should. The world wouldn't stop turning. Chaos wouldn't descend. What was the worst that could happen?

She could get a slap on the wrist at work, maybe more.

She could get her heart broken.

But she could have a hell of a good time in the process.

Landry sprawled in his chair, his long legs stretched out under the table. "So what's the story? You were new to town and didn't know the history of the area when you bought your house?"

She angled her own chair toward him, sliding back a few inches, giving herself room to cross her legs without bumping her knee on the tabletop with every breath. She didn't miss the shift of his eyes to her legs or the smoky look that glazed his eyes for an instant. "Oh, I knew. Jimmy told me, and the real estate agent stressed repeatedly that the neighborhood had had its share of trouble."

She smiled a thanks to Tish when the girl brought their drinks and took a cooling sip before waving at a couple across the bar. "That's Sam and his wife, Shawntae. He's an FBI agent, and they live down the block. The house over there belongs to Jamie, the man behind the bar and owner of O'Shea's, and his wife, Karen. They just moved their women's shelter out of the house and into an apartment building down the street. Their son,

Reid, helps out both here and at the shelter, and his wife teaches in Serenity's very own private school.

"The couple sitting on the top step at Jamie's are Nicholas, a lawyer who does pro bono work for families, and his wife, Lainie, who used to be an FBI agent but now volunteers around here herself. Remy Sinclair, the special agent in charge of the local FBI office, and his wife are raising their family on Divinity, and Smith Kendricks, the US Attorney for the Eastern District of Louisiana, and his wife, Jolie, an investigative reporter, live four doors down from me. Smith's and Remy's best bud, Michael, is an NOPD detective who moved into the house at the very end of the block a couple years ago, and his wife also teaches at the local school."

"And though DiBiase didn't stick around, you did."

She nodded. "Jimmy's really not a home owner kind of guy. He doesn't like doing maintenance or yard work or not being able to pick up and move on a whim. Buying the house when we got married was his idea, not mine, but it turned out to be a much better fit to me than him. This is the first time in my life that I've lived in the same state, let alone the same house, longer than three years."

That acknowledgment gave her pause. Frequent moves were a staple of an NCIS career, same as the navy. Some agents would stay at a command as long as possible to avoid pulling their kids out of school too many times or because their spouses' careers weren't easy to pick up and start over in new locations, but she'd never thought she would be one of them. She'd already been here longer than she'd expected, with no clue when orders might come down.

Later rather than sooner sounded good at the moment.

"Anyway," she said with a shrug, "my point is that

things have changed around here. Serenity's not perfect, but people are doing their best to get it a little closer. There's a lot of good folks living here."

"I'll take your word for it." He took a long, lazy drink of pop before adding, "But I bet you sleep with your gun nearby."

"I keep my gun nearby no matter where I am. There are criminals everywhere, even in Paradise." After a pause, she clarified. "Which, for the record, is located on the coast of Hawaii. Any coast. Year-round."

"One of those places you lived less than three years?"

"Two years, eleven months, three weeks. I fell in love with surfing, SPAM and a boy called Kanani. I was in third grade when we moved, and I thought my heart would never heal, though I was never quite sure what I missed most—Kanani, the surfing or the food."

"I'd lay my money on the food," Landry said drily.

Thinking of the number of times the ocean had sent her and her board tumbling and of the dark-eyed little boy who'd held her hand during recess through all of second grade and part of third, she sighed. "You're probably right. I blame my mom. Food is an important part of Vietnamese culture which she definitely passed on to me. She loves to cook, and I love to give her feedback."

"What's your favorite dish?"

"Che ba ba," she said without hesitation. "It's a dessert. Sweet potato, taro, tapioca. Incredible."

"I've had it. Mama Tranh makes it."

Alia had made a mental note of Mama's Table, a restaurant in the Quarter run by Mama's daughter, Huong. A glance at her watch showed it was too late to visit tonight, but she was free for lunch tomorrow. Maybe Landry was, too. "What's your favorite dish?"

"Anything with lemongrass."

Alia was convinced that one of her mother's reasons for disliking Jimmy had been his dislike of her native food. Lien Hieu Kingsley loved fixing dishes that reminded her of home and was accustomed to similar passion in everyone who ate them. She would love a man who already had shared that passion.

If they ever met. If they ever had reason to meet. It was way too soon to make a guess about that.

"How did you discover Vietnamese food? I can't imagine you picked it up from your parents."

"I went out with Huong a few times before I introduced her to her husband. One day I met her at the restaurant, and her grandmother insisted on feeding me, and…"

He shrugged as if there was no need to go on, and for Alia, there wasn't.

"So Huong's married now." Sure, Alia always tuned in to food matters, but she'd heard the important part of the nonfood conversation, as well.

"With two kids. They're the light of Mama Tranh's life."

Of course. "You plan on having kids someday?"

Landry's gaze was directed past her, thoughtful but unfocused. It took him a while to offer another shrug. "I don't know. Fifteen, ten, even five years ago, the answer was absolutely not. The older I get, though… What about you?"

"I tell Mom if she wants grandbabies, she'd better adopt them. I'm not exactly warm and fuzzy with helpless little bald creatures."

He laughed. "I hear it's different when it's your own bald creature."

"That's what Mom says. Seriously, I've never held a baby, fixed a bottle or changed a diaper. My friends laugh hysterically at the idea of me with a miniature human. They would leave their kids with their dog before they'd trust me with them."

"Aw, I used to babysit my nieces all the time when they were *both* in diapers. It's easy."

She exaggerated her shudder for effect. "And yet you have none of your own and aren't sure you want any."

"Not because of the kids themselves. My parenting role models should have run fast and far from even the idea of bringing another life into their world. Jeremiah never taught me anything about being a father except through his actions, and those all fell under the category of things *not* to do to a child."

He didn't want to be a father unless he was sure he could be a good one. The realization touched Alia—and, of course, made her wonder yet again about the relationship he'd had with Jeremiah. Had Jeremiah been one of those fathers who couldn't bear to not be the strongest, the smartest, the most successful, who would crush his son's ego to puff up his own? Had things between them changed as Landry grew up, or had it always been ugly? Did Landry have one single good memory of his father?

"He may not have intended to teach you anything," she said quietly, "but he did. He taught you the *don't*s to raising a child. By elimination, the things left are the *do*s." When he looked skeptical, she added, "There's not much difference between being a good uncle and a good father."

After his noncommittal gesture, the conversation lightened. They compared favorites. Sports: his, football; hers, baseball. Movies: his, action movies; hers, comedies, the dumber, the better. Books: his, mysteries; hers, thrillers. Music—blues and jazz—and food—Cajun for him, everything for her—were the only things they agreed on.

It didn't bother Alia, because there was one other thing they agreed on, and it was the most important one: each of them liked the other.

Which led to another important thing: with the situation—and her job—in mind, how far could they explore that?

Chapter 8

The time was nearing midnight when they left the bar. Since Alia had driven, Landry offered to walk back to the Quarter; Alia offered to walk with him. "If something happened to you on the way home, it would taint your image of my neighborhood forever," she said with a smug smile.

"Your feet hurt."

"My house is right over there." She gestured vaguely, but he didn't bother to look. He preferred to watch her face and her body and the way she moved. Just something as simple as lifting her arm to point off into the night was enough to leave him in an off-balanced daze.

"I'll change shoes."

He agreed to that much, not because he really expected her to walk with him but because he wanted to see where she lived. Which of these small, stately houses had she liked enough to live in, both with DiBiase and without? What kind of house appealed to a woman who'd never lived more than three years in one place?

So he followed her to the car. Again, she kicked off the heels, this time ignoring the seat belt as she reversed down the street and around the corner, then headed for Divinity ahead.

The block was quiet, the streetlights buzzing, each one surrounded by a halo of bugs, while at least one light showed in every house. One of Landry's neighbors played the TV loud every night; another was a huge fan of Miley Cyrus at eardrum-piercing levels. When he stood on Alia's sidewalk, he didn't hear anything but a few birds, a dog or two, an occasional car a few blocks away.

"Home, sweet home." Alia joined him, heels cradled in her arms with her purse. "Would you have picked it out as mine?"

Landry glanced from her to the house. It was a cottage with a little Creole influence, a little Gulf Coast influence and a few embellishments from a typical Victorian. A half dozen broad steps led to the deep porch that stretched from end to end, with the door off center in the middle. Typically in a cottage of this style, every room had an exterior door to improve airflow, but here the second door had been replaced with a full-length window. The wood was painted pale yellow with shutters and trim the color of lime sherbet, and it sat on a good-sized lot of lush green grass in need of a mow.

It was fairly small, probably only four rooms downstairs and maybe two up. Great for a woman alone or a couple, but cramped once you added a toddler or two.

"It suits you better than those bigger places." He gestured toward a row of three-story minimansions across the street. "But if I'd been guessing where you lived, my money would have been on a riverside condo."

"I get that a lot. I don't know why. I'm not rich. I'm not elegant. I'm certainly not all about modern sterility." She climbed the steps and unlocked the door, pushing it open to reveal a living room filled by only two pieces of furniture: a huge sectional sofa and a square wood coffee table that looked as if it had been reclaimed from someone's falling down old barn. Above the fireplace was the flat-screen TV, and built-in shelves to the right held an old-style turntable and a sizable collection of record albums.

Forget the riverside condo, he thought as he stepped inside. There was something about the place that fitted her just fine: the comfort, the solidness of everything, the coziness, even the faint leather/wood/vanilla scent that stirred in the still air. He could easily see her stretched out on the sofa, feet propped on the back cushions, an old Etta James record spinning on the turntable.

"Quick tour," she said, and headed from the room. There were no hallways on the first floor. A small bathroom opened up next door, stairs climbing to the next story, the kitchen beyond that, and a doorway from the kitchen led into a tiny laundry room, then the front room opposite the living room. That room was an office: computer, scanner, two printers, file cabinets, framed photos and her college degree. Back in the kitchen, glass jars filled with candy and snacks lined the counters, and the table, like its smaller twin in the living room, appeared to have escaped the barn but not before the roof collapsed on it. The aged wood had some serious dings.

"Let me grab some comfortable shoes."

Before he could tell her he was big enough and brave enough to walk home alone, she was disappearing up the stairs. Rolling his eyes, he stopped in front of the bookcase and flipped through her record collection. She'd claimed blues and jazz as her favorites, and they did make up the bulk of the selections, but her tastes were much broader. Country, zydeco, classical, gospel, rock, and everything else shared the smaller of the bottom two shelves.

A few thunks and thuds filtered from above before Alia came down again. She'd changed not only shoes but clothing, too, from the minimalist dress to a pair of snug-fitting running shorts and a tank top that left even less to the imagination than the dress had. Her shoes were, by far, the most substantial thing she wore.

Landry's gaze skimmed the running shoes, then slowly glided upward. Soft, smooth, bronzed skin—one of his weaknesses. Long sexy legs—another. A flat belly, a gentle curve from hip to waist, the roundness of her breasts, strong arms...

The crazy thought drifted through his mind that he didn't need an escort home. He could just stay here until dawn, appreciating everything that went together to make her so damn appealing. He could even just look and not touch...though he wanted to touch, to stroke, to hold and kiss and see where things went from there.

Which would be pretty much nowhere. She was a cop. She was working a case that, lucky him, kept bringing them together. She wasn't about to risk her job—or disappointing her father, the admiral—by messing around with him.

"You're not really planning to walk home with me."

"Why wouldn't I?" She didn't pause in the act of

shrugging into a nylon shoulder holster—cooler, he assumed, than leather on a muggy night. Once she'd adjusted it the way she wanted it, she pulled a lightweight
hoodie on over it.

He swallowed hard. He'd never been drawn to delicate women in need of a big strong man to protect them,
and Alia was a prime example why. She damn well protected herself, and he found that way sexier than a damsel in distress.

Beads of sweat were gathering across his skin, sliding down the center of his spine, and they made his
voice thick, even though he tried to hide it with teasing.
"What's the plan? If we get mugged, you'll hold them
off while I run for help?"

She smoothed the jacket over the holster, then flashed
him a measuring look, from his worn T-shirt all the way
down to the ratty sandals on his feet. Her gaze was warm
and heated him from the inside out. "I don't know how
fast you can run."

"Doesn't matter. I only have to be able to outrun *you*."

She smirked. "Not likely. I'll tell you what, if we get
mugged, I'll handle the bad guys. Then you can thank
me later."

He knew exactly what form he would want that
thank-you to take. Blocking the image from his mind,
he snorted. "I think getting to kick bad-guy ass in front
of me would be reward enough for you."

"It is my favorite activity," she agreed as she opened
the door, locking up behind them. For a moment, she
stopped on the porch, still, a shadow among other shadows, the only sound her slow, even breaths. She stood,
eyes closed, listening, and he watched her, also listening.
Slowly other noises joined her breaths: his own breath-

ing, a baby crying next door, the soft steps of the fattest orange cat he'd ever seen stalking across the neighbor's porch. A helicopter buzzed overhead, navigational lights blinking in the dark sky, and a motorcycle roared a few blocks away, the two engines combined so powerful they seemed to vibrate the ground under their feet.

The whole quiet of it was relaxing. Give him a drink and a few hours' use of one of her comfortable-looking chairs, and he couldn't think of much else he might want.

Besides her.

Landry didn't know if he broke the spell or she did. She drew a loud, sudden, shaking-herself-back-to-action breath at the same time he moved down the first step. Without speaking they walked to her car, backed out of the driveway and drove out of the neighborhood, leaving behind Serenity, Divinity and Trinity.

A few minutes later, she pulled to the curb on Bourbon Street, blocking his driveway, and gazed at him. She wanted to say something, or wanted him to. He didn't know. He opened the door and swung one foot to the ground, then turned back to her. "Lunch tomorrow?"

Her faint smile was echoed in her eyes as she nodded. "Noon? Here?"

Another nod.

He slid out, then bent down to look at her. "I'll see you then."

He watched until her car disappeared into the shadows down the street, the red taillights the only sign of it, then they were gone, too. He breathed deeply of garbage and beer and sweaty people partying on a miserably hot night. He listened to the competing music from nearby bars, the loud voices of tourists passing by, the sound of a siren down the street, the clank and wheeze of an air conditioner losing the fight to the heat, and he smiled ruefully.

Five minutes of Bourbon Street made him miss the evening of peace on Serenity. He never would have believed it.

Alia wasn't a shoe whore. She had a few pairs of killer heels—in ways both good and bad—but she would never buy a pair of shoes that cost more than her monthly mortgage, and she didn't need an excessive number of them. Other than three pairs of good running shoes, the rest of the shelves were filled with shoes ranging from reasonably priced pumps, boots and sandals to dollar-sale flip-flops.

Clothing, however, was a different matter.

She stood in the closet—formerly known as the guest bedroom—Sunday morning and surveyed her choices for lunch with Landry. There was a rack filled with dresses like last night's, some reaching to her ankles, others barely covering her butt, all of them snug-fitting and flattering. There were pants, skirts, suits, sundresses; jeans, capris and shorts; shirts and tees and tanks, covering.the gamut from casual to nice-restaurant-worthy.

And there were a lot. They filled the racks around the perimeter of the room and the drawers of the two dressers that stood back to back in the middle. Never let it be said Alia Kingsley had nothing to wear.

She pulled a pair of capris from their hanger. They were the exact shade of her favorite lime sherbet, loose-fitting and cool, and she'd had the luck to find a print scoop-neck top that matched. That and a pair of well-worn sandals, plus dangling earrings and a couple of thin bangles, and she was ready to—

Her cell phone interrupted the thought, a standard ring—not her mom's or dad's. She pulled on the shirt on her way to the bedroom and snatched the cell off the bed, noting Jimmy's number on the screen before answering. "I'm off today."

"Yeah, so am I. But not everyone has our good luck, sweet pea. What are you doing?"

She turned on the speaker, then dropped the phone so she could wiggle into the cropped pants. "I'm getting ready for lunch. What do you need?"

"Maybe I'll join you. What are you having?"

"Vietnamese," she said sweetly.

"Yeah, maybe some other time," he responded, just as she'd expected. "Listen, I got a call from Jack Murphy. Remember him?"

"Sure. Best detective NOPD has." Intense, damn good-looking, loved his wife, adored their kids and had an admirable solve rate.

"Yeah, well—hey. I thought I was the best."

"You keep thinking that, Jimmy."

"You're hard on a man's ego," Jimmy said in a wounded tone. "Anyway, Murphy caught a case this morning. Woman came home from early services at church and found her husband dead in his office."

Alia fastened her watch, then sprayed a cloud of perfume around her. "And that has to do with me how?"

"The guy was Bradley Wallace."

She knew that name: it had appeared on the lengthy list of Jeremiah Jackson's associates. According to Mary Ellen, Wallace had been one of her father's nearest and dearest friends. They, along with three others, had grown up together, gone to college together, lived within blocks of each other their entire lives. Their wives had been friends, their kids playmates, and Brad Wallace had been devastated by Jeremiah's death, according to the interview the police had done with him.

Taking the phone off speaker, Alia held it to her ear as she started downstairs. "How did he die?"

"Stabbed multiple times in the office in his Garden District home. Wife hadn't seen him since she went to bed last night. He'd stayed up to work, never did go to church with her anyway, so she wasn't expecting him. Today she went to roust him for brunch with some friends and found him." Jimmy paused. "There were cuts and stab wounds pretty much everywhere, and when they moved him, his tongue fell out of his mouth."

"Well, that's interesting." Alia picked up her purse and keys, then let herself out of the house. After the coolness inside, it was like stepping into an oven set on broil, with the added discomfort provided by the humidity. It reminded her of the first facial she'd ever got, back when she was barely a teenager, when the tech had spread a hot, steamy towel over her face, sucking the air right from her lungs.

"Jeez, Alia, a man gets sliced and diced, and you think it's *interesting*?"

"Don't you?" she retorted.

"Well, yeah, but you're supposed to be a better person than me. Where's your feminine sympathy?"

She snorted at that. "Are you going to the scene?"

"Hell, no, it's my first day off in nearly a week. Murphy only called because of the connection between his victim and ours. He'll keep in touch in case it turns out there's something there. Enjoy your lunch. I'm gonna go find me a rare steak." He said a cheerful goodbye.

Alia tossed the phone on the passenger seat. Leave it

to Jimmy to describe a gruesome murder, then happily turn his mind to raw meat. Not that the same gruesome murder had had any effect on her appetite, either. What did that say about them?

As she drove away from her house, she considered the information. Was it coincidence, two old friends being murdered in the same manner less than a week apart? Possibly, but everything in her doubted it. Wallace's death wasn't a robbery gone bad. Burglars might kill if surprised by the home owner, but take the time to inflict extensive stab wounds? To sever his tongue? No way.

Like Jeremiah Jackson, Brad Wallace's murder was a rage killing. It was personal. Given their friendship, it very well might have been committed by the same person.

So they had four murders—she said a silent apology to Constance Marks and Wilma and Laura Owens, whom she was convinced had just been in the wrong place at the wrong time. Camilla Jackson's death had been cruel but not in the sense of her husband's or his friend's. It didn't take nearly as much anger or strength to lock a woman away where she would likely die as it did to viciously, repeatedly stab two grown men. As for Miss Viola, hell, her murder had been simplest of all: a hand on her frail back, giving her a shove.

The two men, though…that had been overkill. They had been the real targets, while the women had died because… Maybe because of something they'd known about the two men?

What had Jackson and Wallace done?

If Alia hadn't made plans with Landry, she would head to the Wallace house, seek out Murphy and get his permission to wander through and look at the crime scene. She would talk to Mrs. Wallace and the couple's grown children and the people the new widow had called to comfort her. She would find out what kind of man Wallace was—husband, father, businessman—and she might even warn Mrs. Wallace to take up residence elsewhere for a time.

But she *had* made plans with Landry, and it was her first day off in nearly a week, too, and it was Murphy's case, not yet officially tied to her own. She could get a report and/or talk to Murphy tomorrow.

Today she was just going to be a woman having lunch with a man she liked a whole lot.

And, knowing herself, finding out everything he knew about the newest victim. Unsolved puzzles just didn't go away and leave her alone. She'd been that way a long time and didn't expect to change anytime soon. But she would still have plenty of attention for Landry and lunch and whatever he had in mind after lunch.

Pulling to the curb on Bourbon Street, blocking Landry's car in its reserved space, she shut off the engine and opened the door just as he walked through the gate. His cargo shorts were dark gray, his T-shirt white, his flip-flops looking as if they'd passed the thousand-mile mark a long time ago. Dark glasses shaded his eyes, an Ole Miss ball cap covered his hair and beard stubbled his chin. He looked... *Damn!*

"You can park in my boss's space if you want to walk," he said as she slid out. "It's just down that way. The restaurant, I mean."

She moved the car to the space on the right, locked up, then slid her keys into her pocket. "I'm hungry. Lead the way."

They walked the first block in silence. It was barely

noon, but all the detritus from last night's partying had been swept up. The street was fairly quiet, waiting for today's revelry to start once everyone had recovered from last night's.

Though she usually found silence between them comfortable enough, that wasn't the case today. Her mouth kept opening, questions about his father and Brad Wallace trying to spill out. It could wait until after they'd eaten, she silently insisted. She hadn't had a home-cooked Vietnamese meal in a long time, and Mama's Table was the closest she was likely to get. She intended to enjoy it.

Then share the news.

Don't let the place fool you, he'd said when he'd first told her about Mama's Table. It was in the middle of the block, a narrow storefront between two abandoned shops. The menus had hung in the windows so long that the food in the photographs was washed-out and strangely hued, but the smells when he opened the door were heavenly.

"I've passed this place dozens of times. How did I miss it?"

Landry shook his head. "I thought you could track food like a bloodhound." He pulled off his glasses and ball cap and ran his fingers through his hair. "I usually sit there."

He directed her to a small table for two halfway to the back and not ten feet from the cash register. Did Mama and Huong like to keep an eye on him?

Alia opened the menu and gave a happy sigh. "I think I'll start with one of everything and see where to go from there." Catching his amused look, she grinned. "Such a goal might break a lesser person, but I am strong. I will survive."

The waitress—not Huong, apparently, and far too young to be Mama—brought them glasses of ice water and took their orders for tea and appetizers. Alia chose *goi cuon tom*, shrimp and rice noodles wrapped in rice paper with veggies and peanut sauce, while Landry asked for *dau hu chien*.

"You get points for eating fried tofu," she told him with her best teasing smile.

"I've eaten stranger things."

"I lived in Hawaii. I've eaten SPAM. On purpose. For breakfast, lunch and dinner. In tacos. With gravy. As sushi. Fried, baked, grilled and cold from the can." She gave him a *top that* sort of look, then turned back to the menu as the waitress arrived with drinks. For lunch, she decided on *tom rang muoi tieu*, crispy in-shell shrimp stir-fried with bell peppers, onions, garlic, chili and other seasonings.

The waitress turned to Landry, and so did Alia, curious about his order since she would likely end up tasting at least a bit of it. She always did.

"Now she's going to make fun of me." He directed his words to the waitress, lifted his menu and pointed. "I want that."

Alia stretched to see. "What is it?"

"Bun thit nuong," the girl said.

"Ooh, pork vermicelli noodle bowl. I love noodles. And pork. And pickled daikon."

Landry handed the menu to the girl, then asked, "Is Huong here?"

"No, she comes in late on Sunday because of church. But Mama's in back. I'll tell her you're here."

Alia touched one hand to her tightly braided hair. She hadn't acknowledged it while getting dressed, but she'd wanted to look good for meeting Landry's ex-girlfriend. Hence, the clothes a few steps above her usual summer outfit of shorts and tee, and jewelry and brain cells fighting hard against the tug of hair roots.

It wasn't that she was jealous of… Well, yes, she was. She was jealous of every woman who'd had a relationship with Landry, or who could have one if she wanted. Every time she felt a jolt of pure womanly appreciation for the man, she envied every female, available or not, whose job didn't stand in the way of a relationship.

Hers didn't have to. If she were no longer assigned to this case…

"It's about time you showed your pretty face here." Mama Tranh's voice echoed in the small space an instant before a short, lean gray-haired woman grabbed Landry in an enthusiastic hug.

"I was here last Tuesday."

Mama made a dismissive gesture. "And where were you Wednesday, Thursday, Friday and yesterday?" Her gaze shifted from him to Alia, and her dark eyes lit up. "It's about time you brought a pretty friend," she said slyly. She offered her hand and gripped firmly when Alia took it.

"Chào, bà Tranh. Tôi Alia."

The old lady's eyes widened, then crinkled as a smile split her face. "Ah, Landry, you found a girl who speaks to my heart. *Nó là tốt đẹp để đáp ứng bạn.*"

They spoke a few moments more, Alia's Vietnamese slower and not as sure as Mama's. It felt good to be speaking it, though, bringing back sweet memories of her childhood. When Mama returned to the kitchen, Alia slid the paper from her straw and used it to stir sugar into her tea. "My mother's parents own a restaurant in Chicago. Every summer when Mom and I visited them, I hung out in the kitchen and practiced my Vietnamese with the employees. I don't get to use it much these days."

"Mama's tried to teach me a few words, but I have no talent for languages. She thinks I should at least be able to pronounce the names of the dishes I order, but I figure that's what the pictures are for."

Alia wondered as he sprawled comfortably in his seat if he'd ever called Camilla mama, or if he'd ever spoken of her with such fondness. He was obviously generous with his affection. How hard had it been for him growing up in the Jackson household? How hard had it been to leave?

Not very, she suspected, especially since he'd had Miss Viola's support.

But what had prompted a fifteen-year-old boy, even with support from a surrogate grandmother, to move out and basically turn his back on his parents? What had made life at home so unbearable?

And did it have anything to do with the murders?

She didn't bring up the subject until they'd left the restaurant, her stomach full, her taste buds' cravings happily satisfied. They'd strolled along the sidewalks, talking little, dodging foot traffic, until they found themselves at Jackson Square. She didn't know if it was because she'd been speaking her mother's language or eating her mother's food, but she found herself copying her mother's pastime: people-watching, admiring some outfits, coveting a few others and wondering what in the world possessed some people to dress the way they did. It made her homesick.

They wandered into the square and off the sidewalk into a patch of shade, where they settled on the grass. Despite the warm temperature, every bench in the park was occupied, and plenty of people sat or sprawled on the lawn. The sidewalks surrounding the square were crowded, as well. Life as usual in the Quarter.

Landry plucked a blade of grass, flattening it between his fingers. "So you're half-Vietnamese."

"And half-Nebraskan. Dad wanted to see someplace besides the plains, so he joined the navy right out of college. Mom's parents wanted to see something besides war and strife, so they immigrated to the USA when she was seven. We've still got family in both places, though, so we visit."

"And you like most of them?"

She thought about his parents, the grandparents he'd hardly known, the aunts, uncles and cousins he'd hardly seen since moving out. Would he have had more sympathy from them if they'd known the details? Or less?

"I adore most of my family. We have some odd ones—the hellfire-and-brimstone preacher, the hypochondriac, the serial marry-er, the my-kids-are-geniuses moms. But mostly they're good. My dad's brothers are farmers. My mom's brother is retired from the Marine Corps, and her sister runs an internet jewelry business. They're decent people, and for the most part, their kids are decent people."

She watched a diaper-clad baby with sweet blond curls circle his family's quilt on his tiptoes, grinning at every person who looked his way. She had this vague impulse to think, *aw, how cute,* the way she did with puppies, but it was never in an *I want one* sort of way. "The good thing about family is if you don't like the one you're born into," she said quietly, "you can always make one of your own."

"Advice I got from Miss Viola."

"Did you take it?"

He tilted his head to one side. "Yeah, I guess I did. I've got friends—good friends. And I still see Mary Ellen and her family a lot."

But judging by his expression, a surrogate family left something lacking. Letting go was the key. He had to let go of his past and everyone in it to fully accept his present and future. Murders, she imagined, made that hard to do.

So it was time to bring up one more. "Do you know anyone around here by the last name of Wallace?"

The name echoing in his head, Landry watched the kid Alia had focused on earlier. Skinny body, long legs and arms, rounded belly and a perpetual grin, he—or she, hard to tell—was apparently comfortable in his role as pampered prince in his own family. He was cute enough to make Landry smile. Not cute enough to stir a longing for a little prince or princess of his own.

As he forced his gaze back to Alia and her question, his jaw tightened fractionally. His shrug was jerky, his casual tone phony. "There was a great blueswoman named Sippie Wallace. Given that she died of natural causes in the '80s, I doubt she's the person you're asking about."

In fact, he knew she had to be asking about Brad Wallace, or maybe his wife, Adelina, or his children, who had played with Mary Ellen and Landry when they were kids. The whole family had been at the funerals last week, minus the youngest. Adelina had cried a lot, the two girls had been stone-faced and Brad, the lying bastard, had been strong and stoic.

Landry had wished more than once that Wallace would drop dead before the services were over.

The grass he'd been messing with was limp, its color broken down to dark green, its chlorophyll smell on his fingers. He tossed it aside, drew his knees up and rested his arms on them. "You want to know if I remember Brad Wallace. The answer is yes. I haven't seen any of the Wallaces in years, except for Jeffrey, the youngest kid. Last time I saw him, it was winter and he was sleeping in a doorway a few blocks from here. Why?"

"He was homeless? Or just sleeping off a drunk?"

"He had skipped out of rehab for the fourth or fifth or tenth time, so he wasn't welcome at home. I took him home with me, fed him, let him crash on my couch for a few days. I came home from work at four one morning, and he was gone. I haven't seen him since."

It had been a shock when he'd recognized the dirty, barely coherent man as his childhood friend. Jeffrey was younger than Mary Ellen but looked twenty years older. He'd been scrawny and twitchy, and his eyes... They had been uncomfortable, flat, empty.

Ten years ago Landry had seen that look in his own eyes too many times to count, that desperate need to escape. Sometimes it got so bad, living in his own head, that he'd been tempted by booze and drugs. Instead, he'd seen a shrink.

Another deep, deep debt he owed Miss Viola.

Alia's voice came, soft and sympathetic. "Did he get along with his father before the rehab?"

He smiled faintly. "The short answer is no."

"And the long answer?"

"You'd have to ask Jeffrey or the old man."

"Do you know where to find Jeffrey?"

"Nope, but anyone in town can tell you where to find the old man." Living in a mansion in the Garden District, working in a luxurious penthouse office on Canal Street, partying with the rich and respectable, when he ought to be burning in hell.

Alia hesitated, her eyes going dark and shadowy, her mouth thinning. "Actually, I doubt many people can. Brad Wallace was stabbed to death sometime between last night and early church services this morning."

Something twisted in Landry's gut—not regret, damn sure not sorrow. It wasn't even shock. Just a vague satisfaction that common sense said he should feel guilty for but couldn't. "Good," he murmured. "He got what he deserved."

Alia's shadowy look and thinned lips didn't change as he glanced away from her. He didn't care whether she heard his next word but said it anyway, just for himself. "Finally."

Too late for Jeffrey. Too late for a lot of people. But hallelujah, the son of a bitch wouldn't hurt anyone else in this world.

"Do you think it's connected to the other murders?"

Alia's shrug was so tiny, he would have missed it if he hadn't been watching her from the corners of his eyes. "Do you believe in coincidence?"

Landry lay back in the grass, staring at the leaves above him. His gut was still tight, and he was getting twitchy like Jeffrey—his body responding to what his mind didn't want to acknowledge. Coincidence was a marvelous thing…but two best friends, two sick bastards, dying within a week of each other, both stabbed?

Justice, vengeance, a good thing for everyone who knew them—sure. Coincidence? Not likely.

Alia laid her hand on his arm. "Landry, were Jeremiah and Brad Wallace guilty of something that led to their deaths?"

He didn't want to talk about this, not to anyone, but especially not to her. People were allowed to keep secrets, weren't they? No one was obliged to share all the ugly details of his life. And these weren't his secrets alone. They included, affected, other people. They weren't entirely his to tell.

Except people were dying because of them. Jeremiah and Wallace had deserved it. Camilla bore some responsibility, too, but by God, Miss Viola had done what she could. She hadn't deserved a shove down the stairs.

Would telling Alia everything stop the killings? Maybe not. Maybe Jeremiah and Wallace had been into things Landry knew nothing about, things equally worth killing over.

Before he figured out whether he was rationalizing so he could stay silent, Alia's cell rang. He considered his cell phone a convenience for himself. He didn't make a lot of calls, rarely texted and always screened his calls. He had no desire to be reachable on a whim. Alia's phone, on the other hand, was a business tool. She was probably getting more information about Brad Wallace's murder, more gruesome details, more questions.

And she was probably going to ask some of them of him.

He sat up, mimicking her position, though he deliberately focused on not listening to her end of the conversation. He'd had pretty much nothing on his mind but murder the past seven days. He wanted to be done with

it. Wanted to go back to life as normal. Wanted to work
and fend off overly friendly tipsy tourists and play with
his nieces and maybe even go on a date or two.

With Alia. And *date* wasn't exactly where he wanted
to go. *Bed* had a really good sound to it.

She ended the call, easily stood and offered her hand.
"That was Detective Murphy. He's investigating Brad
Wallace's death. We're going to meet at his house to talk
for a few minutes."

Landry laid his hand in hers and pushed himself up,
bearing most of the effort himself. "You can leave your
car where it is as long as you want."

She didn't release his hand. "You're coming with me.
It's just a few blocks from here. Then we can find something to eat."

His gaze slid down her body, all soft skin and muscle, then back up to her face. "We just ate enough food
for four."

"We didn't have dessert." She pointed to the right of
the cathedral. "Jack's house is over that way."

He followed her, mostly because she still held his
hand, partly because damned if he didn't like the feel of
her slender, strong fingers wrapped around his. The sen-
sation was split somewhere between reassuring and sensual, and he could use massive doses of both right now.

Murphy's house wasn't quite what Landry expected
for an honest New Orleans cop: large, historic in age,
well maintained, multiple stories, a lush green courtyard out back just visible through a wrought iron gate.
Another unexpected surprise: a sign hanging above a
small door opposite the main entrance that welcomed
customers to Evangelina's to have their palms read and
their futures foretold.

New Orleans had its legitimate psychics, and way more than its share of frauds. This seer married to a police detective—which did she claim to be, and which was she really?

"I hear she's legit," Alia remarked after ringing the bell at the main entry. "I don't know. I've never had much interest in that sort of thing."

If Evangelina Murphy was the real thing, maybe she could answer all of Alia's and her husband's questions and leave Landry with a little dignity intact.

He would have made Murphy for a cop if the guy had come into the bar. It wasn't the gun on his hip or the badge on his belt. He just looked like a cop: law-and-order, tough, had seen a lot. Alia introduced Landry to him, then Murphy introduced his wife, Evie, on her way out the French doors into the courtyard.

"Would you like to join us outside, Landry?" she invited. "We've got cookies and lemonade."

Landry was pretty sure he saw Alia's ears perk up and her nose wrinkle in an appreciative sniff. "You talk shop," he said with a wink. "We're gonna go have cookies."

Chapter 9

"You miss lunch today?" Murphy asked.

Alia brushed her chin to make certain she hadn't begun to drool. She loved cookies and lemonade. And cupcakes and limeade. And pies and tea, cakes and coffee, ice cream and root beer, chocolate and anything.

"No, I ate," she admitted. "I just tend to eat all day. How'd you get home so quick after catching a homicide?"

"I'm just killing time. I'm meeting with the oldest daughter and her husband in an hour at their place on Chartres, then with the younger daughter two hours after that."

"What about the son?"

Murphy's dark eyes widened. "I didn't know there was one. The wife only mentioned the two girls."

"Jeffrey. Landry said he has a substance abuse problem." Had Jeffrey died since Landry had last seen him?

Or had he disappointed his parents so deeply, they pretended he no longer existed? Or maybe disappointed his *father* so much, *he* pretended he didn't exist?

Murphy toyed with a bandage on his index finger. It was lime green with purple dinosaurs on it. "Why would a woman who just found her husband stabbed and mutilated forget to mention she had a third child?"

It was a rhetorical question: because she thought he might have committed the murder. Mrs. Wallace might have blamed her husband for Jeffrey's problems, for his failed rehabs, for not allowing him to come home.

If Jeffrey was guilty, that likely meant no connection between this murder and the others. Jeffrey might hate his father, but why would he hate Landry's father?

"How many stab wounds did your guy have?" Alia asked.

"Fourteen."

"Mine had more than thirty."

"Mine had his tongue cut out."

"Okay, you win on that. Why? A message to keep quiet about something?"

"That's the usual idea."

"You think there's something *un*usual here?"

Murphy gave her a sideways look. "You navy people must get way more interesting cases than we do if *you* don't. By the way, Landry Jackson…isn't that Admiral Jackson's kid?"

"Yeah."

"He a suspect?"

She shook her head. "His boss alibied him. We just had lunch," she went on. "He knows a place that makes great Vietnamese food, and I needed great Vietnamese food."

"Hey, you don't have to explain to me. I'm not in your chain of command." Murphy disappeared into the kitchen, then returned with a paper plate of cookies and a plastic glass of lemonade. "Sorry for the dishes. Our kids are hell on breakables."

They settled at the dining table, Alia reaching for a cookie before her butt was fully in contact with the chair. They were home-baked—sniffing out home versus commercial, fresh versus day old, was one of her talents—and they were dotted with yellow specks of lemon zest. Incredible. She might marry for an unending supply of cookies this good.

"I called DiBiase to compare notes, but he was, uh, busy. He gave me your number."

Alia snorted. She knew too well what Jimmy's *busy* looked like on his days off. "That's okay. I'll make him squirm for the details tomorrow." She took another cookie. "How did the killer get into the Wallace house?"

"There was a broken glass in the back door. The alarm wasn't armed."

"Same as Jackson's. Weapon?"

"Knife from the kitchen."

"Narrowed the time of death any?"

"Likely between 2:00 and 5:00 a.m. Same method of entry, same weapon, same approximate time." Murphy scowled. "I'll find out what I can about Jeffrey, but a doper going all psycho on his father is one thing. Going all psycho on one of his father's friends…"

They shook their heads at the same time.

"You know, Jackson and Wallace were good friends all their lives. Maybe something they did years ago has come back to bite them in the ass." Alia took a sip of lemonade sour enough to pucker her mouth, sweet enough to make her taste buds do a happy dance.

"Any idea what?"

She glanced out the French doors on the far side of the room. Landry and Evie were sitting on the broad veranda, paddle fans overhead stirring the air. Two kids played in the yard while a third bounced on Evie's knee.

Something had happened to drive him not only out of the family home but out of the family, as well—something damaging enough that he didn't want to talk about it all these years later. Could it be related to Jackson's and Wallace's murders?

She looked back at Murphy and forced a smile. "My head is entirely too full of ideas, Detective. It's weeding them out that's the problem."

Landry had never been dissatisfied with the apartments where he'd lived since he was fifteen. They'd always been a bit on the shabby side, like much of the French Quarter. They were old, run-down and lacked amenities such as air-conditioning, heat, a bedroom—except for the current one—and furnished with third or fourth-hand stuff. Failings aside, they'd been *his*. Besides the landlord, he'd had the only key to the lock; no one could come in unless he invited them.

Privacy like that made up for a lot of shortcomings.

But there was something awfully pleasant about sitting on Evie Murphy's veranda, smelling the flowers, hearing the fountain, listening to the kids' giggles and shouts. What he'd seen of the inside was luxurious compared to his own place, and what he'd seen of the outside, well, he could spend a whole lot of time in that courtyard.

He and Evie had talked about the kids, about New Orleans, her psychic business, even a little about himself, while they shared cookies and lemonade. Now, with the youngest of her three dozing fitfully in her lap, she said, "I'd ask you how the son of a murder victim wound up with the NCIS agent investigating the case, but then I'd feel obligated to tell you how I wound up married to the detective who once arrested me."

His brows rose even as he corrected her misimpression. "I'm not *with* Alia."

Her snort was similar to Alia's, though softer, more delicate. "She's a beautiful woman, isn't she? Obviously, I didn't know her when she married Jimmy, or I would have told her not to because of that faithfulness problem."

"Did the spirits tell you he couldn't keep it zipped?"

She gave him a chastising look. "Womanly intuition did. Sometimes you can just tell. He's a good detective, though."

"Then between him, Alia and your husband, they should be able to figure out what's going on."

Her chair creaked a few times as she shifted the girl to rest against her other arm. "It would help if the people they question were forthright."

She wasn't looking at him when she said it, and there was nothing pointed or accusing about her tone—just a general statement offered in a careless voice. Landry was no fool, though. He sensed what she didn't put into words or tone.

"What makes you think I haven't been forthright?"

She gave him an innocent smile. "I didn't say that." A pause. "Sometimes you can just tell."

On the front steps, Alia had said she didn't have much interest in psychic sorts of things. Landry never had, either, though he knew people who did. Several of the waitresses at the bar would sooner miss paying their rent than have to cut out their readings, and Miss Viola had once confessed that she'd consulted a psychic on a number of occasions.

"Some things are meant to remain private," he said evenly.

"And some aren't, even if we think they should."

"It doesn't have anything to do with the deaths."

Evie's gaze settled on him, sharp, steady but kind. "How can you know that?"

His mouth thinned. He wanted to believe he was right, but he didn't know it. There was only one thing, to his knowledge, that linked Jeremiah, Camilla, Miss Viola and Brad Wallace that was important enough to kill over. But that one thing had happened so long ago. Why now? After all these years, why would it lead to murder?

"How many people have died?" Evie asked.

He didn't have to take a moment to count. The number was there, in the back of his mind, dark and ugly. "Seven."

"Seven, three of them innocent bystanders. How many could there be?"

Briefly he considered turning her question back on her: *How could I know that?* But if the killings were tied to the past—his past—he could make an educated guess. Instead, he corrected her. "Four of them were innocent." But that wasn't totally true. Miss Viola hadn't deserved to die, but she hadn't been entirely innocent. She'd known something and done little about it.

What she'd done had saved him and Mary Ellen and that was all he'd ever really cared about. But apparently it had also got Miss Viola murdered. And Camilla. Who else was on the killer's list? How many besides the obvious targets? Was he there? Was Mary Ellen?

"Miss Viola meant a lot to you, didn't she?" Evie asked softly.

He nodded while watching the older kid, Jackson, dangle his sister's doll over the fountain.

"She died because she helped you."

His gaze flickered sideways to her. Had DiBiase told Murphy that, or was she reading whatever it was psychics read? "Probably."

"Her help allowed you to get to a place and a time where you could help yourself. If you help find justice for her, your debt to her will be repaid."

Debt. Miss Viola had never looked at it that way. Everything she'd done, she had done because she loved him. She'd told him that whenever he'd brought up how much he owed her. She had loved him, and she had died in part because of him, and it didn't matter who else shared in his secrets. Justice for Miss Viola was more important than keeping their pasts buried.

It was more important than protecting Jeremiah's reputation.

It was damn sure more important than Landry's own privacy, because if not for Miss Viola, he doubted he would have any sort of life worth keeping private.

Keeping his voice even, he said, "Your son's about to dunk your daughter's doll in the fountain."

Evie smiled. "She's not innocent herself. I'll bet she's threatening the same with his favorite toy."

Landry leaned to the side to see that she was right. The pretty little girl, who looked angelic in a white dress and bare feet, was holding a gaming system inches above the water.

"Jackson, Isabella, stop it right now." She didn't raise her voice or even look to see if they obeyed. It had been that way in the Jackson household, too, but it had been fear that made him and Mary Ellen instantly obey. The Murphy kids did it out of respect for their mother.

The French doors behind them opened, and Alia and Murphy came out. He stood behind Evie, his hand on her shoulder. With the baby in her arms, they made a picture that stirred something like envy inside him. He had never had that kind of commitment or…serenity in his life. Under the circumstances, he thought he was pretty well adjusted. He had his share of one-night stands and short-term relationships. He'd even had a few long-term, when he'd been as close to loving a woman as a lot of men ever got.

But he'd never really committed to those women. He'd never imagined them in his life because he'd never told them what that life included. He'd never told them the truth.

The truth shall set you free.

It might find Miss Viola's killer. It might protect Mary Ellen.

It might change the way Alia looked at him, because for a lot of years, it had damn well changed the way he had looked at himself.

He tuned back into the conversation in time to hear Alia say, "…appreciate your time. Can we get together in the morning with Jimmy and go over everything?"

"Sure. Give me a call."

Landry stood and found himself closer to Alia than he'd expected. She radiated heat and the aroma of lemon-flavored cookies and something subtler—sweeter, more erotic. Something sultry.

They said their goodbyes and left through an elaborately worked gate that opened into the alley a few yards from the street. Silence settled between them, lasting until they'd reached the sidewalk, until they turned left toward Bourbon Street. Finally, he dragged in a deep breath, swallowed hard and said, "Let's go for a drive."

She didn't ask where he wanted to go or why. She simply said, "Okay."

Within minutes they were outside the bar. He dug his keys from his pocket and beeped open the locks. Heat rolled out of the car, shimmering and breaking an instant sweat on his skin. He cranked the engine, turned the AC to high and rolled down the windows. It took a few moments to back out, what with the steady flow of foot traffic, then he headed out of the Quarter.

"What did you think of Evie? Real or fraud?"

He glanced at Alia, her smile failing to hide the fact that she was seriously interested. "No fair," he replied. "It's not like she was doing a reading."

Though she'd done just that, sort of. Maybe her husband had filled her in. Maybe she had just been making guesses. Maybe it was a psychic's job to learn things.

"She bakes great cookies. I would marry her for those cookies."

Was it that easy? All he had to do was get Evie's cookie recipe and Alia would be his? If life were only that uncomplicated…

"Did you know that at one point, Murphy arrested her for some suspected involvement in a murder case?"

"Really." Alia considered it then. "He doesn't seem the type."

"If you'd ever had reason to arrest Jimmy, wouldn't you have?"

"If I'd thought I could get away with it, I'd've killed Jimmy."

"You ever get personally involved with someone in a case?"

"Once."

Stopping at a red light, he looked her way again. "How'd that work out?"

She met his gaze, hers steady and serious. "Verdict's still out."

The words repeated in his brain until the blast of a car horn made him realize the light had turned green.

He eased his foot down onto the gas and crossed Canal, then a few blocks later, Poydras. He had one of two possible destinations in mind, and both were drawing nearer with each block. He drove along Saint Charles Avenue, watching tourists as the trolley passed on its Garden District tour, sweaty and hot, red-faced but mostly smiling, having a good time, and he saw a few residents facing the afternoon the way a good Southerner should, doing nothing, escaping into cooler places, waiting for the sweltering sun to set so life could resume.

His decision on where to go was simple enough: he turned into the driveway of the first house he reached. Miss Viola's.

The house looked exactly the way he'd seen it thousands of times: all neat and trim, drapes opened on the lower windows, lace panels making it difficult though not impossible to see inside, fresh flowers hanging from baskets on the porch and filling pots that lined the steps. Nothing had changed since the time he'd visited last Monday, not a thing, but everything *was* different.

This house had always been his refuge, his safe place—rather, it had represented those things. Miss

Viola had been the true refuge and safety. Without her, this place that had been so important was nothing but walls and a roof.

The thud of Alia's door closing woke him from his staring at the draped and lacy empty windows. He let go of his own car door, shoving it with his hip to bang more loudly that he'd intended.

Alia climbed the couple steps that led to the house, but he ignored them and walked to the garden gate instead.

He didn't know if she wondered, but he offered assurance anyway.

"Miss Viola's kids won't mind if they find us here."

Alia walked through the gate he held open. "Even if they did, you'd be surprised how much influence a badge carries."

He gave her a narrow look. "I've lived in New Orleans all my life. Nothing about that would surprise me."

The garden was still lush and growing, though everything seemed parched, diminished by the absence of Miss Viola. He stopped near the house to turn on the hose, then watched as soaker hoses buried beneath mulch sent tiny sprays of water bubbling to the top.

After circling the garden to make sure the system was working, he sat down on the bench in the corner, the seat cool and shaded by tall shrubs.

Alia leaned against the post that supported the front corner of the pergola, hands folded together. "I'm guessing you want to talk."

"Not particularly." But…justice for Miss Viola, he reminded himself. Protection for Mary Ellen.

Making the decision to tell Alia what she wanted to know had been hard enough. Knowing how to begin… that was a lot tougher. He'd only ever told two people:

Miss Viola and Dr. Granville. Miss Viola had cornered him when he was weak, his defenses down and his panic way up. She'd coaxed him into telling her everything, had held him in her arms and dried his tears and promised to take care of things. Dr. Granville had told him, "Just spit it out." At two hundred and fifty of Miss Viola's dollars an hour for her services, he'd done just that.

But Miss Viola had been his surrogate grandmother and godmother all in one, and Dr. Granville was a shrink. He'd been guaranteed some sort of privacy with them both, and he hadn't had to tell anyone else's stories that they didn't, wouldn't, couldn't want told.

Anything he told Alia would be passed on to everyone involved in the case, including DiBiase. It could make it into the media, maybe the courts. Public record for any and all. The others would hate him, would probably deny it, and he'd be considered some kind of freak.

Miss Viola wouldn't ask him to talk. She hadn't saved his life to have it destroyed over her death. And Mary Ellen...he would make sure Scott kept a close watch on her, beefed up security, maybe even hired a bodyguard.

"What do you think the Fulsom kids will do with their mother's garden?"

Alia's voice was conversational, her question unexpected. He'd guess her motto was *When in doubt, discuss food.*

"The market on Serenity would love to have produce like this," she went on. "Because they keep prices so low, some of the neighbors plant big gardens to share with them. I tried a couple times, but it just proved Mom was right—it really does help to have a clue what you're doing."

"I'll mention it to my cousins."

He sounded stiff and wooden, even to himself. Apparently, not telling wasn't going to be any easier than telling.

After shifting her weight a few times and feeling the third trickle of sweat coursing from her nape all the way down to her panties, Alia joined Landry on the bench. It was big enough for two in today's supersized world, so they fit comfortably with room for one or two of Murphy's kids between them.

"Murphy's interviewing the older two Wallace kids this afternoon," she began quietly. "Mrs. Wallace didn't even acknowledge a son. Maybe he died after you last saw him."

As she hoped, Landry felt obligated to answer. "Maybe. But who knows how many times Jeremiah answered the kids question with, 'Yes, my daughter's the light of my life' and forgetting that I existed?"

At least once, Alia acknowledged, according to her own father.

"We know the admiral and Brad Wallace had three other good friends. Did you know them?"

Landry dragged his fingers through his hair, leaving it pointing every which way. With the dark skin and casual clothes and careless style, he could pass for a beach bum if he could just get rid of the ghosts in his eyes.

"Yeah, I knew them. The families hung out a lot. The men had a name for themselves, for their little merry band of drunks and reprobates, but it was secret. No one knew but the five of them, not even the wives."

Drunks and reprobates. It sounded a fitting description. The bar in the Jackson house had been extraordinarily well stocked, both in the main parlor and in his study. And he was the type to carry a huge sense of entitlement. Between his position in the admiralty and his background and family wealth, he'd probably been able to do anything and get away with it. Not all flag officers took advantage of that ability—her father certainly hadn't—but Jeremiah Jackson seemed a prime candidate to do so.

"The admiral knew them a long time."

"Their whole lives. They all lived within a six-block radius. Same schools, same church, same interests."

"What sort of interests?" Alia asked.

Landry breathed deeply, his nostrils flaring. "The usual, to start. Sports. Drinking. Mischief." He gave her a sidelong look. "That was what the parents and the police called it then. Today, it would be auto theft, vandalism, DUI, assault." He reflected for a moment, a cynical smile quirking his mouth. "Or maybe not. Family name and money still go a long way in New Orleans covering up crime."

Alia could easily imagine Jeremiah and his friends—spoiled, indulged, handsome, irresponsible—being rowdy and wild with no one to answer to but the parents who'd done the spoiling and indulging. Then the irrepressible Jeremiah had sought a commission in the US Navy, and suddenly he'd had a reason to behave. Family reputation might have protected him from consequences in the real world, but it hadn't carried any weight in the navy. He'd found himself in a position where he'd had to work and accept responsibility, where he'd been judged on all aspects of his life, except family name, and he'd had to straighten up.

If he'd stayed in the civilian world, would life have been easier for Landry? Instead of being rigid and unforgiving, would Jeremiah have allowed his son the same carefree life he'd lived?

"To start, you said. They'd had the usual interests to start. What did those interests become?"

He studied his hands a long time, and she lowered her gaze to them, too. His hands were large, his fingers long, the nails trimmed short. There were a few ragged cuticles, a few calluses, a scar that was several shades lighter than the surrounding skin. They were good hands that could give pleasure and soothe sorrow and cradle his young nieces and make a woman feel safe. Like any hands, they could cause pain, too, but she was sure they didn't.

And although she took care of her own safety, she could use some pleasure and soothing and cradling.

She suspected he could, too, especially once this conversation was over.

"Like I said, they had a name for themselves, like they were some sort of covert society. Over time, that was what they became. I don't know when it started, only when they dragged me into it. I had just turned eleven."

An initiation? Had the men brought their sons into the group to tutor them on their way to becoming drunken reprobates? What would such an initiation entail? Alcohol, certainly. Sex, most likely. A prostitute, bought and paid for, *happy birthday to you*.

"The old man took me to a run-down place they'd rented at the end of the street in a run-down neighborhood. There was a living room, a kitchen, a bathroom, and the rest of the rooms were bedrooms barely big enough for a bed. There were bars on the windows and heavy-duty locks on the doors."

A bad feeling twinged in Alia's stomach. Maybe the

admiral hadn't wanted a prostitute to initiate his son into sex. Maybe he'd chosen someone closer to Landry's age, someone a boy might pick for himself, a pretty girl, a virgin herself, who wouldn't go along willingly.

The men's *mischief* had included assault, he'd said. Maybe rape, too? Kidnapping?

She was regretting all the lemon cookies, rumbling quietly in her stomach as she waited for Landry to go on. One glance showed his stomach was just as unsettled; his face was pale, his eyes stony, and his hands were trying to curl into knots. Only his strength of will kept them flat against the bench.

Experience told Alia to remain quiet and let Landry continue at his own pace. The woman inside wanted to encourage him, to clasp his hand in hers, to show the sympathy and anger rising inside, to give him a safe place while he related an ugly experience.

She didn't do any of that. She clenched her own hands together, and she waited, time crawling like tiny unseen bugs over her skin.

Clouds passed over the sun, bringing an added layer of shade, at the same time the breeze picked up. She would like to think a shower was coming, long enough to lower the temperature but brief enough not to interrupt the day. Hardly a breath later, though, the clouds moved on and the sun shone hotter than ever.

Finally she spoke. "I could call Jimmy if you'd feel more comfortable."

"God, no. This is hard enough without adding someone else to the audience." He exhaled loudly. "Okay. Jeffrey Wallace and I called them drunken pervs. They met every Saturday night that all five were in town. It was a night for revelry, they said. In the beginning, they brought food, booze and girls. Women. Hookers, I guess. A few times I saw Wallace give them money when the night was over. But not the first night. The first night…"

This time his fingers did curl into fists, bent so tightly his knuckles turned white.

"All five families were so damn *important*. They took what they wanted, and to hell with anyone who interfered. It didn't matter whether they wanted property or a position or money or someone else's girlfriend or sex with each other's—"

The words damming, he got abruptly to his feet and walked away. Alia sat motionless.

Oh. God.

She bent forward at the waist, breathing deeply, of damp earth and maturing vegetables and faint scents of fertilizer. She inhaled good stuff, exhaled bad. Inhaled the smell of cucumbers on the vine and breathed out the filth that just kept growing inside her.

When she was sure she could stand without puking, she did so. With one arm, she swiped sweat from her face, tightened her shoulders and stiffened her spine, then went in search of Landry.

She found him kneeling between rows of tomatoes, plucking weeds, pushing back leaves, searching out fruits. He laid a couple of large green tomatoes in a dusty basket he'd picked up somewhere, then added a handful of grape tomatoes.

"Miss Viola always had trouble estimating how many plants to buy. If one tomato plant was good, then weren't ten ten times better? She used to send Mary Ellen and me home with bags stuffed with corn on the cob, beefsteak tomatoes, cucumbers as big as our arms and enough strawberries to stain every piece of clothing we owned.

I asked her once why she planted so much, and she said, 'I just don't know when to stop.'"

"She never stopped looking out for you, did she?" Obviously, it was Miss Viola who helped him out of the nightmare Jeremiah the self-centered pervert had put him in. All the love and support, emotional and financial, she'd given him...

"No, she didn't." He pulled out a few more weeds, wiped off the mud on his shorts, then plopped on his butt on the mulched path.

"Like I said, I don't know how it started or how long it had been going on. Two of the men—Steven Anderson and Gary Grayson—are cousins, and word was, they'd been messing with their younger cousins for years."

Alia forced a breath, forced her emotions back and drew on the analytical part of herself she relied on. Though Alia-the-woman was still there, still reeling, Alia-the-investigator was taking charge.

"What is the gender breakdown of boys to girls among the five families?"

"Mary Ellen and me. Jeffrey has two sisters. Anderson had one daughter, and Grayson had two. Marco Gaudette had three girls and one boy."

Poor kids, betrayed by the people they should have trusted most. If that was the reason for the murders, and she felt sure it was, how many potential suspects were there? Three remaining pervs, four wives, twelve victims and anyone they'd confided in. Boyfriends, girlfriends, spouses, counselors, cops, priests or ministers. Even friends had been known to seek vengeance before.

"What about the wives? What did they know?" Alia lowered her voice. "What did Camilla know?"

Landry rested his wrists on his knees and held her

gaze. "I don't know. But as far as I can recall, her fondness for mainlining gin started about the time of that birthday. We never talked about it. When I could pretend it never happened, I did. The closest we came to discussing it was when I asked her to leave him. He'd just left town, and I thought we could disappear while he was gone. All she had to say was yes, but instead she poured another drink."

It had been a hell of a life: abuse, pain, disillusionment and a mother who did nothing to help.

Alia wasn't an overly emotional person. She always related to her victims' suffering, but in a cool, detached manner. Right now, just for an instant, she wanted to put her head down and cry. She wanted to wrap her arms around her mom and dad and thank them profusely for being such great parents. More than that, she wanted to wrap her arms around Landry and hold him until everything was all right.

Things might never be *all right* again for him and the other kids involved.

God, she felt naive. She knew it happened. Her first juvenile sex crimes case had been one too many. She knew sometimes fathers did horrible things and sometimes mothers let them. Hell, she knew sometimes those roles were reversed.

But God in heaven, she didn't, couldn't, understand it. Any person standing by when a child was abused boggled her mind. A *parent*, the person who gave that child life, whose blood ran through his veins, knowing and doing nothing...

Camilla Jackson had got no more than she deserved.

And Alia wished she could be naive again.

"How old was Mary Ellen when she was included?" she asked when she was sure her voice would be steady.

"Ten. They had *standards*, you know." He spit out the word.

"Does she remember?"

Her question surprised him, his eyes widening slightly. After a moment, he shrugged. "I don't know. I always thought so. I mean, how do you forget something like that? But we've never talked about it, ever. Not even before I moved out."

Kids *could* forget something like that. They could push it into the back of their minds, bury it deep beneath trauma and fear and pain and denial. They could go on with life, function normally, appear to have a loving relationship with their abuser. As emotionally fragile as Mary Ellen was, Alia was pretty sure that was exactly what she'd done. It had been her only way to survive.

"What about the other kids? Do you know what happened to any of them?"

He scrubbed his jaw with one hand. The muscles there had tightened before the conversation began and weren't showing signs of relaxing anytime soon. "One of the Wallace daughters is married. The other's been divorced a few times. Anderson's daughter killed herself when she was eighteen. Mary Ellen had just come back from boarding school, and it hit her really hard. Surprising, given that outside the family things, they hadn't been friends. Mary Ellen started boarding school when she was thirteen, stayed until graduation."

More of Miss Viola's doing, Alia supposed. She couldn't have helped Landry escape and left Mary Ellen to endure alone.

Maybe Mary Ellen had related to the girl's decision.

Maybe she'd found herself contemplating the same decision.

"I've heard that some of the kids were in and out of jail. The rest…" Landry shrugged.

Suicide, drugs, criminal activity and serial marriage. Alia was sure there were even more interesting problems hiding in their backgrounds.

Abruptly he stood, brushed the seat of his shorts, then extended his hand to her. He pulled with more force than she expected, and she stumbled to avoid stepping on the basket of fruit. She was just inches from him. It was the kind of closeness a woman should take advantage of when it presented itself, and if she didn't, the man should. But she didn't, and neither did he, except for continuing to hold on to her hand while his gaze searched hers. He looked hard, intent, seeking—she wasn't sure what. Pity? Compassion? Revulsion?

Did he think that admitting he'd been raped would affect the way she felt about him?

It did, but not the way he might expect. It stirred up all kinds of emotion—anger, sadness, a fierce need to protect him. Compassion, admiration. She respected the way he'd lived his life, not letting his bastard father destroy it, being who he needed to be, doing what had needed doing. Jeremiah Jackson III had basically told Jeremiah Jackson the demon to go to hell, and she was proud of him for it.

Whatever he saw or didn't see apparently satisfied him. He let go, picked up the tomatoes and handed them to her, then said, "If you're lucky, I'll find some ripe corn and fix you my special grilled dinner."

"With fried green tomatoes?" she asked hopefully, relieved to set the seriousness aside for a moment.

"When I grill, I grill everything." He elbowed her. "Don't pout. They're even better that way. We'll have to stop at the store and get a few things."

"Hey, I'll happily do all the shopping for a man who cooks. Just lead the way to the corn."

Chapter 10

After a stop at the market, Landry took Alia back to his apartment, where they had about a minute's debate to decide to cook dinner at her house. She had a great grill, she said, used only during her parents' visits, and since he wasn't sure when he'd last washed dishes or cleaned the apartment, he was happy to go elsewhere.

The cottage didn't have a back porch, just a broad set of steps that led to a yard with grass and a small clump of crape myrtles to one side. The grill was off to the side, too, where Landry left it for the time being. He was sprawled on the steps with a cold beer in hand, eyes closed, and letting the breeze rustle across his skin.

It hadn't been so bad, confiding in her. He'd thought he would never tell his story to another soul, that Dr. Granville had been absolutely the last. She'd told him it was nothing to be ashamed of, that she wouldn't advise opening conversations with strangers with it, but the only one paying the price of secrecy, she'd insisted, was him.

In a sense, she'd been right. It must not have haunted any of the bastards responsible. But she'd been wrong, too. Two who'd done it and two who'd known were dead. They'd paid for what they'd done or, in the case of the women, not done.

And he felt better for telling.

He felt better for Alia's response.

The screen door closed with a bang seconds before she sat down beside him. She had a cold drink, too—something turquoise blue in a tall glass—and carried a handful of mini candy bars, offering him one. "I called Murphy and asked him to hold off on interviewing the Wallace daughters. He rescheduled for tomorrow afternoon."

Landry acknowledged the news with a nod. He hadn't spoken to either of them since he'd left home and wasn't likely to ever get a friendly word from them once they realized he'd told their secret, too.

"I also checked the names you gave me."

Since they'd arrived at the house, he'd put the chicken in a brown-sugar-and-cinnamon marinade, cleaned the corn on the cob, sliced the tomatoes and kicked back with a beer, while she'd been on the computer. Shifting to one side, she pulled a piece of paper from her hip pocket and smoothed it one-handed. It was covered with blocks of chicken-scratch writing so tiny he couldn't make out much more than a name here and there. He counted ten blocks. He and Mary Ellen, apparently, didn't rate inclusion, he presumed, because the cops had already looked at them.

"Of Wallace's three kids, the oldest is married, no

children, does all the same social stuff as her parents. Nothing questionable or notable about her. Daughter number two has been divorced six times, no kids and does none of the same social stuff as her parents. She's got a few DUIs, a couple of arrests for public intox and a fondness for making a lot of public scenes. Jeffrey has a dozen drug busts, nothing major, and has apparently disappeared off the grid. No activity on his Social Security number, driver's license is expired, nothing for a couple years."

Was he dead? God, Landry hoped not, but he'd been so damned lost the last time he'd seen him.

Another sin to lay at their fathers' feet.

Plus a prayer that Jeffrey had cleaned up, changed his name and moved to a nice little town where he'd met a nice little girl who healed hearts and souls.

Alia deciphered the next set of scratches. "The Anderson daughter committed suicide, like you said. Straight-A student, all kinds of activities—everyone loved her, teachers and students alike. She'd been scheduled to begin classes at Tulane that fall. Too close to home, maybe?"

"Wouldn't it be for you?"

Her expression darkened, became implacable and driven and just a little bewildered. That was the part of her, he knew, that was asking, *How could they do this?*

He'd asked *how* and *why* a thousand times. Had begged them to stop at least a thousand times.

Clearing her throat, she went back to her notes. "Grayson's daughters. The older one is married to another of New Orleans's golden boys. Her husband has very public affairs, but she keeps a stiff upper lip and stands by her man. She has a ten-year-old son who's been kicked out of two schools and is currently enrolled in a military-type boarding school. Her daughter is seven and goes to private school. The family goes to church with Mom and Dad, is regularly seen at Commander's Palace with them for Sunday brunch and lives a block or two away.

"Daughter number two is a barely functioning alcoholic. Divorced twice, one son who's five and living with his father's family. Doesn't work, apparently supported by her family—a little blackmail there, you think?—and though she claims New Orleans as home, she spends most of her time traveling elsewhere."

Man, they were a depressing bunch, Landry thought. Coming from fine, respectable families, backed by power and influence and wealth—and a dozen loser kids.

Except Mary Ellen. All she'd ever wanted was to get married and raise babies and be happy. It had taken a while, but she'd achieved those dreams.

And he was all he'd ever wanted. He had a job he liked. He took care of himself. The only family he wanted was the one he chose for himself. The past was, most of the time, in the past, where he no longer had nightmares about it. His only true regret at this very moment was Miss Viola's death.

How many men could claim only one regret?

Well, make that two, he thought with a glance at Alia. She was off-limits now but maybe someday…

"The Gaudette kids," she said, her tone sounding as if she was glad they were getting to the end. "The oldest daughter went to college in Virginia, married a man from London, moved there and stayed. According to Facebook and the mommy blog she does with her friends, she's happy and productive and fiercely vocal on the matter of child abuse laws, there, here, everywhere."

That one's going to run the world, her mother used to proudly say at those family dinners.

Or ruin it, her father had always muttered to the other men, who'd laughed.

"The second kid still lives in the area. She runs a no-kill animal shelter with her girlfriend. Her only presence online is for the shelter—fund-raisers, features on adoptable pets. She's never been arrested, keeps her life private. She visits her sister in London once every year or so but doesn't seem to have contact with her parents. The parents do, however, make a sizable donation to the shelter every year. Gets them platinum status on the website."

"Her father always believed if you threw enough money at a problem, it would eventually go away."

"Last ones. Daughter number three isn't on the radar, not since she spent two years in a psychiatric hospital about five years ago. She left Louisiana for California—that's where the hospital was—and never moved back. She's living a totally unremarkable life there with a boyfriend and four cats. The son never married, has three kids, all in the custody of their mothers. He was in an accident a few years ago—motorcycle versus semi—and is a paraplegic. He lives, God love him, with Mom and Dad."

"Is that his punishment or theirs?"

"You could make an argument either way." Alia folded the paper again, creasing the lines. "You're surprised by how much you remember."

Draining the last of the beer, he pointed the bottle at her. "I tried for years to forget every last detail. After years of therapy, I found a balance I could live with."

"Until the past week upset the balance."

"It did that." He shook his head ruefully.

After a moment, she met his gaze. "It seems you and Mary Ellen and the mommy blogger and her sister survived the best. No drugs, no arrests, no drinking—"

He held up the beer bottle.

"—to excess, and no messes in your personal lives. Excepting the murders."

"Those pesky little murders do tend to get messy."

She leaned back against the steps and drew a long suck of drink through the straw. She looked about fifteen years old. Maybe it was the Kool-Aid, or the absence of her weapons and badge—on the counter just inside the door—or her hair falling loose from its braid.

She was the kind of girl he'd stopped dreaming about when he was fourteen. It was hard for a boy who was getting sexually assaulted every few weeks to think about normal boy-girl stuff like having crushes, holding hands, kissing with tongues. It had been impossible for a long time to even imagine willingly getting intimate.

He'd made up for that during and after therapy. He'd been intimate, maybe with too many women, to forget how his first few years of sex had gone.

He wanted to get intimate with Alia. How did that work, given her job and his relation to four murder victims? Could it even work? Was she interested?

His ego said yes. It wasn't standard policy for her to spend so much time with someone like him. He didn't see Jimmy DiBiase coming around on his time off or hear Jack Murphy sharing the details of his personal life.

There was more than the job between him and Alia. He felt it. But the job between them was one hell of an obstacle. No more television than he watched, he knew cops weren't supposed to get personally involved with the subjects of their investigations.

And yet it sometimes happened. Jack and Evie Murphy were proof.

Abruptly, as Alia popped another candy bar into her mouth, he asked, "Am I a suspect in these crimes?"

She chewed the chocolate and crumpled the wrapper into a tiny ball. "You're on my list, but your alibi keeps you from getting a big red question mark beside your name."

After a moment, he asked, "Do you really have an actual list?"

"Yep."

"With red question marks?"

"Yep. I'm a visual person." She ate the last candy bar, then checked the time on her phone. "Aren't you getting hungry?"

He considered saying no, making her wait for another hour, but he'd be lying. He was always ready for corn on the cob and green tomatoes, hot off the grill. Besides, who knew how cranky she'd get if she was really hungry?

While she watched, he removed the grill cover, lit the burners, scrubbed the grates and wiped them with oil-soaked paper towels. Together they brought out the food and utensils, then she stood nearby while the chicken sizzled in the hot spot, the corn browned and melting butter caused flare-ups under the grate. The tomatoes, basted with oil, went on last.

"I'm surprised. I didn't peg you for a cook."

"I'm not a cook. I'm a griller. Easiest way in the world to fix a burger, steak or fish."

She snorted. "Sometime I'll introduce you to my

binder full of take-out and delivery menus for every restaurant in a ten-mile radius."

He shook his head, and she gave him a warning finger. "Don't try to make me feel guilty with that look. My mom gives it to me often. She's the expert at it."

Her gaze settled on the food, and an expression came across her face—and it wasn't admiring the crosshatch lines on the tomatoes, the black bits on the corn or the lovely sear on the chicken. The case was forefront in her mind again. Soon there would come a comment or a question he wouldn't have an answer to, but he didn't mind. He didn't have a giant red question mark on her list, and that was enough for him.

"Why kill Camilla first? Why not Jeremiah?"

And there were the questions. Taking her glass, he pushed the straw aside and took a long drink of sweet liquid. "I don't know. Opportunity? Jeremiah told people she was out of town. Maybe she really was planning on leaving, so that made her first."

She acknowledged the possibility with a nod. "I wonder if she *was* first. If there have been any other deaths associated with these people besides the daughter's suicide. Maybe we just don't know."

Landry carefully flipped a piece of chicken to the cooler side of the grill with tongs, then said, "Maybe Camilla intended to tell someone. Maybe it was finally time to clear her conscience."

Alia considered that. "Confession is good for the soul, they say. A friend, a pastor, a psychologist? And she could have unwisely—"

She said the last word tactfully, but he corrected it. "Drunkenly."

"—admitted her plans. Your father—any of the men, all of them—could have put her in that crypt."

Landry wished for another beer, larger and stronger and colder then the last, then Alia laid her hand on his forearm. That was better than all the cold beer in the world.

"I'd like to think he had some sort of feelings for her that wouldn't let him do that," he said regretfully. "They were married more than thirty years. They had children, grandchildren. But he traded his kids to his friends for sex, so hell, what do I know?"

After a few more moments, he removed the food from the grill, and they settled at the small kitchen table to eat. Much as he liked sunshine and heat, air-conditioning had a lot going for it.

Everything was smoky, the chicken tender, the corn buttery, the tomatoes tangy. He'd cooked enough for three, and all the plates were empty when they finished. Where did she put it all?

She gave a satisfied sigh. "If I married you, would you grill dinner every night?"

He stilled in the act of reaching for dishes to carry to the sink. It was a silly question, based on her affection for food rather than her fondness for him. But it touched the part of him that had found intimacy a problem. It made him feel normal. "Maybe every other night. Odd nights we grill. Even nights we get Vietnamese."

"Excellent compromise." She moved the beers to the countertop, then got a pop-up wipe to clean the table. "With beignets on Sunday mornings and oysters on the half shell every Friday night."

His hands in sudsy water, Landry studied her. While prepping dinner, he'd seen all the candy dishes, had found a cabinet full of potato chips and cereal. There hadn't been much else in the way of food besides canned and frozen vegetables and six half gallons of almond milk. "Your father starved you as a child, didn't he?" he teased.

She stuck out her tongue. "He brought me a scooter pie home from work every single day. When he was deployed, he mailed them to me every day...though now that I think of it, my mom may have just told me to make me happy because they were never crushed or melty."

"And I'm sure your mother fed you as often and as much as possible."

Alia rinsed the first dish he'd washed, then dried and put it away. "Mom says every Vietnamese mother needs a village to feed. I was hers." She gave the towel a warning wave in his direction. "I know what you're doing. Jimmy teased me about how much I ate every single day we were married. You're just a little more tactful than him. He was always saying, 'Damn, girl, you eat a lot.' I do. I always have. Mom says I begged for extra bottles of formula when I was six months old. Jimmy says one day my metabolism is going to fail and my ass is going to explode to two ax handles' wide."

Landry handed the last dish to her. "I like your ass just fine."

After putting the plate away, she swatted him with the towel. "I wasn't fishing for a compliment, but thank you."

Still teasing, he said, "Now you say something nice about me."

"Oh, you *are* fishing for compliments." She hung up the towel, smoothed it neatly, then looked up. "I like you—" After a moment, she changed the inflection and simply, quietly repeated it. "I like you."

* * *

It was nearly ten when Landry rose from the couch and stretched. "I should go."

Yes, you should, Alia thought, but she didn't want him to. Which was exactly why he should. She had already spent way more time with him than she could justify, doing things far better suited to boyfriend/girlfriend than special agent/subject. The only claim she could make with a clear conscience was that things hadn't gotten physical. Yet.

She slid to her feet, turned off the music and walked barefoot with him to the door and outside. Nocturnal insects sang in a chorus of buzzes. A soft breeze carried fragrances from a neighbor's garden, and somewhere distant a train whistle sounded.

They stopped at the edge of the steps, the boards warm and worn smooth against her feet by generations of feet traveling across them. He was near enough for her to feel the energy radiating from him, to touch if she swayed just the tiniest bit to her left. She could lay her head on his shoulder, feel his warmth and strength and breathe in the scent of him. She could then lift her head from his shoulder and find herself exactly where she wanted to be.

Wrapped in intimacy with him.

He gazed at her a long time in the dim glow of the porch light, and she knew—not wishful thinking but *knew* as sure as she stood there that he was thinking the same thing. He wanted intimacy, and he wanted it with her.

Confirming her thought, he leaned closer, a slow encroaching that gave her plenty of time to step back. She didn't. His mouth was only an inch away, almost near enough to kiss, to taste, but before she closed the distance between them, he spoke.

"I like you, too," he murmured in a raspy voice. "So what do we do about it?"

Her breath caught. A frivolous part of her that so rarely showed itself did a silent *Yes!* while another part sighed with relief. If she were a different person, a more overtly emotional person, she might even call it a swoon.

"Do we wait until the case is over and done with and then see…?" He arched one brow.

Tilting her head to the side, she replied, "That's one option."

"It could be weeks."

"Months," she agreed. "Or…"

"Or?"

The thought played in her head, tempting her with the possibilities, stunning her with the idea of making such a commitment to a man who might be nothing more than a short-term fling. Though in her gut, she knew there was nothing short-term about what she felt. What she was pretty sure he felt.

He was waiting for her to suggest option two, still standing impossibly close, his dark gaze locked with hers. A slow smile formed, softening the lines of his face. "Guess I'll have to wait to find out."

She smiled, too.

"I'll be going to the funeral home again tomorrow. I'll give the guy Scott's credit card information and ask him to outdo the old man's send-off." Hands in his pockets, he gazed into the night. "The good thing about them finding her body when they did…with the year-and-a-day rule, she can't be buried in the same crypt as him. Her life with him might have seemed like an eternity in hell, but at least she won't have to really spend eternity with him."

"Thank God for small favors." Alia wasn't wild about the aboveground crypts or sharing her final resting place with a bunch of other people, but the idea that, one year and a day after she was interred, the workers could pop open the vault and slide someone else in, frankly, made her skin crawl in a major way.

"Come by the bar tomorrow evening if you get a chance." His hand fumbled for hers, and he gave it a squeeze, then let go.

She was still nodding agreement when he reached his car. She watched until he drove away, then moved a few steps back to sit. Getting comfortable, she drew her feet into the seat, wrapped her arms around her legs, then sighed softly, thinking about that second option again.

When she realized that the bump pressing against her hip was her cell phone, she pulled it out, stared at it a moment, then dialed. Though it was her mom's cell she'd dialed, her dad answered. After thirty-five years together, neither needed nor wanted much privacy from the other.

Alia caught him up on the public aspects of the case before her mom came on the line. "Tell me what's new, *chica*."

"That's *cô bé* to you."

"Don't get sassy, girl. Have you had a date since we last talked?"

Alia ran through her encounters with Landry, but none of them technically qualified as a date. Except… "A man cooked dinner for me this evening."

In her mom's book, that was beyond dating and darn close to being engaged. "*Really?* What did he fix?"

She recited the menu, then teasingly added, "That was after he took me out for Vietnamese for lunch."

"Ooh." Lien sounded somewhere between envious and thrilled. "So what are you doing for this man that makes him want to feed you so well?"

For a moment, Alia wished she could give a naughty reply that would make her mother laugh. Instead, she went for blunt truth. "I'm helping find out who murdered his parents."

The silence on the line made clear that her mom's light mood had vanished like a helium balloon in typhoon winds. "He's Admiral Jackson's son."

"Yes."

"He's a part of your investigation."

"Yes."

"You're not supposed to get personally involved with him."

"No, I'm not." Alia watched lights streak across the distant sky and wished they were shooting stars or lightning. She could make a wish or sleep well in her warm, dry cocoon of a bedroom while nature raged outside. But based on their location and movement, she was pretty sure the lights belonged to a medical helicopter, picking up or dropping off a critical patient.

"Landry is a good guy, Mom," she said quietly. "He… he gets me. He likes me. And I like him."

For a moment she was transported back to Hawaii and the day she and Kanani had become official. *Do you like me?* he'd asked solemnly, and she'd shrugged. *I like your toys. And your bike. Plus, I can run faster and jump higher than you, so that's good.*

But I can skateboard better, and I can surf. So d'ya want to be my girlfriend?

Seeing that they'd been pretty equally matched, she'd
agreed. Thankfully, her tastes had matured since then.
She liked Landry's eyes…smile…body. His sense of
humor and his intelligence. The way he could say so
much with only a look, and the way he'd survived a
childhood so ugly that it made her hurt for him. She
figured she could outrun, outjump and outskateboard
him, and she didn't give a good damn if he could surf.

"Have you been intimate with him?"

The question startled a laugh from her. "Aw, Mom,
you sound so proper when you put it that way. No, we
haven't had sex."

"Intimacy isn't just about sex, LiLi."

Alia thought about the story he'd told her that afternoon—trusted her with—and her throat grew thick. "I
know."

"What are you going to do? Ignore your feelings and
do your job? Avoid him as much as you can?"

"I was thinking…" Mouth pursed, she drew a deep
breath, then expelled it. "I might request to be removed
from the case."

That earned another silence from her mother. Alia
wasn't a quitter. When she accepted a responsibility,
she saw it through. Impossible projects, difficult classes,
ugly turns in relationships…she'd learned from her father, whose farming family had been on a first-name
basis with hardship, and from her mother, whose family
had faced life-threatening adversity in their homeland
and made a new home in a new country. Every effort
deserved her best.

"He's that important to you," Lien said.

"I—I…yes."

"Will this adversely affect your career?"

"I don't know." It was an important case; Jeremiah Jackson aside, the sheer number of victims made it important. Any solve made an agent look good. This one would carry extra weight.

"But you're willing to put your feelings for this man ahead of your career." Her tone was cautious. Was she disappointed in Alia? Did she think her only child was letting down people who counted on her—her coworkers, her victims, her parents, herself? All for a chance at an affair that might not amount to anything.

Or could turn out to be everything.

Alia's answer was practically a whisper. "Yes?" That little question at the end had nothing to do with her certainty, just her very personal, very vulnerable admission, and her mom knew it.

Lien let out a heavy breath. "I've been waiting a long time for you to meet someone who is important enough to take precedence over your job. Someone who wasn't Jimmy DiBiase. It's about time. How does Landry feel about children?"

"You're still going to have to adopt your grandbabies." Relief washed over Alia, easing muscles she hadn't realized were tight. Telling her mom, who would tell her father, was the hard part. Talking to her boss tomorrow would be a breeze in comparison.

Of course her boss could refuse. She could remind Alia that everyone was putting something on hold for this case. She could insist that Alia's love life could wait. She could even, as she was good at doing, issue an ultimatum: stay with the case, keep her distance from Landry and be the consummate professional she was trained to be, or else.

But those were worries Alia wasn't dealing with until they happened.

"Tell me something about him," her mom requested.

"Ask me something." When it came to new boy-friends, Alia and Lien were more like best girlfriends than daughter and mother, discussing eye color or dimples or hotness factor rather than anything important.

So her mother's question surprised her. "Does he have a good heart?"

Alia smiled slowly. "He loves his sister and adores his nieces. He treated his elderly cousin with great affection and respect. He helps old friends with nightmares of their own, and he's got more friends, and better ones, than I do."

"Sounds good, LiLi. How does he treat you?"

Letting her feet plop to the floor, Alia slouched down on her spine until she could prop her heels on the railing. "Sometimes he makes me laugh, and sometimes I make him laugh. He took me to meet the old lady who runs his favorite Vietnamese restaurant."

Mom's voice perked up. "Does he speak Vietnamese?"

"Not even enough to order. He points at the pictures like I used to do."

"Yes, but you were seven." Then Lien relented. "At least he knows good food. That other one acted like we were trying to poison him."

That other one wasn't the worst of the ways Lien had referred to Jimmy. Some of them had been very colorful, thanks to Alia's Grandpa Kingsley and her Ông oi Hieu.

"We like the same music, and we like to talk, but we don't have to." That was a good thing, one she and Jimmy had never achieved. If they weren't talking, they'd been having sex or arguing.

She wondered wistfully when she would have sex with Landry.

"He must have issues, with his mother, father and cousin all murdered in such a short time."

This wasn't the time to admit that he despised his father and was a virtual stranger to his mother—though for very good reasons. Her mom wouldn't understand his parents' behavior any more than she did.

She didn't look forward to sharing those reasons with Jimmy and Jack Murphy in the morning. Just the thought made her stomach tumble.

"You know, you don't want to take your career lightly," her mother said. "But when a man like this comes along—a man of substance—you can't put him aside and hope he waits until it's convenient for you. Now the sweet-talking weasel—of course you'd never risk anything for him. He's just a right-now kind of guy. But if you really think Landry is the forever kind, you owe it to yourself to find out."

The forever kind of guy. She'd teased with her mom that her dad was the last one of that kind ever made. It scared her that Landry might be one—might be *her* forever guy. Special Agent Alia Kingsley, never fazed by murderers, rapists or thugs of any kind, was quaking deep inside at the possibility.

"Try to help Daddy see it that way, will you? I don't want him to think that I'm going with my hormones instead of my brain."

Her mom snorted. "Your father's gone with his hormones instead of his brains plenty of times. In the end, though, all he wants is for you to be happy."

"And to eventually be the director of NCIS."

"Ah, he's just living through your accomplishments. We both are."

Alia laughed. "There's a frightening thought."

"Be happy and give us grandbabies. That's all we really want from you. And—" Lien turned totally serious. "I'll deny I said it, but truth is, the grandbabies are optional. You happy and healthy—that's all that matters." She paused. "Do you feel better?"

Silently Alia scanned through her emotions. "I do."

"Good. That's how it should be when you talk to your mama. Love you, sweetie."

"Love you and Dad." Alia disconnected the call and stared into the sky. Had Camilla Jackson ever called her son *sweetie*? Had she told him she loved him? Had she really felt that love?

Alia was an equal-opportunity assigner of guilt: if one parent hurt a child and the other didn't stop him/her, they both failed the minimum standards of decent parenting. But there was still something inside her, old-fashioned maybe, that felt the mother was a little more to blame. Camilla had carried Landry for nine months; she had incredibly intimate contact with him every day for forty weeks. She'd nourished him, diapered him, sat up nights with him. She'd had a mother's obligation, a connection that even a father couldn't match in the most primal of ways.

And yet she'd forfeited her responsibility. She'd turned that monster of a father loose on her children and closed her eyes while he and his bastard friends hurt them. Raped them.

She should have drowned in that gin bottle. But that would have been too easy a passing. She would be punished in the hereafter, but it gave Alia some warped satisfaction to know she'd suffered in this life, too.

Chapter 11

The supervisory special agent in charge of the NCIS office was a formidable woman. Slender and able to intimidate agents far more experienced than Alia, Sheila Martinez listened to Alia's request to give up the multiple homicide. Now she sat, studying Alia, her expression giving away nothing of her thoughts.

Alia was doing her best to appear just as impassive. She didn't think she was anywhere near succeeding.

After an eternity, Sheila broke her silence. "You want to be excused from a major investigation because you're involved with one of the subjects—the admiral's son, in fact."

"I'm not—" Alia broke off. *Involved* didn't always include sex. There was no way she could deny emotional involvement with Landry. Hell, she couldn't even deny the hope that it did include sex. Soon. "Yes, ma'am."

"How far has it gone?"

"Nothing physical." *Yet.*

"Yet." Sheila spoke the word Alia had only thought. "And his alibi is reliable?"

"For the first murders."

"How sure are you that the murders are all connected?"

"I'm convinced of it."

After another long silence, Sheila grudgingly said, "Make sure DiBiase has your notes and tell him he'll be working with Zoe—" Her dark gaze narrowed. "Make that Marcus Trent."

Oh, so you've met Jimmy, Alia wanted to say, hiding a grin at the change from pretty blue-eyed Zoe to grumpy loner Marcus.

"I'll do that this morning, ma'am." Alia rose, wiping her palms on her pants under the guise of smoothing the fabric. She was halfway to the door when Sheila spoke again.

"We do an important job here, Alia. It's not like handing off an account at an insurance agency or assigning a teacher to a different classroom. We need continuity in our cases. We can't have agents deciding their cases interfere with what they really want to do."

Feeling about ten years old again, Alia was searching for an apology when Sheila went on.

"The job demands a lot. It can be hard to find the right balance between it and your personal life. Some people are cut out for it, especially," she added with a rueful smile, "if you're ambitious and determined to be not only the first black but also the first female NCIS director.

"But that kind of single-mindedness can be awfully lonely at times." Sheila saw Alia's gaze flicker to the photos on her desk. "Nieces and nephews. I never married. I'm not one of them who found the right balance."

Unsure what to say, Alia remained silent.

"I hope the young Mr. Jackson is everything you want and more." Sheila turned stern again. "Because you don't get a second chance like this. Understand?"

"Yes, ma'am. Thank you, ma'am."

Turning on her heel, Alia swiftly left the office. Within half an hour, she was at the police station, seated at a conference table just down the hall from the office Jimmy and Murphy shared with a half dozen other detectives.

"Well?" Jimmy prodded after a moment.

The sick feeling was back, tying her stomach in knots. Even when Murphy slid over a zippered bag of lemon cookies, a gift from Evie, she couldn't have forced even one bite. She'd known this would be hard. She just hadn't known how hard.

With a deep breath, she forced out the words. "I think I know why our victims were killed." Willing her voice to remain empty of emotion, she told them everything Landry had told her. She barely slowed even when the men spoke—*Aw, jeez*, Jimmy said while Murphy muttered, *Damn*. She didn't stop until the story was done.

Silence echoed in the room for a moment, then Jimmy sighed. "It's a hell of a motive. I'd've killed the bastards myself if I'd known."

Murphy agreed. "Puts a whole new slant on the questions I'll be asking the Wallace daughters this afternoon."

"Narrows the suspect list, too."

"Speaking of that…" Alia pulled out the notes she'd

made last evening and slid the wrinkled paper across the table.

Jimmy scowled at it. "What? You thought you'd scribble a few lines in your spare time?" In an aside to Murphy, he complained, "She used to give me lists like that to do the shopping, then get pissed because I couldn't figure out what the hell she wanted."

Murphy took the paper and snorted. "Perfectly legible to me." He read off a few bits of info to prove he could, then shrugged. "You want to come with me to interview the daughters?"

Yes. She'd never been taken off a case before, voluntarily or otherwise—had never had to let go and be cut out of the loop. Most of her cases, she was proud to say, she'd closed. A few had been consigned to the cold case file, though she still looked them over from time to time.

But this one was now officially out of her hands. The acknowledgment came with both relief and regret. "No, actually, I'm no longer assigned to this investigation."

Jimmy stared at her, but Murphy didn't appear surprised. Maybe he'd seen more than she'd realized yesterday, or maybe it just took a hell of a lot to surprise someone who'd been a cop as long as he had.

"Martinez yanked you off?" Jimmy demanded.

"No. I asked to be reassigned."

"Why?"

"Conflict of interest and all that," she said blithely.

"Oh, hell, what you're doing with Jackson doesn't have a damn thing to do with how you're working the case."

The disgust in Jimmy's voice sent warm affection through her. "I'm glad you have faith in my ability to separate the personal from the professional."

He flushed faintly. "I always thought you were a hell of a cop, Alia. Besides, damn, who among us hasn't slept with someone involved in a case?"

She was the only one to raise her hand. But she hoped to remedy that soon.

Gathering her stuff, she stood. "By the way, Jimmy, SSA Martinez assigned another agent from the team to work with you."

His eyes brightened. "Zoe?"

"Marcus Trent." She couldn't help but laugh at his disappointment. "Good luck, guys. If you need anything, you know where to find me."

As she walked down the hall, she pulled a cookie from the bag and bit into it. Damn, it was even better than the half dozen she'd eaten yesterday. Maybe she would beg Evie for the recipe and learn to make them.

Better yet, she'd beg Evie for the recipe and persuade Landry to make them.

Though the temperature was hovering somewhere around *broil* when she stepped out of the building, the mere thought of how she might *persuade* Landry was enough to make her shiver.

Mondays were slow nights in the bar, though *slow* was a matter of perception. If it was located anywhere besides Bourbon Street, Landry would say they had a good crowd. Given that they were on Bourbon, it was slow.

It was nearly seven o'clock, not even halfway through his shift, when Alia walked in the door. He wasn't the only one who noticed her, glancing about as a dozen male heads swiveled in her direction. They watched her stride across the room, admired her as she easily slid onto a stool, then went back to whatever had occupied them before.

Except him. He leaned on the bar in front of her, separated from her by her purse—tiny—and a plastic bag—huge. He didn't need the whiff of warm bread, spicy meats and olives to know the bag contained food.

Folding her hands together, she smiled. The strength of it hit him in the midsection like a fist. "Hi."

"Hey. Is that smile for me or the food?"

"It's a toss-up. I've got muffalettas from Frank's. Plus potato salad, tabouli and extra olive salad."

"That's worth smiling about." He popped the top from an icy beer and set the bottle in front of her. "You look like you had a good day."

"It had its moments. How was yours?"

He shrugged. "I went back to visit the Cadillac man. Camilla's service is set for Thursday."

Though he'd expected her smile to fade, he was sorry when it did. She was beautiful no matter what her expression, but she actually glowed when she smiled, as if life couldn't possibly get any better.

He wasn't sure when or if he'd ever smiled like that.

"I saw Mary Ellen and the kids afterward. She's doing better."

"Good. Great. I can only imagine how hard this is for her."

It was the same for him. Somehow, after everything, Mary Ellen had stayed close to their parents. She had truly loved them, and now she truly mourned them, while Landry couldn't summon any grief. Only regret.

"Did you talk to DiBiase and Murphy?" He didn't want to ask the question, didn't want to know the answer. Admitting that he'd been a victim was hard enough.

Admitting that he'd been a victim of rape… His face flushed hot with shame. Men rarely reported sexual assaults, Dr. Granville had told him, just for that reason, because they found it humiliating, emasculating. It was neither, she'd insisted. He'd been a child, a victim, in no way responsible for what had happened to him. He'd had nothing to be ashamed of.

After a long time, he'd learned to believe her. But sometimes old habits were easy to slip back into.

Though he was avoiding looking at Alia, he sensed when she moved, laying her hand over his. "I told them everything. They'll handle it with all the sensitivity it calls for."

He snorted. "Sensitivity? DiBiase?"

"Jimmy used to be a sex crimes detective. His cases were primarily rapes, and he was very, very good with the victims." Her voice lightened a fraction. "I know, I know. Surprised the hell out of me, too."

Landry studied her hand on top of his, her fingers bare of jewelry, her nails neatly curved and painted with pale pink tips. Her watch emphasized the delicacy of her wrist, its gold gleaming against her brown skin.

He'd done a lot of hand-holding in his life, first with Camilla, then with Mary Ellen. He liked that Alia was strong enough to not need it, strong enough to offer it to others, yet soft enough to accept it if she'd wanted it.

He had to pull away to wait on a customer. When he returned, he asked, "Are you just going to let your sandwich sit there and get cold?"

She glanced at the bag, and that familiar gleam came into her eyes. "I was hoping you'd get a dinner break at a decent hour. I brought plenty to share."

He didn't normally eat dinner until closer to ten…but

normally he didn't have a muffaletta and Alia waiting for him. Catching the attention of the other bartender, he said, "I'm taking my break. I'll be upstairs if you need me."

Circling the bar, he picked up the food, gave Alia a hand down from the stool, then led her outside and through the gate into the courtyard. Her flip-flops punctuated their steps as they climbed the stairs.

"I envy your commute."

"It comes in handy, but it limits the excuses when you're late to work."

"Ah, yes, no matter where I live, I can always claim traffic as an excuse. Well, unless they send me to a ship."

Landry looked at her over his shoulder while he unlocked the door. "Is that possible—being sent to a ship?"

"You think crimes don't occur on board ships?" She shrugged, a lazy sensual movement that came totally naturally to her. Granted, he found pretty much everything about her sensual. "Sailors and marines are people like everyone else. They commit crimes and are the victims of them. Of course, for a shipboard crime, you have the advantage of a limited suspect pool."

He opened the door and stepped back to let her enter first. As she looked around, he tried to imagine the apartment through her eyes. It was a little over seven hundred square feet, two-thirds of it devoted to living room, dining room and kitchen, the remaining third a bedroom and bathroom. The floors were wood, the windows facing the courtyard were floor-to-ceiling and two paddle fans swirled the warm air.

"How long have you lived here?" she asked as she took the plastic bag from him.

"Ten years? Twelve? I don't remember."

She nodded knowingly. "Nice job of decorating."

"What do you mean? I haven't—" Breaking off, he laughed. "Be happy it has furniture. I wouldn't have bothered with more than a mattress on the floor if Miss Viola and Mary Ellen hadn't nagged so much."

She set her beer on the coffee table, then began unpacking the food bag. She pulled out the small containers of side dishes, held up a bag of Evie Murphy's lemon cookies with a grin, then removed the sandwiches. She'd hadn't bothered with the quarter or half-sized sandwiches, a meal all in themselves, but had gone for the full ones, each about the size of a dinner plate, loaded with meats, cheeses and that incredible olive salad. They'd been toasted so that everything was warm and melty and the edges were crispy, and they reminded him how long it had been since lunch.

He got plates, silverware and a long wicked-sharp knife, plus a pop for himself, then joined her on the couch. "You said your day had its moments," he reminded her as he cut a wedge from the sandwich she'd handed him. "What were the good moments?"

She had already taken a bite of her sandwich and now edged a chunk of olive from her lip into her mouth. After chewing slowly with her usual look of food-orgasm, she shrugged again. "It's kind of hard to tell the good ones from the bad. I met with my boss, and that was kind of tough but good, and I met with Jimmy and Murphy, and that was kind of tough, too, but also good."

Landry talked with his boss every day, but he imagined meeting with the special agent in charge of a whole field office was different in a lot of ways. His boss, Maxine, held a lot less power over his life than Alia's boss did over hers. The worst Maxine could do was fire him, and he could have a new job by closing time. Alia didn't have a *job*. She had a *career*.

He wondered when her career would take her from New Orleans. Wondered how lonely he would be when she was gone.

They'd met under damnable circumstances. By rights, they should never have crossed paths, never have talked beyond the first or second interview. He shouldn't know anything about her, shouldn't feel anything for her.

But he did.

She scooped portions of each side dish onto her plate, heaped more olive salad onto the next bite of her sandwich, then casually said, "I asked my boss to remove me from this investigation."

Landry was swallowing a drink of pop when her words sank in, and he choked, grabbing for a napkin, coughing to clear his throat. "You what?" A croak was all he could manage.

Her look was level, steady. "You heard me."

"Why?"

She pinched off a piece of sandwich and took a delicate bite. "I told you last night there was another option."

I like you, too, he'd told her. *So what do we do about it? Wait until the case is solved?*

She'd asked to be taken off a major case because of her feelings for him.

He didn't know how to react. This couldn't be a good career move. Major cases put major marks in the advancement column. He imagined solving the murder of an active-duty admiral, to say nothing of the other six victims, would be a giant gold star for everyone involved. And she'd walked away from it. For *him*.

No one had ever made that kind of sacrifice for him. He didn't know if he deserved it.

But *damn*, she'd walked away from all that for *him*. He was…flattered. Humbled.

She was watching him, her gaze still steady and level, but he saw just a flicker of vulnerability. She'd made a big sacrifice to give this thing between them a chance and was wondering now if she'd misread the situation, if she'd derailed her career for nothing.

Slowly he set his sandwich down, wiped his hands, then slid across the cushion separating them. He took the bit of sandwich from her hands, used the same napkin to wipe them, then for a long moment, he just looked at her. Whatever she saw in his face must have reassured her because the vulnerability faded and was replaced with something smoky and warm and dark.

He touched her face, brushing a long strand of hair back, tucking it behind her ear, then let his fingertips brush her skin. So soft, flawless, stretched across high cheekbones, warm enough to sear his fingers. He recalled the first time they'd talked, wondering if she'd dressed to downplay her looks. He hadn't realized then that clothing was just a wrapper, that nothing could downplay the delicate lines of her face, the shape of her eyes, the arch of her brows, the stubborn line of her jaw, the kissable shape of her mouth.

Most of her hair was in a braid, but some of it loosely framed her face. It was as silken and sleek as he'd expected, wrapping around his fingers before effortlessly sliding free again. Reaching behind her, he pulled the band loose, then combed his fingers through as it fell loose.

Alia lifted both hands to his face, cupped her palms

to it and kissed him. Damn, but he liked a woman who took what she wanted.

Her hands were hot, her touch sure. There was no hesitancy, no tentativeness. Her mouth covered his, and her tongue slid inside, bringing with it the taste of beer and food and something medicinal like a breath mint. Bringing with it hunger and need and a sort of unsteadiness in his gut that he remembered all too well. The first time he'd had sex with a girl, the first time he'd had sex with a woman who meant more than usual to him, and now the first time with Alia. Big moments in his life.

Too soon, she ended the kiss and put a little space between them, not much, nothing either of them couldn't close by leaning forward an inch or two. "Now we have another option," she said quietly.

"Keep our distance until the case is over or forget the case and have wild, hot, crazy sex every chance we get? In the real world, which of those is an option?"

She smiled, sweet and sly and a little devilish. "I was hoping you'd think that. So…you want to finish dinner or show me your bedroom?"

Landry picked up her left hand, keeping her from getting up if that had been her intention." My bedroom isn't bad. It has an air conditioner and a massive old bed that Miss Viola gave me when she found me sleeping on the mattress on the floor. It even has some stuff— some decor—hanging on the wall." He gave the word *decor* a twist, making fun of her earlier remark and his own lack of ability and interest in making the place look nicer. "However—"

She faked a pout. "I hate that word. It usually means I won't get my way."

He stroked her palm, making her shiver once, then

twice before she curled her fingers over his. "However," he repeated, "I have to be back at work in fifteen minutes. That's not even enough time to finish one kiss."

"The last kiss didn't take fifteen minutes."

"That's because you were doing the kissing. I need more than that. I like kissing, and I'm really going to like kissing you."

Her pout deepened. "I work all day. You work all night. I don't see time in our schedules for kisses lasting more than fifteen minutes, to say nothing of anything else, until Saturday." After a moment, she sighed acceptingly. "What time do you get off?"

"Three a.m."

"I have to get up at five if I'm going to run before work." Drawing a set of keys from her tiny purse, she peeled off a house key and gently squeezed it into his hand. "I'll leave some lights on for you. Don't do anything foolish like wander around the house or use the bathroom before you let me know you're there. I sleep with a weapon."

"So I've heard." He didn't look at the key, but the shape of it was practically burning into his palm. He'd never had a key to anyone else's house before, not even his parents'. Camilla had been willing to trust him with it by the time he started middle school, but not Jeremiah. The housekeeper was always there during the day, and in the evening, Jeremiah assumed, Camilla always was. It had been her, Landry's and Mary Ellen's secret that sometimes when their father left town, their mother went out on it.

Alia trusted him with her key. Trusted him to come into her home in the middle of the night, when she very

well might be asleep. *Trusted* him. That was a damn
good feeling.

They polished off their dinner, and he turned down
an offer of a cookie. He liked sweets but not the way she
did. Even his nieces the sugar demons didn't like them
the way she did. She could indulge her sweets craving
in the cookies.

He would indulge his in her.

His fifteen minutes had passed five minutes ago when
they finally locked up and went downstairs together. Just
outside the gate, where her car was parked in his boss's
spot, he slid his arms around her and pulled her near,
feeling the bump of her pistol at her waist beneath her
shirt. "There it is," he teased.

"Mmm-hmm. The handcuffs are on the other side."

"I bet a lot of guys, when they find out you're a cop,
ask you to use the handcuffs on them."

"Um. But you'd be the first one I might actually say
yes to."

The streetlights were starting to come on, buzzing
like giant insects, and foot traffic had picked up on the
sidewalks. Music came from the open doors of the bar,
a decent rendition of "The Sky is Crying," competing
with something heavy metal across the street. It was a
good evening for taking a lazy walk through the Quarter,
sitting in a restaurant courtyard over a leisurely meal…
or laying down a beautiful woman and exploring every
centimeter of her lovely body.

Soon.

Not soon enough. But he'd taken too much time off
the past week, all for bad reasons, and would be off the
day of Camilla's funeral this week. Alia was worth waiting for, damn, as long as he had to.

He leaned close to her, nuzzling her neck, smelling the faint fragrance of perfume, the fainter scent of lemon and sugar. "You sampled Evie's cookies on the way over," he murmured, his lips barely brushing her skin.

"Murphy gave them to me this morning. It's nothing less than a miracle that I hadn't inhaled them by noon."

With a laugh, he kissed her mouth, quickly, reining in the passion and need. "Thanks for dinner."

"You're welcome." The look she gave him was filled with something far more than the routine gesture the words denoted, something more like a statement of fact. An invitation.

With a reluctance that matched his own, she pulled free and went to her car. Before sliding inside, she gave him a glance, a tiny wave, and murmured, "I'll see you."

"Absolutely." He watched her get in, back up, then drive away down the street before he went inside the bar.

Nothing less than a miracle, she'd said. Simple words applied to a lot of things that, honestly, weren't the least bit deserving of the designation. But feeling the way he did, after all the ugly emotions in his past...

That really was nothing less than a miracle.

And its name was Alia.

The ring of the cell phone an hour later jerked Alia out of a lazy, satisfied, full-stomach-glass-of-wine stupor. Drying her hand on a towel, she picked it up from the table next to the tub, glanced at Caller ID, then turned it to speaker. "Hey, Jimmy."

"I didn't wake you, did I?"

"If I'd been asleep, I wouldn't have answered."

"Liar. Are you busy?"

"No." She gazed at the few remaining jasmine-scented

bubbles dotting the surface of the water. She nudged the faucet with her toe, turning it to full blast to both revive the bubbles and reheat the water.

"Are you taking a bath?" he asked at the sound of the rushing water. "Hell, sweet pea, that's not fair. How am I supposed to talk business when I've got this image of you in my head all naked and wet and soapy?"

She ignored the question and sank a little deeper into the water as it warmed. Her hair was piled on top of her head, but strands of it trailed in the rising water. "What business? I'm off the investigation, remember?"

"Does that mean two old friends can't talk about their work?"

She was about to point out that they weren't friends, but the realization that they really were stopped her. How had that come about? She'd loved him, hated him, wished he would disappear off the face of the earth. But, yeah, in their own way, they'd become friends.

"You know I'm supposed to be out of the loop now," she reminded him.

He snorted. "You know I decide who belongs in my loop. That's why I never became a big-time fed like you. I live by my own rules."

He did. He had his own code of honor, and his first priority was doing right by the victims of the crimes he investigated. He broke rules and took shortcuts, but he got the job done, and truth was, if she was ever the victim of a crime, she couldn't think of a better cop to handle the investigation.

"Did you go with Murphy to interview the Wallace sisters?"

"I did. It was like refereeing a bare-knuckle fight. Older one's a coldhearted snake, and the younger one acts like a spoiled-rotten teenager having a bad day. They were spitting and hissing at each other the whole damn time. Older one did most of the talking. Younger one did all of the drinking."

"Did they admit to the abuse?"

"Number one flat out denied it ever happened, then began cussing at number two for making up more lies about dear beloved daddy. Her reaction was so over-the-top it was obvious Murphy hit a nerve. The second one didn't admit it, either, though. She'd just say things like, 'He never learned that actions have consequences,' and 'You reap what you sow.' Enough of an admission for me."

For her, too, Alia acknowledged. In that sense, the Wallaces weren't so different from Mary Ellen and Landry. She pretended nothing had ever happened, and he'd found it impossible to pretend but damn hard to admit.

"Do you think either of them could be the killer?"

"You know my philosophy—anyone can kill for the right reason."

So if he was conspiring with the others, why implicate himself by confiding in Alia?

With her free hand, she rubbed an ache between her eyes. "If the abuse is the motive—" and she believed that with every gut instinct she had "—why now? Mary Ellen's the youngest of the kids, and she's in her late twenties. Presumably the abuse ended when the kids were in their late teens, graduating from high school, going off to college, gotten old enough to lose their appeal. What happened now to cause the murders?"

"Here's a scarier question," Jimmy said grimly. "You and I both know pedophiles don't just stop abusing kids because their victims get too old. They go out and find new victims. Where have these bastards been getting their thrills since their own kids grew up?"

Just the question was enough to tie Alia's stomach in knots. One more thing for the team to look at: what contact did the men have with kids in the right age group? They could volunteer at church, coach a sports team, lead a social organization, mentor at-risk youth, prey on young cousins, nieces, nephews or neighbors… The possibilities were depressingly endless.

"Well, now that I've brightened your day…" Jimmy heaved a sigh, and she knew from experience that it was accompanied by fingers raking through his hair. "I think I'm gonna call it a night and give Nina a call. You should do the same."

"Nina's not my type," she said drily.

"You know what I mean, sweet pea. Call Landry. He owes you after what you did for him."

"He *owes* me? You think that's the only reason he would want to spend the night with me, because he owes me?"

He laughed at her incredulity. He'd laughed a lot when they were married, whether her outrage was real or feigned. "Aw, hell, darlin', you know that's not what I meant. I'd spend the night with you if you'd just ask." His tone turned hopeful. "You think you might be asking anytime soon?"

"When I've gone stark raving stupid. Good luck with Nina tonight."

"I'm good. That's why I don't need luck."

It was her turn to laugh, but she sobered quickly. "Hey, Jimmy. Thanks for the call." Quickly, before he could think of a comeback, she hung up, set the phone aside and pulled the old-fashioned stopper from the tub. She was tired and would be getting up—at least, waking up—two hours before her regular time. She needed to rest…and store energy.

After a shower to rinse away the suds, she dried off, wrapped a towel around herself and went to the closet, rooting through dresser drawers for something to sleep in. She was a fan of snug-fitting tanks and girl-cut boxers for pajamas, but surely she had one nightgown, one silky-satiny-sexy sort of thing left over from her marriage. God knew, she'd been given plenty of them at her wedding showers, all wasted on Jimmy, who could get turned on by a woman in a hobbit costume.

But the sexiest thing she found was a nightshirt, way too big, with a crazed-looking rabbit on the front. A wedding-night gift from her mom, it made her laugh out loud before she stuffed it back into the drawer.

The hell with it, she decided, grabbing a pair of lavender-striped boxers and a pale gray tank. Landry wasn't coming over for her clothes; he'd seen the way she dressed. He wanted to see *her*. Naked.

Some emotion—anticipation? nervousness?—sucked the air right out of her lungs.

Her last night with a man—one night in an anonymous hotel with an anonymous visitor to the city—hadn't been her proudest moment. Tonight she was aiming for a whole other outcome.

Tonight she was hoping for more. Like long-term, a-future-and-more.

After tugging the tank over her head, then freeing her hair, she sank onto the padded stool in the middle of the room. She'd really done this, hadn't she? Gone and fallen for Landry, crazy-mad, wanting, God, anything and everything they could have. She had figured she would fall in love with someone after Jimmy; she'd just thought it would take a good long while—a few decades sounded about right—for all the shudder-inducing memories of her marriage to fade.

Mr. Second-Time Right had never had a face in her future-gazing. She could have described him with three words: different from Jimmy. Another NCIS agent, she'd supposed, or maybe a sailor or Marine. Someone with a career of his own that meshed well with hers.

Not a bartender. Not in New Orleans. Not within five years of the divorce.

Not someone she'd give up a case for. Not someone she'd give up the job for. Not someone she would stay in New Orleans for.

A sigh that was both anticipation and nervousness, along with a little bit of fear, rustled through her.

She jogged downstairs, double-checked the locks front and back, clicked on the lamp next to her reading spot on the sofa, a light on the stair landing, a third in the upstairs hallway. Then she slid into bed, sure she wouldn't sleep well.

Within five minutes, she was out. Never let it be said that Alia Kingsley missed food or sleep for anything other than a dire emergency.

It was hours later when she found herself just as suddenly awake. Drowsy and sleep-befuddled, she rolled onto her back as lightning flashed outside the window, illuminating the entire room. She figured her neighbors deserved curtains on her bedroom windows, even if the only goings-on were sleeping, but she loved nighttime storms, so the curtains were pale and sheer. In the middle of a storm, it was like turning on a couple three-hundred-watt bulbs.

It wasn't just the storm that had awakened her, though. Down the hall, the third stair from the top creaked; a moment later a solid footfall sounded in the hall. A size-eleven sneaker, she suspected, and a little bubble of pleasure popped inside her.

She slid up until she was leaning against the head-board and brushed her fingers through her hair. A shadow fell across the floor in the hallway, then Landry stepped into the doorway, hands in the air. "Is it safe to come in?"

She raised her own hands. "Pistol's on this nightstand. Taser's on the other." She glanced at his wet hair, at the T-shirt molded by moisture to his chest, then nodded toward the windows. "I take it we're getting rain."

He toed off his shoes before looking around.

"Bathroom's next door down."

He disappeared again. When he returned, the shoes were missing, no doubt, draining on the bathmat. His shirt was gone, too, probably hanging over the shower curtain rod, an image powerful enough to make her shiver. She'd missed those little telltale signs that said a man lived here—or, at least, got naked here once in a while.

Seconds ticked past as they stared at each other, their views brightly lit by each flash of lightning, then cast into shadows unreached by the light in the hallway. After a particularly loud clap of thunder that vibrated the floor beneath them, her breath caught in her throat, and heat surged through her.

She pushed back the sheet, swung her feet to the floor,

then reached into the nightstand drawer, pulling out a handful of condoms. "I forgot to ask…"

With the barest of smiles touching his mouth, he shoved his hand into the pocket of his cargo shorts and drew out another half dozen. "Until I make up my mind whether I want to give fatherhood a shot, I stay prepared."

A lump formed in her throat. It made her voice hoarse as, with hands folded primly in her lap, she asked, "You have any particular preference right now?"

Slowly he pushed away from the door frame and began walking to her. "It's still up in the air. But someone I like very, very much told me I already knew what I needed to be a good father. It's made me think." He shrugged negligently. "Meeting the right person can make you rethink a lot of things."

She didn't waste more than an instant wondering if she would have to rethink the issue. It wasn't as if she was going to toss the condoms into the trash, wasn't something to decide right this moment.

Instead, she slowly stood, curled her fingers around the hem of her tank and peeled it off. It fell from her hands, brushing her leg on its way to the floor, then she did the same with her boxers, stepping out of them, shivering as the air-conditioning kicked on.

Or was it the intensity of his gaze that made her skin ripple with goose bumps?

"Damn," he murmured, his gaze never leaving her even as his fingers undid his zipper, then worked the wet fabric over his hips, freeing his erection, drawing her gaze slowly downward. His skin was a few shades paler than hers, tawny gold, lightly dusted with hair across his chest. His shoulders were broad, his chest muscular, his belly flat and his hips narrow. Long, lean legs and a long, hard—

She swallowed greedily and said—*once more with feeling*—the same thing he had. *"Damn."*

Chapter 12

Landry hadn't been teasing when he'd said he liked kissing. It was sweet and tender—something he hadn't associated with sex until long after he'd moved out on his own. He liked the textures and the tastes and the intimacy. Incredible intimacy, more than the act of sex itself.

He especially liked kissing Alia, his tongue stroking over hers, the soft sounds she made in her throat, the huskier sounds he made. He liked the feel of her lips and the touch of her hands and the heat from her body...but not enough to spend the very next quarter hour kissing and nothing more. That would have to wait for next time, after he'd satisfied this need for her. In a day, a week, a year, another lifetime.

Lightning lit the room, brilliant enough to glow against his eyelids, and a breath later thunder rattled the old house. Immediately both repeated, thunder still roll-

ing while lightning zagged across the sky. They were in
the heart of the storm, their breathing ragged, her hands
roaming, his body straining.

Blindly he found a condom on the nightstand and
ripped open the package as he edged her toward the bed.
His arms around her, he tumbled her onto the mattress,
and they fell together, a laugh escaping her.

As he began to put on the condom, she slid her hands
from his back to his groin, pushing his own hands away.
She fumbled, teased, stroked, until he couldn't breathe
or hold himself steady, until every muscle in his body
trembled. "You're not helping," he choked out, and she
laughed again.

"You want me to stop?" She was trying to duplicate
the innocence that was in her voice in her expression,
but she looked entirely too wicked.

"Oh, hell, no."

Sweat was beaded on his forehead before she finally
slid the condom into place. He eased her onto her back,
then shifted over her. His arms still trembled, heat still
pumped through him in place of blood, need still clawed
inside him, but he held himself motionless and stared
down at her, memorizing everything about her.

He wanted her more than air, but that was nothing
new. He'd wanted other women the same way. The new
thing, the different thing, was that he *needed* her. *Needed*
to feel her, touch her, kiss her, hold her, protect her, be
protected by her. *Needed* her in a way he'd never needed
anyone, in a way he couldn't imagine ever needing anyone.

Her eyes darkened with passion—not just lust, but
more—and gently she touched her fingers to his mouth.
Twisting his head, he kissed them, then slowly slid deep

inside her, and it was like finding the place where he belonged, the woman he belonged with. It was like finding home.

And he was welcomed.

Alia lay on her side, facing the windows, Landry's
body curved against her, her back to his front. The storm
continued to rage, as if the system had liked what it had
seen in the city and settled in for a while. High winds
buffeted the windowpanes and rain thundered against
the roof, the intensity of both energizing her.

Truth was, great sex did that all on its own. The storm
was just icing on the cake.

The thought of cake—or, hell, just icing—made her
stomach rumble. Landry's drowsy chuckle vibrated
through her. "Are you really thinking of food at a time
like this?"

"I always think of food. Well, almost always." Sighing with more pleasure than she remembered feeling
in ages, she snuggled back even tighter against him.
"Though there were a few moments there where food
was the last thing on my mind."

"Next time that'll be my goal. To make you forget
about it completely."

Next time. How had she never before noticed the loveliness of those two words side-by-side?

"What time do you usually get to bed?" she asked,
in the mood for the smallest of small talk, so her body
didn't have to reassign a single cell from enjoying the
pure satisfaction still trembling through her.

"Three-thirty. Maybe four." He nuzzled her hair. "I
take it you're not getting up at five to run if the storm
doesn't pass."

"I like to run, but I'm no fool. Getting struck by lightning seems a really bad way to start the day." A pause filled with a yawn. "What time do you get up?"

"Ten. Eleven. Sometimes noon. Depends on how well I sleep."

"Do you usually sleep well?"

He was silent for a time. She might have thought he'd drifted off in the middle of her question except his breathing was too unsteady and shallow for sleep. At last, he said, "Pretty much. Before…" His shrug rippled through her.

Before. When life had been a living hell, and even when it wasn't, when he'd been learning to deal with it and put it in the past. As much as a past like his could be kept there.

"How about Mary Ellen?" she asked quietly. So much for enjoying pure satisfaction, but the question had popped out on its own, and darkness, relatively speaking, seemed as good a time to ask as any. "Does she have trouble sleeping?"

"I asked her today if she ever thought about what had happened when we were kids, and she—she just gave me a strange look. Like she didn't know what I was talking about. I added, 'with Jeremiah,' and she said nothing happened to think about and changed the subject."

Alia wasn't surprised. Mary Ellen was frail; pretending her childhood had been ideal was far preferable than acknowledging the ugly truth. The older Wallace girl was nearly ten years older than Mary Ellen and, according to Jimmy, not the least bit frail, but she lived in denial, too.

"Mary Ellen went to boarding school when you moved out, didn't she?"

Landry shifted onto his back and pulled her onto her

other side so her head rested on his shoulder. "I couldn't just leave her there." He waited through another rumble of thunder before continuing. "I couldn't take it anymore. I knew talking to Camilla wouldn't accomplish anything, and the old man had already warned me that no one would believe me. He was a Jackson, a distinguished naval officer, a well-loved, respected member of the community, and I was a snot-nosed kid. He couldn't have cared less if I disappeared. But he never would have let Mary Ellen go with me."

"What did Miss Viola say?" Had the old lady wanted to call the cops? Maybe for Landry, it would have been a case of he said/Jeremiah said, but Miss Viola had been a better-loved, more-respected member of the community, plus she would have had that sweet-old-lady thing going for her. Her credibility surely would have surpassed Jeremiah's.

He wrapped a strand of her hair around his fingers, let it uncurl, then did it again. "She wanted to go to the authorities, but I was convinced they wouldn't believe me. All she knew was what I'd told her; she'd never actually seen anything. And Jeremiah's parents bought him out of trouble all the time when he was a teenager. He knew how much to offer and who to offer it to. And if the cops didn't believe me, he'd never let me see Mary Ellen again. He would punish us both."

"So Miss Viola helped you move out and...?"

"She bluffed Jeremiah, made him think that her visit was just out of courtesy, just a warning. She told him that she knew all about their little group and that the chief of police himself—her husband's best friend—would know about it come Monday, and God help him and his band of perverts then, because no man in the city would. She said the only thing that would stop her from telling the chief was if Mary Ellen went off to boarding school that very weekend. She'd pulled strings with the school her own daughter had gone to and got Mary Ellen accepted on Saturday, and on Sunday she was on the plane." He smiled faintly. "Money talks. A lot of money talks a lot."

Alia wondered just how big a donation a one-day admission policy required. She had a few friends who'd gone to exclusive boarding schools like Mary Ellen's, and their parents had submitted their applications before the ink on their birth certificates was dry. There were probably Fulsom family wings, endowments and scholarships still feeding off that initial donation.

"It must have been a relief for Mary Ellen to escape the abuse."

"You'd think that, wouldn't you?" He gave her a wry look. "She hated it. Hated leaving home and her friends and Mom and Miss Viola and me. Hated the weather, the activities, the classes. She even hated the food. Said her Louisiana-bred stomach couldn't tolerate it." His voice turned hollow. "She blamed me. She insisted she could have handled things at home, but I never gave her a chance. She hated it so much that she was sick the first six months she was there."

Now she insisted there had been nothing at home to handle. Alia could sympathize. Intellectually, she could sort of understand, but realistically she didn't get it. Landry and Miss Viola had offered her a way out of a nightmare. Sure, she'd been homesick; of course, she'd felt as if she'd lost everything and everyone of importance to her. But to make herself sick, then to put the details of that nightmare out of her mind as if it had never happened…

"Did you see her during that time?"

Landry shrugged. "A few times. We didn't talk like we used to. Things were getting better by her senior year, but she got upset all over again that I wouldn't go to her graduation. Miss Viola offered to pay my way, but our parents were going. It would have been the first time I'd seen Jeremiah since I moved out. I couldn't do it." He sucked in a loud breath. "I was a coward. I was praying I'd never see him again as long as I lived."

A coward? For not wanting to face his brutal father? It saddened her that he'd ever thought such a thing.

"You were a brave kid, Landry, and stronger than most people ever become. And now you won't have to face the bastard ever again. The Jackson/Davison family can be normal again, one big happy family. One set of birthday parties, one set of holidays." Mention of holidays reminded her of something Jimmy had brought up earlier. *Where have these bastards been getting their thrills since their own kids grew up?*

The thought sent a shiver of dread through her, despite the heat radiating from Landry's body. In the thirty hours or so between him telling her about the abuse and Jimmy asking that question, her entire focus had been on the victims in the distant past. She'd never given a second's thought to later, probably even current, victims.

Rising to lean on her right arm, she gave him a troubled look. "Those birthdays and holidays Mary Ellen spent with your parents…" Oh, God, she didn't want to ask, didn't want to put even the whisper of a possibility into his mind, but it was a valid question. An urgent question. "Were they limited to Mary Ellen's family and your parents? How did the admiral interact with the kids? How much time did he get…alone…with…"

Rage darkened Landry's face, his body frozen with it, his breathing stilled by it. "No," he said, but it wasn't even a whisper, no voice, no substance, just denial. "No. She might pretend it never happened, but surely somewhere inside she knows better than to leave him alone with her babies. She would never, ever let anyone hurt the girls. Never."

He stopped abruptly, his face taking on a sickly tinge. "They've been doing it all this time, haven't they? It wasn't some sort of game they played while it was convenient, then gave up when it wasn't. They've been finding other kids…"

He lunged out of bed and for the door. A moment later, Alia heard the retching as he emptied his stomach in the bathroom. She sat up, sheet tucked under her arms, her eyes closed. There was a reason she'd never made a go of child sex crimes investigations. Her days would have been filled with heartbreaking interviews with victims, kicking the living crap out of suspects, losing her job for use of excessive force and puking out her guts every night. There were people, thank God, who did it, who had that strength, but she wasn't one of them.

After a moment, he came back into the room, walked to the windows, pushed aside the curtains and stared out. He seemed unaware that he was naked, lightning giving tempting views of his lean muscled body before shadow enveloped him again. He was gorgeous. Glorious.

And he was breaking her heart.

"The first time…" Between the wind, rain and thunder, his voice was barely audible.

"I wanted to die."

Alia drew her knees to her chest and hugged them tightly. Every breath of the woman inside her wanted to go to him, wrap her arms around him, tell him he didn't have to go on, tell him everything would be all right and bring him back to bed.

The cop in her held back. Talking was one of the hardest things any victim ever had to do. If he was able to share these ugly, painful memories with her, the least she could do was listen.

"Finally I learned to just take it." His voice was heavy with derision.

"One Saturday evening, just before my fifteenth birthday, he told me and Mary Ellen to be ready by eight. Mom was already so drunk she couldn't stand up by herself. She got that way a lot when he was home for weekends. Mary Ellen whispered that she didn't feel good and asked Mom if she could stay home. Camilla just looked away from her, as if she didn't even hear, but her face turned bright red, as if she was ashamed of herself."

Alia let herself imagine the conversation: the exclusive neighborhood, the beautiful house, the lovely room filled with priceless antiques, the three tormented people and Jeremiah, Satan in disguise. She could smell the gin and the anger and the fear, could see the tension vibrating the air.

"Mary Ellen started to cry. That always set Jeremiah off in a rage, so I stepped up and said, 'I'm not going.'"

What a shock that must have been to the admiral, so accustomed to giving commands and seeing them followed. That his own son would dare say no, would make a stand, must have touched off every spore of his rich-white-male-officer sense of entitlement.

"I thought he was going to kill me. I grabbed Mary Ellen and dragged her upstairs and locked us in my room.

He would have caught us before we made it to the door, but Mom jumped from her chair and stumbled against him. He had to get her out of the way before he could follow us, and by then we'd barricaded the bedroom door with the dresser. It was the only time she ever intervened." A note of surprise, even wonder, softened his voice as he turned to look at her. "I'd forgotten that."

Bleakly he lowered his head, scrubbed his face with his hands. "She should have done more, but at least she tried that time."

"She should have cut his genitals off years ago and fed them to the gators."

He smiled faintly. "Not a bit bloodthirsty, are you?"

She smiled, too, just a little. "My job is to protect people who can't protect themselves."

"Your passion," he clarified.

"Yes," she agreed. Unfolding her legs, she slid to the edge of the bed, trailing the sheet behind her until it fell loose, and she went to stand in front of him. "That, and you."

He laid his palm against her cheek, warm and callused, and for the longest time just looked down at her. Bringing his forehead to rest against hers, he gave a long, soft sigh as if releasing the tension inside him. "I'm a lucky man, Alia," he whispered.

Alia wasn't the girliest of girls. She'd been a rough-and-tumble kid, and not a lot had changed as an adult. She carried a gun. She ran like the wind. She lifted weights and subjected herself both to being tasered and pepper sprayed. She could hold her own in a physical confrontation against men who outweighed her two to one. She didn't get all gooey-soft inside, didn't have a sentimental bone in her body, and couldn't remember the last time she'd cried.

At least—she sniffled and held tightly to Landry—until now.

Landry was still awake when the alarm on the opposite nightstand went off. Alia stirred in his arms, reaching blindly behind her, silencing it, then settling into even, steady breathing again. Her hair fell across her face, trailed across his shoulder and chest, shifting lightly with each exhalation.

Just a few hours ago, he'd told her that he didn't have much trouble sleeping anymore, but since then he'd lain awake, one subject running through his mind: he should have gone to the police, the way Miss Viola had wanted, all those years ago. Maybe they wouldn't have believed him, but at least the suspicion would have been planted. Word would have got out—the city loved its gossip—and maybe a few people would have kept their kids away from Jeremiah and his buddies. Maybe a few kids could have been spared. But no, he'd been selfish, afraid to try, concerned only with himself and Mary Ellen. He hadn't given a damn—hadn't even spared a thought—about anyone else involved.

The guilt was nagging, sharp edged, but he found a little comfort in Dr. Granville's regular theme: *You were a kid. A victim. You're not responsible.* He did bear part of the responsibility, but not as much as the men did. And maybe it wasn't enough, but he could help stop them. They wouldn't hurt any other kids.

The alarm beeped again, and with a groan, Alia shoved her hair back from her face, then slowly, sleepily smiled. Without makeup, her hair a tangle and weariness etching lines on her face, she was beautiful. Warm. Solid. Naked. "Good morning."

"Good morning."

She sat up, turned off the alarm, then stretched her arms high above her head. The movement gave him an incredible view of her back, spine straight, skin soft and caramel in color, muscles flexing, waist narrowing in, hips flaring out. Bending, she found her pajamas and pulled on the top, then shimmied into the shorts. "When did the storm stop?"

He glanced at the windows, hearing the rainfall but no thunder, seeing no lightning. "A while ago." It was just a guess. He'd been too preoccupied to notice.

"Sorry about the alarm. I'll be quiet getting ready so you can go back to sleep." She pressed a kiss to his cheek, then shuffled out of the room.

He should put on his damp clothes, go home and sleep in his own bed, but the idea seemed entirely too much work when he was already naked and in bed and so damn tired. Besides, he liked the idea of sleeping in Alia's bed, of smelling her scent on the pillow and sheets, of being surrounded by the feel and the thought and the memory of her.

His eyes drooped shut as he turned onto his side, one arm resting on her pillow. He was vaguely aware of water running, bare feet padding past the door, clothing swishing and heels tapping by again, the aroma of coffee drifting on still air. A sense of well-being seeped through him, of comfort and belonging and safety, as his mind finally shut down and he drifted to sleep.

It was hours before he woke up, still in the same position. The continuing rain cast the room in shadows, but he came alert with instant awareness of his surroundings. Alia's house. Alia's bed.

It took a moment to realize it was the cell phone that had awakened him. Sometime before leaving, she'd emptied his pockets on the night table—keys, wallet, fewer condoms than he'd left home with and the cell that was ringing again—and taken his damp shorts from the room. He stretched across to reach the phone, settling into the now-cooled sheets where she'd lain earlier, and said hello to Mary Ellen.

"Did I wake you?"

His gaze flickered to the clock. It was a few minutes till twelve. "Yeah, but it was time to get up anyway."

"I don't know how you manage, working all night and sleeping through the morning. My girls would have a fit if I tried."

"I don't have girls," he pointed out. He only had the one, and she'd left hours ago.

"The blessings in my life." After a moment, she added, "You and Scott, too, of course. Could I interest you in lunch?"

It had been a long time since last night's muffaletta, and he'd expended a fair amount of energy since then. "Sure. Where do you want to go?"

"Oh, it's rainy and wet and the girls are visiting friends. Why don't you come over here, and Geneva will fix that squash casserole you like."

Yellow squash, onions, butter and bread crumbs... It was worth getting out of bed and going out into the rain for. He told her he'd be over soon and hung up, but it took him another ten minutes to get up and dress. He took the stairs two at a time, stopped abruptly at the bottom, then went into the kitchen, where he found a notepad beside the refrigerator with a pen. He needed another five minutes to decide what to say, finally settling on two words: *Call me.* Tearing off the sheet, he anchored it on the counter in front of the candy jars, where Alia was sure to find it.

The house was quiet but not in an empty way. Alia's energy was everywhere, seeped into furnishings and rugs and old cypress boards. He felt its absence the instant he locked the front door behind him. He missed it.

But he would be back.

After a stop at his apartment to change clothes, he drove across town, wipers swiping away the rain every few seconds. He arrived at Mary Ellen's house to find her waiting for him on the gallery, looking pretty as a picture. *Southern Belle at Leisure.* Her hair was pulled back, her makeup applied, her dress flattering in a deep rosy pink. It was the best he'd seen her look since the day Jeremiah died.

She led him through the house and into the sunroom, where a wicker table was set with china, crystal and silver, familiar patterns that he'd seen at every meal here. Soon she would be making room for their mother's dishes, probably giving them the place of honor simply because they were Camilla's.

"I saw Daddy's lawyer this morning," she said once they were seated and Geneva had served the salads. Her smile was plaintive. "I told him I want half the money to go to you. Half ownership of the house, too."

Landry stared at her, totally surprised on the surface. His subconscious, though, had half expected this. She was sweet and giving, and she'd never blamed him for not getting along with their parents.

He hesitated, touched beyond words, before gently,

quietly saying, "I appreciate the thought, but I don't want his money, Mary Ellen, or the house."

"You're his son. You're entitled to it. Keep it, give it away—I don't care, but this is something I have to do. I've already signed the paperwork, so it'll do no good to argue with me." Her hand shook as she prodded the salad greens with her fork. "What should we do about the house? I hate to let it pass out of the family, but I couldn't possibly live there, not with the memories it holds now."

Landry's fingers clenched the fork. She was so fragile that he found it easy to forget that she had bulldog traits, as well. Sometimes she got an idea in her head and there was no distracting her. She worried at it—and him— until she was satisfied they'd done the discussion justice.

What to do about the house? He'd left seventeen years ago and had zero desire to return. He didn't give a good damn whether she sold it, let it stand empty until it crumbled in on itself or burned it to the ground. But neither of those last answers would satisfy her. While he was still considering what to say, she spoke again, idly, with a hint of pleasure.

"You and your bride could live there."

His gaze lifted, his brows arching. "I'm not even dating anyone." No, he and Alia had totally skipped that first relationship step and gone straight to the good stuff.

"You will someday. You'll fall in love and get married and maybe even have kids, and what a great home to provide them when that day comes."

Not nearly as great as a cute little Creole cottage in Serenity, which didn't even have a second bedroom, thanks to its owner's fondness for clothes.

"I don't know about the marrying and kids part—" though he was less sure today that it wouldn't happen than he'd been a week ago, even a day ago "—but I wouldn't live there."

"Do you know how many people are just waiting for a chance to buy a Saint Charles Avenue mansion?"

He was sure there were plenty. The Saint Charles name had always been special in the Garden District. As far as he was concerned, any one of them could have it. But he didn't want it. "You have good memories of the house," he said carefully. "I don't. As Jeremiah started telling me when I was about six, I wasn't cut out to be a Jackson. I'm certainly not cut out to live in the Jackson mansion."

Whatever lightness had made its way into her expression slipped away, leaving her melancholy and regretful. "Landry, he set terribly strict standards for you, and he was wrong. He never acknowledged that you weren't like him and never would be, and that was unfair of him. But if he'd known he was going to die, he would have mended things with you. I know he would."

She looked so hopeful, trying to convince herself that it was true. Of course Jeremiah had known he was going to die someday, but he'd still never shown any interest in Landry. His son had written him off, and by God, Jeremiah had erased him from existence in his world.

Geneva took away the salads, though neither of them had eaten more than a few bites, and served the meal on plates translucent with age: shrimp-stuffed chicken breasts, squash casserole and green beans fresh from someone's garden. Mary Ellen thanked her with a fond smile, picked up her fork, then set it down again.

"I miss him so much, Landry," she whispered, tears glistening in her eyes. "Mama, too, of course, but Daddy...I was with him the night before he died, and he was happy and healthy and so strong, and then... It breaks my heart the horror they went through."

At least Landry had got a taste of Geneva's squash casserole before Mary Ellen finished talking. Now there were knots in his stomach, and his heart was breaking, too, for his sister's denial, for her continued insistence that their parents had deserved love and respect, for himself because he couldn't share her delusion.

They were dead, for God's sake—killed for their sins. Somewhere inside her, Mary Ellen had to know that. Couldn't she acknowledge it even a little? If not, if the memory was that deeply buried, couldn't she at least keep it to herself?

Immediately he felt guilty. Grief should be shared, not hidden away in shame. Maybe he didn't feel love or respect or even regret for their father's death—and not much for their mother's—but he loved Mary Ellen. He owed her support if nothing else.

Abruptly her fork clattered to the plate, her fingers trembling, twitching. "How can you not miss them, Landry?" The sorrow was gone from her voice, replaced by something flatter, cooler. Something...angry? "They were your *parents*. Your *mother*. Your *father*. Without them, you never would have existed. How can you sit there without even a single tear of sympathy or grief for them?"

The emotion caught him off guard—both hers and his, because that was definitely anger simmering inside him, just underneath the indifference, the uncaring that bothered her so much. Setting his silverware down, he pushed the plate back a few inches, then folded his hands in his lap.

He schooled steadiness into his voice. "I did my crying for them, because of them, a long time ago, Mary Ellen. I cried so damn hard and so damn often that I ran out of tears."

"Things never had to get so bad." Her tone, her smile, her very self, seemed brittle as if the slightest jostling might break her. "Daddy was hard on you, but all he wanted you to do was try. Go along. Make an effort now and then to be the son he wanted you to be. But that was too much to ask, wasn't it? You had to do things your way, even if it meant destroying our family. You moving out, me being sent off to that horrible place, Mama and Daddy brokenhearted—all because you couldn't bear to let him win. Well, you know what, Landry? It was never a game! There weren't any winners. Just losers. Even you lost out on having parents who loved you in your life."

Ice pumped through Landry's veins. Denial must be a cozy, snug place. He would have loved to live there for a while, but he'd never been able to turn his memories off long enough to settle in.

Rising from the chair, he dropped the napkin on the table before facing her. "It's been a hell of a week, Mary Ellen, and I'm not going to fight with you. You believe what you want, I'll believe what I know and neither of us will try to change the other's mind. Deal?"

He turned with a squeak of his flip-flops and headed for the front door. He'd reached the foot of the stairs when her steps click-clicked on the floor, when she called his name and threw herself into his arms the instant he turned.

"I'm so sorry, Landry! I don't know what got into me. I'm just so tired and sad, and the doctors have me taking so much medicine, and I just feel like things are never going to be normal again! Please don't go away mad! I didn't mean to upset you. I just…" Her voice lowered to a whisper. "Oh, God, things have gone so wrong, Landry."

He held himself stiff a moment, two, before his muscles relaxed of their own accord, his arms pulling her closer, his hand patting her back. "It's okay," he murmured over and over until her tears stopped and her trembling eased. "I'm not mad. I've never been mad at you."

Her snort was unexpected, a response he could easily imagine from Alia but never from Mary Ellen. "Bull," she whispered, followed by a hiccup of a laugh. "You've been mad at me dozens of times. You just can't *stay* mad because I'm so sweet and you love me so much." She lifted her head, wiped her eyes with her little finger, drying them without smearing her makeup, then gave another shaky laugh. "I love you, too. I couldn't live without you."

Under normal circumstances, though they were close, they weren't touchy-feely with each other. Her words made him feel a little of the old comfortably familiar awkwardness. He hid it with a grin. "I plan to be around a long time."

Pulling out of his arms, she took his hand in both of hers. "Stay longer now. Geneva can reheat our lunch, and she made a fabulous cobbler with peaches picked from her own trees, and there's vanilla ice cream, too. Please? I promise, no more talk about Mama and Daddy and the house."

Because he knew she wouldn't likely keep her word— how could she avoid talking about the biggest tragedies in her life?—he was reluctant to say yes, but leaving would only hurt her feelings. He was a grown man. He could listen to her, could bite his tongue if necessary.

And Geneva's peach cobbler was a thing of wonder.

"Lead the way back to the table." As he followed Mary Ellen down the hall again, he realized he was starting to think about food the way Alia did. The thought made him smile.

Chapter 13

The rest of the meal passed pleasantly enough. Landry and Mary Ellen talked about the kids, how Scott was taking them to Baton Rouge after work that afternoon, where they would stay with his parents until the Sunday after Camilla's funeral. They discussed mutual acquaintances and the weather and how lucky Mary Ellen was to have Geneva, who, along with Mama Trahn, was the best cook in the city. He would have to snag a dinner invitation for him and Alia with this same menu. She would fall in love with Geneva after the first bite and be wanting to marry her once she tasted the peach cobbler.

It gave Landry pause, imagining his sister and her family, Alia and him gathered around the dinner table. He'd never brought a woman to any family get-together—had always kept his love life separate from his family life. But Alia fit perfectly into that image. Mary

Ellen would like her because he did, Scott because she was so damn likable, and the girls would love her and want to be just like her when they grew up.

It felt very right.

After dessert, he and Mary Ellen took glasses of iced tea onto the gallery, sat under the protection of the broad roof and watched the rain for a while. It had settled to little more than a sprinkle, a fine rinse that washed everything clean and made it gleam. Tiny drops beaded on the grass blades and the flower petals and made him feel lazy, as if all he wanted to do was sit here until Alia got off work, then go to her house and sit on that porch with her.

Or just take her straight to bed.

He was considering that, his body temperature rising, his muscles getting twitchy, when Mary Ellen broke the silence.

"I know I said I wouldn't…"

He bit back a sigh.

Staring into the distance, she heaved her own sigh, heavy and reluctant. "Yesterday you asked if I ever thought about what happened when we were kids. What were you talking about?"

The question hung between them in the air, as if the humidity had caught it and wouldn't let it fade away. He shifted to look at her, but she continued to stare off, her expression stark, her body absolutely motionless. For just an instant, skin pale, unmoving, distant look, she reminded him more of a statue than a living, breathing person. Then she met his gaze. Hers was filled with shadows and emotion that scraped her raw, that scraped him raw, too.

He didn't want to tell her. Didn't want to uncover

memories she'd buried more than half a lifetime ago. Didn't want to tarnish that love and respect for their parents that had irritated him so a few hours ago.

He was tired of talking about it, thinking about it, feeling the betrayal and the pain and the shame and the anger and the bitterness. He wanted, just this once, to forget as thoroughly as she appeared to have done.

But she was going to find out. The police had talked to the Wallace girls yesterday. They would get to the Grayson and the Gaudette kids soon, if they hadn't already.

And they would come to Mary Ellen. They would want to corroborate Landry's story, would want the details of her own abuse. Was it better to let them spring it on her out of the blue or for him to bring it up?

"What did you mean, Landry?" she repeated, her voice plaintive and shaky and just a little bit scared. "Why did you leave us? Why did you make me go away for so long? I know that was because of you. Daddy reminded me every time we talked. What happened?"

Liquid splashed over his fingers, and he realized his hands were shaking every bit as much as hers were still. He set his glass on the table between them, dried the wet spot on his shorts and swallowed hard. "Do you remember all those Saturday nights we spent with Jeremiah and his friends?"

Something flickered through her eyes, and a muscle tightened in her jaw. Her mouth worked, as if a spontaneous denial was trying to work its way out but failed. "I—I—" Clamping her mouth shut, she shook her head hard. "No. No, the only time I saw those men was when our families got together. I never…"

He didn't say anything. He just watched her head shake get faster, more emphatic, her lips thinner.

"Nothing happened. Of course nothing happened. Daddy wouldn't allow—" Panic joined the fear in her eyes. "Mama wouldn't allow—" Now there were tears, too, not falling yet, just gathering, like the raindrops on the tips of the flower petals.

"Why would you say such a thing, Landry? Why would you think—" Her mouth formed an O, and the tears started falling. "Oh, my God, Landry. How could he— I'm so sorry! Oh, Lord, I'm *so* sorry!" She reached a trembling hand toward him. "Why didn't you tell Daddy? He would have protected you! Hell, Landry, he would have *killed* anyone who hurt you!"

He sat, stiff and cold and so damn sorry. "He didn't protect me, Mary Ellen. He arranged it all."

Horror lit her face as she went statue-still again. He thought of his earlier caption for the picture she'd made and changed it now to *Southern Belle in Torment.* It was too much to take in. She was…shattered.

He should stand, take her in his arms, tell her it was all a lie, but any comfort he might offer would be too little, and it was too late to take back his words. "I'm sorry, Mary Ellen," he whispered, his words barely audible over the steady drip of the rain. "But you asked, and I needed to tell, and the police will be questioning you…" Piss-poor excuses, but all he had to give.

He waited for hysterics, more tears, wails, collapse, but she didn't surrender to any of those. Slowly she lowered her hand, wrapping those fingers over the hand that held her iced tea, and she gave him a dry-eyed look that was surprisingly strong. "You told the police this?"

He nodded grimly.

"You told them everything?"

His nod this time was even grimmer.

"Why?" One word, not sharp, not angry, not teary, just very controlled. It surprised him again. He'd never seen her so controlled in an emotional situation. It must be the medication, he thought numbly.

"Why do you think they were killed, Mary Ellen? Jeremiah and Camilla, Miss Viola and Bradley Wallace? Because of what they did, because of what Camilla and Miss Viola knew."

A shudder ratcheted through her as she raised one hand to her forehead, pressing the skin there as if to relieve an ache. "I didn't know…I don't… Why don't I remember that?"

Relief swept through him. It wasn't an admission, but it was a start. "You were young. Sometimes our brains push ugly things into a corner and cover them over so we don't have to deal with them." Sometimes he wished for a brain like that.

"But you remember." Unexpectedly her lips turned up in a tremulous smile. "I know, I know, you're stronger and braver than me. You always have been."

"You're strong in your own way, Mary Ellen."

"I don't feel strong. In fact, if you don't mind, I'm going to take one of the doctor's magic pills and lie down for a while."

"Of course I don't mind." He stood and offered his hand. She laid hers in it, all long, thin bones and porcelain skin, her fingers cold, her nails polished a shade of pink so pale that it was barely a color. Carefully he pulled her to her feet, then walked to the door with her. He thanked her for lunch. She thanked him for coming, and then she hugged him tightly.

He watched her go inside before turning to the steps. He'd just reached the bottom when she called his name once more. Turning back, he found her standing in the doorway, hands clasped, gaze sliding to, then away from his. "I hate to ask…especially now…but…"

Take a breath and spit it out, Jeremiah used to say when he'd had enough of what he'd called her dithering—which was usually about three words into it. But Landry didn't chastise her. He just waited.

She did take a breath, forcing it to fill her lungs, blowing it out again. "There are a few pieces of jewelry I wanted to put with Mama. I told Mr. DeVille I would bring them over first thing in the morning, but Scott won't be home until late, and I don't think I can face the house alone, not this soon. I—I—"

He could go with her. Hell, he'd arranged *and* attended Jeremiah's funeral solely for Mary Ellen's sake. He could damn well go into the house for the few minutes it would take to get the jewelry. "Do you want to go now?"

The ginger press of her fingertips to her forehead again accompanied the shake of her head. "I can't just yet. Can I call you? Will you be able to take a little time off?"

"Sure. Just let me know."

The smile that wreathed her face was sweet and grateful. "Thank you."

As Alia pulled into her driveway, the sun finally broke through the clouds that had covered the city all day and glistened off the windows of her house, the wet paint and grass, the puddles that had gathered in low spots. On its downward slide over the horizon, it would probably heat the air enough to make things steam, filling the air so full of moisture that it would be like rain that just floated rather than falling. If she'd had anything planned for the evening besides being lazy, it might be miserable, but she didn't.

Unless Landry had some suggestions.

She let herself into the house, sighing at the tremendous difference between the chilled dry air inside and the hot heavy humidity out. She'd entertained herself on the way home with the fantasy of finding Landry there, having forgotten to tell her that Tuesday was his day off, grilling dinner, planning to spend an entire evening and a lovely night with her.

There was no sign of him, though, and the fragrance she inhaled in the air was either left from that morning or wishful thinking.

Kicking off her shoes at the end of the couch, she pattered into the kitchen to get a couple pieces of candy to see her through changing her clothing and found the note from him on the counter. A grin split her face ear to ear, melting away the fatigue of the extra hour and a half she'd put in at work. She popped one of the Hershey's Kisses in her mouth, took the cell from her jacket pocket and dialed his number as she went up the stairs.

Damn, it went to voice mail. "Leaving notes with my candy stash," she teased. "Oh, you know me well. I called, as commanded. Feel free to do the same when you get a minute."

She'd changed into running clothes, though she had no intention of running this evening, and fixed herself a glass of Kool-Aid when the cell rang. She answered without looking and swallowed a sigh of disappointment when she heard Jimmy's voice on the other line.

"Heard the news?"

"Hi. I'm fine. How are you?" she asked sarcastically.

"Someone attacked Marco Gaudette about ten this morning."

Forgetting common phone etiquette, she grabbed a handful of candy from the kitchen, then sank onto the sofa, bare feet propped on the coffee table. "Attacked how?"

"Caught him in the office parking garage. Apparently ambushed him from behind a big concrete pillar, stabbed him a couple times, but got scared off by a car parking nearby."

"Is he dead?"

"Sadly, no. Get this, the guy's first blow went right through Gaudette's left eye. Bastard didn't see a thing 'cause he was too busy screaming and covering his eyes. *Damn.*" Jimmy made a disgusted sound. "The driver of the other car didn't see anything, either, until he found Gaudette crying like a girl on the ground between the pillar and his car. Of course, stick a knife through my eyeball, and I'm gonna cry like a girl, too."

Alia unwrapped a Kiss, brushing away the bits of foil that fell onto her lap, wadding the paper flume tightly into the remaining foil, and put the chocolate in her mouth. "So the Jacksons, Miss Viola and Wallace are killed in the middle of the night, and the killer goes after Gaudette in the middle of the morning?"

"Are you eating? Jeez, Alia, can you not hold off while we're on the phone? We're talking about a skewered eyeball, for God's sake."

"And I cringed appropriately. But I worked late. I just got home, and I'm hungry."

He snorted before returning to the conversation. "How do you figure Camilla's killed in the middle of the night?"

"Because somebody would have noticed her being stuffed into the crypt, either unconscious and unwieldy or screaming and fighting, during daylight hours."

"Yeah, right. Even in the middle of the morning, we got no more evidence or witnesses than we have from the middle of the night. That garage has exits on three different streets. Anyone could have walked in there."

"Security cameras?"

"No view where the attack took place. We got a picture near the stairs. A navy blue rain slicker with the hood pulled up, jeans, running shoes. We can't even tell how big the guy is 'cause the slicker's way too big."

"Have you warned Anderson and Grayson?"

A grin came into Jimmy's voice. "Did that personally this afternoon when we served search warrants on 'em. Grayson pretended the murders and Gaudette's attempted murder couldn't possibly have anything to do with him, and Anderson looked like you on a cruise with no seasick medicine."

His reference to the first two days of their honeymoon cruise—her stuck in the cabin developing an intimate relationship with the toilet—made her grimace. She hadn't been able to eat a thing those days, which had turned bad luck into cruel and unusual punishment. As if being married to Jimmy hadn't turned out to be cruelty enough.

"I did the search at Gaudette's house and didn't find anything incriminating, though we haven't even made a dint in his financials. We've got teams on everyone else's houses and offices. Oh, yeah, Wallace's youngest daughter showed up at Murphy's desk this morning, too drunk to walk straight. She confirmed what Landry told you. I guess she had to take the edge off—and get out from under her sister's evil eye—to be able to talk about it."

Alia felt a bit of relief that someone was standing by Landry's story, along with a whole lot of sadness. How many lives had the bastards ruined? Landry would be okay—was okay. But what about Mary Ellen? This girl? All the others? Would they ever recover enough to live normal lives themselves? And the one who'd suicided right out of high school—she never even had the chance to try.

"Did she have any idea where they were getting their current victims?"

"Murphy asked her that, she got hysterical and he didn't get anything else out of her. Had to have an officer take her home."

"I broached the subject with Landry, and it freaked him out. He'd just assumed it started and ended with their own kids. He didn't have a clue that they were probably still doing it." She heaved a sigh. "The only thing he could say was that his nieces were safe because of their ages."

Jimmy was quiet a moment, other voices in the background. She would bet he was still at work, paperwork covering his desk, file cabinets and the wall behind him, looking for some little detail that had eluded him. She understood the compulsion. She'd love to get a grip on that little detail, too.

"Speaking of Mary Ellen…"

They hadn't been, but she'd mentioned the nieces, so that was close enough.

"I take it he didn't tell you that she tried to kill herself at that fancy school."

Alia's eyes opened wide. She pictured the only Mary Ellen she'd seen: sorrowful, naive, gentle, adoring her family. And yet, at thirteen, she'd hated her life so fiercely that she'd wanted to die. Hadn't just thought so, but had acted on it.

"No. He said she hated being away from home, but nothing about that."

"Maybe he doesn't know. That family was damn good at keeping secrets. It was about three months after she got there. She washed down a handful of pills with a bottle of gin, but her roommate found her. She did the next few months of classes under the care of the resident psychiatrist."

Camilla's drink of choice, Alia thought. *Like mother, like daughter.* "A resident psychiatrist…jeez, they say being rich comes with its own problems, but at least they can afford to deal with them."

"When they want to. Look at our guys. All richer than sin, all crazy sick perverts, and they didn't use a dime of their fortunes to cure themselves. Just to cover up their crimes. Funny thing about the suicide attempt—" of course there was no humor in his tone "—she denied she did it. Not just lied about it, but swore she hadn't taken the pills or drunk the booze. Swore it on her life, and no one could change her story."

Jimmy took another quick break from the conversation to talk to someone else, and Alia considered his last words. Shame for Mary Ellen that she'd given in to the weakness? Humiliation? Or did she really not remember her actions?

When he came back, he said, "You know, my gut says there's not going to be any physical evidence, unless maybe one of these guys liked to take pictures so he could relive it later. We didn't find anything incriminating in a search of Jackson's or Wallace's homes or offices or anywhere else as of now."

That meant the sexual abuse, if the prosecutor even chose to file charges, would come down to the victims' word against the suspects'. So far, the only victims who'd come forward were Landry and a woman who needed generous amounts of alcohol to let herself remember.

Alia wanted with everything in her for the men to be publicly vilified, humiliated, convicted and sent to prison. She would prefer death—yes, as Landry had pointed out, she was a tad bloodthirsty—but she would settle for prison.

Then she sighed. She would settle for public acknowledgment of the men's crimes, thereby making it more difficult for them to find victims. Hell, if it was the best offer, she would settle for signs in the media, on buses and streetlamps and their vehicles with giant photographs.

"Have fun doing nothing while you wait for your boyfriend to get off work," Jimmy said. "While I wade back into this sick psycho stuff again. If he remembers anything else, call me. I'll be here late."

"I will." She hung up and, even though there'd been no call-waiting beeps, checked the screen to make sure she hadn't missed Landry's return call. She hadn't. He was at work now. Maybe the noise in the bar was too loud for him to hear the ring when she'd called earlier. She called up his number, hit redial and listened to it go to voice mail again.

After flipping through two hundred channels on the television and another round with Landry's voice mail, she pulled out the thick binder of take-out menus that kept her alive, then after a moment's hesitation, put it back. Instead she laced on shoes, tossed her entire purse, her pistol and Taser into a backpack and headed out the door.

She was doing what she did about three nights a week—on the nights she didn't pick up dinner on the way home: going out to pick up something. No big deal. And if she happened to drive past the club on Bourbon and say hello to Landry, no big deal, either. After all, he'd told her to call him, right? And what man wouldn't appreciate her offer to deliver dinner to him at work?

So she made a beeline to Bourbon Street and found Landry's parking space empty. Frowning, she pulled in, then went inside the bar. The music was particularly loud this evening, as was the collection of women on vacation scattered through the room. There were probably twenty of them, a miniconvention of some sort, and they were the too-loud, too-self-involved kind of people that Alia and her friends moved away from in public places.

She sidestepped the three trying to start a conga line and went to the bar, stopping directly in front of the same bartender who'd been there the evening before. "Hey, is Landry here?"

The young man, hair pulled into a ponytail, gave her a disinterested look. "Nope. Said he had family business to take care. Was supposed to be back half an hour ago but hasn't showed."

Sliding onto a stool, she asked, "Did he ask for time off before his shift started?"

"Nope. Got a call, told the boss he needed an hour and left." The man frowned. "I know the guy's got the worst damn luck in the world, but he was off most of last week, tomorrow, the next day for his mom's funeral…I'd like to see my wife once in a while, you know?"

"Yeah, I can bet." She tried to sound sympathetic. "He

didn't tell you anything else? Who called, where he was going, what the problem was?"

"He didn't tell me nothing. Maxine—she's the boss over there—he talked to her."

Alia swiveled the stool to look at the solid woman sitting in the corner, a laptop open in front of her, a bottle of icy water beside it. Neither was doing much to ease the scowl she kept directing at the group of rowdy women. As Alia passed them, she gave them her best imitation of her mother's settle-down *look* before stopping beside the table. "Maxine?"

Pure pissiness looked up through thick red glass frames. "Who you?"

Alia didn't bother pulling her badge from her backpack. "My name's Alia. I'm a friend of Landry's."

"He not here."

"So I see. The guy at the bar said he asked for an hour off for family business. Do you know what that was about?"

"Why I tell you?"

It seemed each person she talked to in the bar spoke in successively shorter fragments. Would Maxine send her to the bouncer, who would grunt indistinguishably to her questions? Alia breathed. "I'm a friend of his. More than a friend. And I know all about the police investigation. I was supposed to call him tonight, and he's not answering."

"Family business. He not answering."

"I know. I just want to make sure he's okay." Impatience sneaked into Alia's voice and earned her a less-than-impressed look from Maxine.

"You wanna talk, you find him. You cop, ain't you?"

Alia fixed a smile on her face. "Find him. Of course,

why didn't I think of that? Nice chatting with you." Spinning on her heel, she stalked back toward the door, getting caught up in the conga line that was now seven, eight, nine, ten women long. The tenth one grabbed at her arm to add her to the dance, but Alia raised one hand threateningly. "You touch me, you're gonna be limping out of here."

"Sheesh," the woman whined, then added in a loud drunken whisper. "Bitch."

Clearing a path, Alia exited the nearest set of doors and tried Landry's number again. "Sorry to keep calling. I'm worried about you, Landry. If you could just let me know you're okay…"

Gripping the phone, she paced the sidewalk. The second time she passed the gate into the courtyard, she acknowledged that she could vault it with little effort. She could kick in his apartment door, she knew. But she wouldn't find him there. He wouldn't be home when his car was gone. He wouldn't handle a family problem at his apartment because who was left in the family to deal with? Mary Ellen, and he always went to her. She would stand out like a sore thumb on Bourbon, especially after dark.

Maybe something had come up at the funeral home. Maybe there was a problem with one of the kids. Maybe Mary Ellen was back in the hospital or someone else had died or—or *something*.

The only way to get any answers was to follow Maxine's advice and go find Landry. If she eliminated all the places he wasn't, then what was left was where he was.

Yeah. Sure. That was going to be easy.

The DeVille funeral home was on Alia's way to the Garden District. She swung into the parking lot, half-filled with cars for another poor soul's visitation. Neither Landry's car nor either of the Davison vehicles was among them. Just to be sure, her next call was to the funeral home to get the deceased's name. No one she'd ever heard of.

From there she drove past Miss Viola's house, looking sadly empty in the middle of its lush lawn. She turned right and found herself a moment later in front of Mary Ellen's house. A few lights were lit against the early darkness—in the parlor, long fingers of light reaching out from the sunroom at the back. The driveway, like at the Fulsom house, was empty.

Alia parked, trotted up the steps and rang the bell, hoping the housekeeper or a babysitter was inside. After ringing it again, she peered through the windows. Everything looked fine, except for the absence of occupants.

She started pacing again as she dialed her phone once more. Jimmy answered, his words garbled by food in his mouth. "Hey, Jimmy, I've been trying to reach Landry. He left work a while ago to take care of a family problem and is late getting back. He's not answering his phone. No one's home at his sister's house. Maybe I'm being clingy—" Jimmy snorted "—but you know what we forgot? He knew what the men were doing, and he didn't do enough to stop it. He looked out for himself and Mary Ellen, but he didn't try to protect any of the others. He could be on the killer's list, too."

"Hang on a minute."

A shudder went through her as she walked from one end of the porch to the other. A doll sat, forgotten, in the chair there, an expensive thing, prissy-looking with perfect ringlet curls and turn-of-the-century clothing. Her name was probably Charlotte or Annabelle, and she

probably looked on with her sky-blue eyes and perfect little open mouth while her owner played with her real toys.

Who was her owner? Faith or Mariela? It was hard
to guess. Alia had never played with dolls herself, but
she would put her money on Mariela. Surely the older
Faith had discovered there were far better ways to en-
tertain herself.

Turning her back on the doll, Alia walked the length
of the porch. Something was poking at her brain, and it
wasn't just worry about Landry. That elusive little detail she'd thought about earlier, that one little clue that
would make everything come together...or might turn
out to be nothing, a coincidence, just a pointless bit of
information.

"Okay." Jimmy had been gone so long, his voice in
her ear startled her. "I called Mary Ellen's phone and got
voice mail. Called her husband, and he's in Baton Rouge
with the kids. He'll be back in a couple hours. Said she
told him she didn't have any plans tonight. She intended
to pick out clothes for tomorrow night's visitation and
would be waiting up for him when he gets home."

"So maybe she ran out of milk. Maybe she went shopping for a new outfit."

Would either have required Landry to take off work to
accompany her? Alia could see him agreeing; after all,
Mary Ellen was the last of his family. But she couldn't
imagine Mary Ellen asking. In the most trying week of
her life, she'd made so few requests of him.

Alia slowed to a stop when chairs blocked her way
and found herself facing the doll again. Whichever niece
owned it must have intended to take it to their grandparents' house, then forgotten it. With her free hand, Alia
picked it up, and a soft-cover book that had been lean-

ing against it flopped onto the seat. Propping the doll in the crook of her arm, she picked up the book with the perfect curls and sky-blue eyes on the cover and opened it. On the left page was written in painstaking lettering: "This book belongs to Faith Davison." On the right, the story began:

My name is Marie Clarice, and I'm ten years old.

Alia sank into the chair. *I'm ten years old.*
Mary Ellen was ten when the abuse began.
Her voice hollow, her hold on the doll so tight Marie Clarice would have protested if she could, Alia asked, "You have your notes there, Jimmy?"
"Yeah. I told you I'd be working late."
"How old is Faith Davison?"
"Hang on a minute… Uh, she's nine. Gonna be ten in… two weeks." His voice turned sharp. "Didn't Landry say they started molesting the girls when they turned ten?"
"We were wondering why now. After all these years, why punish Jeremiah and the others now. Because Faith was about to turn ten. Because he had a brand-new victim to torment. She couldn't stand the idea of her daughter going through what she did. She had to stop it."
"She— You mean Mary Ellen? You think she's the killer?" He sounded both incredulous and thoughtful. "I can see that. Her mother didn't protect her. That's why she killed her first. Then her dad, then the old lady. Once the immediate family was dead, then she could take care of the others."
"But why not—" Alia had to gulp in air to finish the question. "Why not kill Landry when she killed their parents? Why go on to the friends, then come back to him?"

"Because she truly loves him. Maybe she thought she could spare him. Maybe she didn't blame him because he was just a kid, too. Then he went and told their secret to you. The police were involved, it was going to become public, she would become a suspect."

People would know what she had done. Probably more important to Mary Ellen, Alia thought, they would know what had been done to her. Did she think if she killed Landry, the problem would go away? The police would forget his claims? The ugliness would sink back into the past and stay there?

Dear God, she couldn't kill Landry. He was her brother. She loved him. Alia loved him, and he'd done nothing wrong. What safety Mary Ellen had found as a teenager had been thanks to him!

And Miss Viola. And if they were right—which Alia's gut said they were—Mary Ellen had killed Miss Viola.

"Where would she take him?" Jimmy asked.

Too many people around his apartment. Too much mess to use her own home. Too damn big a city to narrow down the choices. Then, suddenly, the answer was there. "Where it all started."

Jimmy swore as the sound of a scraping chair came over the line. "I'll meet you at the admiral's house. Don't you go inside without me, Alia. You understand? You wait until—"

She ended the call. Still clutching the doll and book, she started toward the steps. By the time she reached them, she was running.

Landry had always given himself credit for being a good judge of character. Between his adolescence and years working behind the bar, he'd thought he had a pretty good handle on people. He'd thought the one person he knew best in the entire world was his sister.

He'd been so damn wrong.

He shifted, the thick layers of duct tape keeping him from moving more than an inch or two in any direction. His shoulders ached from being pulled back so sharply, and his head hurt from the contact with a small marble statue that had stood next to his mother's jewelry case for as long as he could remember. Blood trickled down the back of his neck, a tickle that would have been annoying under any other circumstances.

Under the threat of death, it didn't seem so important.

"Mary Ellen."

"Shut up." She didn't look up from the chest where she was rummaging through the drawers one-handed, grasping a long, nasty-looking knife in the other.

He'd met her at the Saint Charles Avenue house a few hours ago by his best guess. She'd been pale and shaky as she'd unlocked the mudroom door, so fidgety he'd needed to steady the key in her hand. Once inside, though, her nerves had calmed. She hadn't trembled at all as they'd climbed the stairs to the second floor, not even when she'd led the way into their parents' room. She had glanced at the stripped-down bed where Jeremiah had died without any reaction at all, and the dried blood splattering across the wall hadn't fazed her.

He hadn't expected it to faze him, but it did.

She'd cried no tears, hadn't said much but had gone straight to the two-hundred-year-old rosewood table where Camilla's jewelry chest sat. He was missing a few minutes after that. The next thing he knew, he was sitting in a chair, wrists and ankles bound, and dripping blood on the petit point upholstery of a chair even older than the desk, and a stranger was inhabiting his sister's body.

It was a hard thing to take in, that Mary Ellen had killed their mother, their father, sweet old Miss Viola and now she intended to kill him. Mary Ellen, who loved kittens and babies and was so fragile and delicate and had never hurt anyone in her entire life.

But all that sweetness and gentleness had just been the outside. Inside, she was more broken than anyone he'd known, and that fact broke his heart.

She moved on from the chest to a bureau made of curly maple that some Landry had brought from France before Louisiana was a state. "What are you looking for?" he asked.

This time she glanced at him, an expression he'd never seen on her face, a coldness he'd never seen in her eyes. "He had a ring. I didn't have time to find it that morning, thanks to Constance coming in to work early."

"What ring?"

"Like this." Shoving a hand into her pocket, she pulled out two heavy gold and onyx rings, identical but for size. "They all had one. This one is Bradley Wallace's. This one is Marco Gaudette's. The lucky bastard survived, but I won't make any more mistakes. A couple more, and I'll have the entire set."

She'd attacked Gaudette? Aw, jeez, Landry's fear grew. "Why, Mary Ellen? After all this time…"

Slowly she came to stand a half dozen feet in front of him. "I was a good daughter. After everything they did to me, I still came over here every week. I had lunches and dinners, I brought the kids to play, I did everything a dutiful daughter should do. And one night, after dinner, after the kids went to play outside with Laura, he smiled at me, and he said, 'Faith will be turning ten before long. I have a special celebration planned for her. Do you remember our special celebration for your tenth birthday, Mellen?'"

Landry had forgotten that was what Jeremiah had called her. Not out of affection but, he'd always believed, because she wasn't worth making the effort to say her entire name.

"I *died* that day, and he was *smiling*. Threatening to do the same damn thing to my baby." She was shaking again, but this time it was rage. It mottled her skin and gave her words a staccato, machine-gun effect. "I talked to Mama. I begged her to do something, to stop him this time, to help protect my baby, but she just brushed me off. Like always. So I took the girls home, but I came back that night. I lured her away—got her to write a note saying she was leaving him—and I buried her inside that damn crypt the way she should have buried me all those years ago." Laughter burst from her. "It was so easy. She was so damn drunk. I said, 'Lie here and rest,' and she did."

Sickness roiling through him, Landry squeezed his eyes shut. He better understood how Mary Ellen had blocked out so much about the past. He was way older, way stronger, and damned if he didn't want to erase the last hour from his memory.

"I was gone for a little while," she said conversationally, seating herself on a lacquered stool, "but when he brought up Faith's birthday again, I came back. I stopped him. I made sure he would never, ever hurt either of my girls or any other girl again."

Landry swallowed hard. "I understand killing him, really I do. And Bradley Wallace and all the others. But

Miss Viola… Mary Ellen, she loved you like her own child. Why did you have to hurt her?"

"Because she knew, and she did nothing."

It was the answer he expected, the one he and Alia had already discussed, but it was no better coming from Mary Ellen. He had hoped for a more satisfying explanation, for enlightenment, but got only disappointment. "She forced him to send you away to school. She got you away from him. She made him stop hurting you."

"By making me more miserable than ever! She took away everything I knew, everything I loved! I died all over again, Landry, while you and she were smugly patting yourselves on the back for saving me! Going to that awful place destroyed what little world I had left!"

He truly didn't get it. He'd known what she was suffering here at home. How could the boarding school have been worse? She'd been *safe* there. She'd had a chance to grow up, grow stronger, to heal, and she hated him and Miss Viola for putting her there?

His little sister *hated* him. Intended to kill him.

Dear God, she had been so much more damaged than he'd ever suspected.

"We were trying to help you. I thought—" He'd thought they were dealing with a reasonably normal girl, given the circumstances, one who would be happy once she was out of the abusive environment, the way he had been. Neither he nor Miss Viola had had a clue that Mary Ellen might have been beyond saving.

"They say I tried to kill myself there." She shrugged carelessly. "I don't know, maybe I did. I was gone then."

That was the second reference she'd made to being gone. Puzzled, he asked, "Gone where?"

"Just…gone. I come when I'm needed and go when I'm not."

She sounded…fractured. As if she'd been living someplace other than the land of denial. Was that how she coped—by *coming* and *going*? Had she created some safe place in her head where she could hide even when in the middle of the ugly things?

He'd done that a few times back then—retreated into his mind, where the pain and humiliation and hatred didn't exist. Where he could pretend nothing was happening, no one was hurting him. But it never lasted longer than the act itself. He'd *always* come back to himself within minutes.

Had Mary Ellen got lost in that retreat?

"I'm sorry, Mary Ellen. I'm so sorry." It wasn't much, but what else did he have to offer?

Grimly he directed his thoughts from the past to the present. If he didn't think of something, there wasn't going to be any future for him. No one knew where he was. They'd missed him at work by now, but she'd taken his cell phone and smashed it. His hands were secured, his ankles even more so. He could knock the chair over, but what good would it do him unless he managed to take her down with him?

Eventually Alia would come looking for him, he was sure of that, but would she be in time? And what would happen if she was? Would she kill Mary Ellen? Would his sister kill her? He knew Alia was strong and well able to take care of herself—those were two of the things he loved about her—but damn if he wanted her to put herself in danger to save him. If Mary Ellen hurt her…

Bleakness settled in his gut. This night wasn't going

to end without someone getting hurt, probably even
dying.

Please, God, don't let it be Alia.

The gate to the Jackson house was open, a lonely
piece of crime-scene tape dangling from one side. Wishing for full tactical gear, Alia secured the Taser into the
waistband of her skintight running shorts, then gripped
the pistol loosely in her right hand. Her cell phone was
tucked inside the ribbed band of the sock on her right
foot, its ringer turned to vibrate.

Jimmy would be here soon with the cavalry, but did
they have that long to wait? Landry had been with Mary
Ellen for about two hours now. He could already be dead.

No. Not possible. If she didn't believe it, it couldn't
be, and she damn sure didn't believe it. Couldn't.

She waited a minute, then half of another one before
she started up the brick drive. She'd driven past the house
before parking at the curb, had seen Landry's car in the
drive, lights on inside. There was no sign of Mary Ellen's car. She must have parked some distance away so
no nosy neighbors could place her at the scene.

There was an eeriness to the quiet. Houses could carry
the essence of their former owners, and Jeremiah's essence had been evil. Knowing what she did, she shivered
as she approached the back door. Her only other time
here, a windowpane had been broken. She didn't need
such measures. When her fingers wrapped around the
cool metal knob and turned with a quiet click, the door
swung inward.

A light shone over the kitchen floor, lighting the
dark bloodstain that marked where Constance Marks
had died. No one had been in to clean the place yet, ex-

plaining the faint mustiness and the fainter blood scent. It replaced the chocolate taste in her mouth with sourness rising from her unsettled stomach.

Careful to walk lightly, she made her way into the hall, then to the bottom of the stairs. The house was too big, built too solidly, for voices to carry, but the light shining from above led her cautiously up each stair.

As she crept along the hall, carpet muffling her steps, she heard the first hum of voices. They came from the master bedroom, where a thin wedge of light spilled through the partly opened door.

"The girls are safe now, Mary Ellen," Landry was saying. "You can stop. No one's going to hurt them."

Alia flattened herself against the wall on the opposite side of the door. She had little view of the room, but she could see Mary Ellen, sitting on a stool, a kitchen knife held loosely in her hands. She was so slender, so damn innocent looking, that a person could be forgiven for thinking she'd never hurt a fly. Harm the brother she adored? Never.

Alia would never forgive her if she succeeded.

"Don't you get it, Landry? They'll never be truly safe. Do you think Daddy and his friends are the only pedophiles out there? Our world was small when we were children, and yet *five* of the men in it were perverts! *Five!* And that's just the ones we know about." She shook her head. "My girls will never be completely safe. But at least these five bastards will never hurt them. I'm gonna make sure of that."

"I don't care if every one of them dies," he said heavily, his voice coming from somewhere directly in front of Mary Ellen. "But what about Faith and Mariela? How are they going to grow up without you? You're their mama. They need you."

"And they'll have me."

"No. They'll catch you, Mary Ellen, and they'll lock you away."

Not in prison, Alia thought, but in a psychiatric hospital, because this was certainly not a sane person in front of her.

"What will the kids think?" Landry went on. "How will they get over it?"

"No one suspects me. No one even really knows me because I come and go." Rising to her feet, she turned defiant, gesturing with the knife to make her point. "And even if I do get caught, at least my daughters will know I was willing to kill to protect them. That's more than you and I ever got from Mama."

Just how much *not sane* was she? No one really knew her? She came and went? Was it possible she suffered from dissociative identity disorder? Was this a separate personality from the Mary Ellen everyone knew and loved, a protector who kept her safe like no one else had ever done?

Alia had no psychological training. She knew not all professionals believed DID was a valid diagnosis. She didn't know how to talk to Mary Ellen in a way that might defuse her rage. She didn't know if she could reason with her.

But she did know how to deal with an armed suspect with a hostage she intended to kill. Lifting her pistol, giving the door a nudge with her left foot so that it silently swung open a few more inches, she stepped into the room, sighted and gently squeezed the trigger.

Chapter 14

The worst of summer was over, though on a hot, sunny October Saturday, it was hard to tell. Landry was sprawled on the back steps of the Creole cottage, a bottle of beer cradled loosely in both hands. He had chicken marinating in brown sugar and cinnamon; he'd microwaved a half dozen potatoes until they were semitender, then sliced them thickly before coating them with olive oil and chopped parsley; and since green tomatoes were hard to come by now, he'd bought the firmest red ones he could find. Different flavor, but still well worth grilling.

All he needed before he put the food on the grill was someone to help eat it.

That changed in half a minute as Alia ran around the corner of the house, arms in the air cheering. Spinning to trot backward, she beamed a smile at her followers. "You made it! You ran a whole mile! Yay!"

Panting and sweaty, Faith and Mariela stumbled to the ground in a heap at his feet. They were dressed like the runners they were slowly becoming, in shorts, tanks and sneakers, picked to match Alia's.

"Why don't you run, Uncle Landry?" Mariela asked.

He gave her a look of horror. "That's Alia's passion, not mine."

"What's your passion?" Faith asked.

"You are. And you—" he nodded at her sister "—and you," he added when Alia sat down beside him. Even though she was damp with sweat, he nuzzled her neck, making the girls giggle.

"Okay, you two, hit the shower," Alia commanded. "Bathe, clean clothes, then lunch."

How could a seven-year-old and a ten-year-old rattle the entire house just by running up the steps? he wondered, then the screen door slammed and he was alone with Alia and he forgot all about the noise.

He smiled at her. "There was a time—" he didn't mention that it was that last day, the day his sister had tried to kill him, the day Alia had shot her "—when I thought those two would love you and want to be just like you when they grow up. I was right."

Her grin was smug. "They are crazy about me, aren't they?"

"So am I."

She rewarded him with a big kiss, then rested her head against his shoulder. They spent a lot of time that way, just being close, touching, not having to talk or anything else. They were the best times of his life.

Well, after the times they made love, of course.

"How's Scott?" she asked.

His brother-in-law had dropped off the girls that

morning, but they'd dragged Alia out for a run before she'd had a chance to say more than hello. He would pick them up tomorrow night after a weekend visit with Mary Ellen at the high-security psychiatric facility where she'd gone shortly after her arrest.

"He's…" Grieving. Shocked. Dismayed. Finding out that the wife he loved dearly had murdered seven people had stunned him right out of his comfortable life. Landry wasn't certain he would ever find his way back to normalcy, but he was trying. For the girls' sake, for Mary Ellen's, for his own.

"Yeah. I know," Alia said, understanding the answer Landry hadn't given. "How are you?"

She asked that question from time to time, tentatively at first, as if making sure he'd forgiven her for shooting his sister. Over time it had become more confident, more of a just-checking sort of thing.

He turned on the steps to face her, taking her left hand in his, gently twisting the engagement ring on her fourth finger. "I see the girls almost every day. My sister is alive and getting help. No more people I know are dying and Jeremiah's partners in crime have been outed to the whole world. On top of that, I'm in love with the sexiest, most beautiful woman I've ever known—"

"And she loves you, too," she confirmed.

"So I'm good." He kissed her, not a lazy fifteen-minute sort of kiss but sweet all the same.

"I'm damn good."

* * * * *

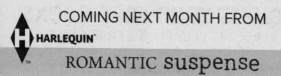

REQUEST YOUR FREE BOOKS!
2 FREE NOVELS PLUS 2 FREE GIFTS!

H HARLEQUIN®

ROMANTIC suspense

Sparked by danger, fueled by passion

YES! Please send me 2 FREE Harlequin® Romantic Suspense novels and my 2 FREE gifts (gifts are worth about $10). After receiving them, if I don't wish to receive any more books, I can return the shipping statement marked "cancel." If I don't cancel, I will receive 4 brand-new novels every month and be billed just $4.74 per book in the U.S. or $5.24 per book in Canada. That's a savings of at least 14% off the cover price! It's quite a bargain! Shipping and handling is just 50¢ per book in the U.S. and 75¢ per book in Canada.* I understand that accepting the 2 free books and gifts places me under no obligation to buy anything. I can always return a shipment and cancel at any time. Even if I never buy another book, the two free books and gifts are mine to keep forever.

240/340 HDN F45N

Name _____ (PLEASE PRINT) _____

Address _____ Apt. # _____

City _____ State/Prov. _____ Zip/Postal Code _____

Signature (if under 18, a parent or guardian must sign)

Mail to the **Harlequin® Reader Service**:

IN U.S.A.: P.O. Box 1867, Buffalo, NY 14240-1867
IN CANADA: P.O. Box 609, Fort Erie, Ontario L2A 5X3

Want to try two free books from another line?
Call 1-800-873-8635 or visit www.ReaderService.com.

* Terms and prices subject to change without notice. Prices do not include applicable taxes. Sales tax applicable in N.Y. Canadian residents will be charged applicable taxes. Offer not valid in Quebec. This offer is limited to one order per household. Not valid for current subscribers to Harlequin Romantic Suspense books. All orders subject to credit approval. Credit or debit balances in a customer's account(s) may be offset by any other outstanding balance owed by or to the customer. Please allow 4 to 6 weeks for delivery. Offer available while quantities last.

Your Privacy—The Harlequin® Reader Service is committed to protecting your privacy. Our Privacy Policy is available online at www.ReaderService.com or upon request from the Harlequin Reader Service.

We make a portion of our mailing list available to reputable third parties that offer products we believe may interest you. If you prefer that we not exchange your name with third parties, or if you wish to clarify or modify your communication preferences, please visit us at www.ReaderService.com/consumerschoice or write to us at Harlequin Reader Service Preference Service, P.O. Box 9062, Buffalo, NY 14269. Include your complete name and address.

HRS13R

SPECIAL EXCERPT FROM

H HARLEQUIN®

ROMANTIC suspense

Elizabeth just found out she's pregnant after a one-night stand with her boss's son. And she's the sole witness to her boss's murder. The only one who can protect her is the last man she wants in her life…

Read on for a sneak peek at Marie Ferrarella's 250th Harlequin installment,

CARRYING HIS SECRET

After getting out of his car, Elizabeth crossed to her own, taking careful, small steps as if she was afraid that tilting even a fraction of an inch in any direction would send her sprawling to the ground.

Discovering her boss's body the way she had had thrown her equilibrium into complete turmoil, and she found herself both nauseous and dizzy.

Or maybe that was due to the tiny human being she was carrying within her.

In either case, she couldn't allow herself to display any signs of weakness—especially around Whit.

At the last moment, just before she got into her car, Elizabeth turned and looked in Whit's direction. "If you need to talk—about anything at all," she emphasized, "call me. You have my number."

"I won't need to talk," Whit told her flatly.

He wouldn't call, Elizabeth thought, sliding in behind the steering wheel of her vehicle. She closed the door and tugged her seat belt out of its resting place. The man could be unbelievably stubborn, but there was absolutely nothing she could do about that except to express her heartfelt sorrow and regret. That and be there if Whit discovered that he did need someone to turn to.

Would Whit take over the corporation? Would he just pick up the mantle and act as if it was all only business as usual?

His manner just now indicated that most likely he would, but the man wasn't a robot or an android. He was going to have to make time to grieve over his loss. If he didn't, eventually it would catch up to him and cause a breakdown.

Whit was too good at his job to allow that to happen. But she was still uneasy. After all, he was a man, not a machine.

She had to find a way to make sure that didn't happen. For his sake, as well as for the memory of Reginald Adair… and the life of her child.

Don't miss Marie Ferrarella's 250th Harlequin installment, CARRYING HIS SECRET!

Available February 2015, wherever Harlequin® Romantic Suspense books and ebooks are sold.